T0279443

The Turban and the Hat

THE ARAB LIST

SONALLAH IBRAHIM

The Turban and the Hat

TRANSLATED BY BRUCE FUDGE

LONDON NEW YORK CALCUTTA

The Arab List
SERIES EDITOR: Hosam Aboul-Ela

Seagull Books, 2022

Originally published as *Al'amamah wal qubba'ah* by Sonallah Ibrahim
Dar al-Mostaqbal al-Arabi, Cairo, 2008

First published in English translation by Seagull Books, 2022

ISBN 978 0 8574 2 980 3

British Library Cataloguing-in-Publication Data
A catalogue record for this book is available from the British Library.

Typeset by Seagull Books, Calcutta, India
Printed and bound in the USA by Integrated Books International

CONTENTS

TRANSLATOR'S FOREWORD

The Turban and the Hat chronicles the story of the French occupation of Egypt (1798–1801) from the perspective of a young man in Cairo. This was the country's first major encounter with European military and technological might, and it came as a terrible shock to the people. But it was hardly the Egyptians' first experience of foreign rule.

In the eighteenth century, Egypt was nominally under Ottoman Turkish rule, based in Istanbul. Real power, however, was effectively held by the Mamluks, foreign-born slave soldiers (mainly from the Caucasus) distinct from the Egyptian people themselves. The Mamluk leaders were known as emirs and often held the title of 'Bey'. As with most ruling elites, their interests rarely aligned with those of the rest of the population, and there was no love lost between the majority of the people and the emirs and their entourages. This situation had obtained for centuries, and it was thus something of a surprise when an extraordinarily powerful and organized force of European invaders arrived on Egypt's Mediterranean shore, announcing that they had come to 'liberate' the people from the heavy Mamluk yoke.

In July 1798, the 28-year-old General Bonaparte of France came ashore at Alexandria, leading what was probably at the time the largest seaborne invasion in history: 335 ships carrying 1,200 horses, plentiful weapons and field artillery and close to 40,000 men (and, as it turned out, 300 women). Passengers included around 500 civilians and over 150 prominent men of science and learning: geographers, mathematicians, botanists, artists and others, along with a good deal of scientific instruments and equipment. They had sailed 4,000 kilometres to Alexandria, occupied the port city, then marched up the Nile to Cairo, capturing cities and forts, massacring villages that refused them food and water, and making quick work of the Mamluk forces at what the French somewhat wrongly call the 'Battle of the Pyramids' which in fact took place north of the ancient monuments, at a place called Imbaba, now a neighbourhood in north-western Cairo.

Needless to say, there were a number of motivations for the French expedition, and liberating Egyptians from Mamluk oppression would have ranked very low on the list, well behind the rivalry with the English and the astounding, audacious ambitions of Bonaparte himself (who would only become Emperor Napoleon I in 1804). Nevertheless, many of his countrymen apparently held dear the idea of themselves as benevolent guardians of those not fortunate enough to be French, and could declare France ready 'to offer a succouring hand to an unhappy people, to free them from the brutalizing yoke under which they have groaned for centuries, and finally to endow them, without delay, with all the benefits of European civilization', as a historian of Napoleon's day put it.

Equally needless to say, few, if any, Egyptians believed in the French goodwill. But Bonaparte went to great lengths to secure the cooperation of major Egyptian scholars and notables. Among those he tried to win over was Abd al-Rahman al-Jabarti (1753–1825), a religious teacher now best known as a historian, who gave us the only major Arabic sources for the occupation: lively, very readable chronicles that give a vivid picture of the chaos of the time. Jabarti and his writings are at the centre of *The Turban and the Hat*.

Sonallah Ibrahim's novel takes the form of a journal kept by a student of Jabarti, a young man who lives with his teacher's family and has learnt some French through an apprenticeship with a European merchant. The novel follows closely the political events as described in Jabarti's chronicles, as the unnamed narrator documents his passage from eyewitness to participant in the events of the day. Ibrahim takes this event of world-historical importance and gives us the view from the ground; he shows us the details of the social, political and religious divisions that complicated reactions to the French. It is a story of the people of Cairo and their responses to the new, non-Muslim foreigners who claim sovereignty over them and their lands. It is, then, a story of resistance but also one of cooperation, collaboration and corruption.

The narrator gets a job at the library of the Institut d'Égypte, the centre of French scientific research; he talks to the scientists and artists, he has an affair with Bonaparte's mistress Pauline Fourès; he accompanies the disastrous campaign to Syria, where he witnesses the ravages of the plague and acts of horrifying cruelty and barbarism. He is astonished by the invaders' lies and propaganda, but he finds that much of what he thought he knew about Egyptians was not correct either. Early on, he resolves to record the truth as he sees it, even if it shows him in a negative light (which, as the reader will see, it does).

In order to tell the truth, he walks the city streets, observing and listening to the inhabitants. And he observes the city itself, showing us the details of daily life: the food, the clothing, the buildings, the streets and neighbourhoods that many readers will know and recognize even now.

A young male protagonist's dispassionate observations of the Egyptian capital and its people will be familiar to readers of Ibrahim's previous works, especially the novels *That Smell* (*Tilka l-rāʾiḥa*, 1966) and *Stealth* (*al-Talaṣṣuṣ*, 2007). The former was his first novel, and its notoriety set the author on the path to becoming one of Egypt's best-known writers. *That Smell* shocked readers with its content (very mild by today's standards) and its style, which is simple and straightforward. Ibrahim has always eschewed what he called 'the conventionally flabby eloquence of Arabic literature', an eloquence that, one might infer, is not compatible with truth-telling. Most of his fiction is set in the present or recent past, and shows a fascination with detritus, material and otherwise. As the critic and translator Robyn Creswell writes:

> [Sonallah Ibrahim's] ideal of the novelist is indeed something like a ragpicker. Sifting through the wreckage of modern life, he rescues its most perishable objects—broken toys, old newspapers, rotten food—and holds them up as so many examples, more or less unwanted, of what we have done and what we will have to answer for (*Harper's Magazine*, 2011).

As part of this detritus-sifting, Ibrahim fills his novels with scraps of everyday life: newspaper clippings, news bulletins, advertisements, political speeches, all of which serve as both a kind of historical documentation and a commentary on the fiction. In *The Turban and the Hat*, he makes use of selected French sources but mainly Jabarti's own work. The documents are more than commentary: they tell the story itself, as a large proportion of the novel is taken directly, often verbatim, from the Egyptian historian's contemporary accounts. (In some cases, for clarity or context, I have in fact substituted Jabarti's original words for Ibrahim's paraphrase.) The novel serves, then, at the very least, as a marvellously readable account of the French occupation through Egyptian eyes.

But *The Turban and the Hat* is much more than a straightforward historical novel. Originally published in 2008, it was written during the American occupation of Iraq, and although there are no direct allusions to current events in the book, most readers will think of the most recent Western incursion into an Arab country and note the similarities: disingenuousness, incomprehension and incompetence, not to mention a certain callousness towards the lives of the natives. (At least the French had their scientific discoveries to boast of, and produced the extraordinary *Description de l'Égypte*, although this has enabled them to label it an *expédition*, rather than the disastrous military *campagne* it really was.)

At one point in this novel, a rumour circulates that Bonaparte is considering making Palestine a homeland for European Jews. This is no anachronistic retrojection of Arab anti-Zionism. In 1799, a French government newspaper printed that Bonaparte had announced such a plan. We do not know if Bonaparte really did make such a declaration but the episode is not the product of Ibrahim's imagination. Bonaparte's intervention in Arab lands was but one of many to come, all of which, from the perspective of the inhabitants, differ in degree rather than kind.

Jabarti's chronicle (and Ibrahim's novel) makes it clear that the French were not the only oppressors, nor was the opposition to them unified. The Mamluks and the Ottomans were Muslims like the majority of Egyptians, but religious fraternity was no guarantee of fair treatment. As a member of the elite, Jabarti looked with open condescension upon 'the common people' and held few ideals about his fellow countrymen. He shows many of his fellow Muslims in unfavourable light and praises French achievements when he thinks appropriate. Jabarti is hardly above reproach, as Ibrahim's novel makes clear. As member of the council of notables and scholars set up by Bonaparte, he benefitted from the French. He then famously (or infamously) rewrote his initial account of the French occupation to curry favour with the Ottoman authorities, removing praise of the French and criticism of the Turks, a fact that finds its way into *The Turban and the Hat.*

Ibrahim has a sharp eye for this kind of hypocrisy and dissimulation. It is another of the hallmarks of his fiction, and of his life as well, in which he has largely proven faithful to his ideals. Arrested in his early twenties as a member of the Egyptian Communist Party in 1959, he spent five of the seven-year sentence in an infamous prison in the Western Desert. When Nikita Khrushchev visited Egypt to inaugurate the Soviet-funded Aswan Dam, Ibrahim and a number of other communist prisoners were released as a goodwill gesture. Since his release in 1964, he has lived very modestly in a middle-class suburb of Cairo, with a few sojourns abroad (journalism in Berlin, film school in Moscow, visiting professor at Berkeley). Unlike the vast majority of his fellow Egyptian writers, he never held a government post. This lifelong commitment to living by his art is exemplified by a moment in his biography that tends now to loom almost as large as his novels.

In 2003, Ibrahim was given the Arab Novel Award by the Egyptian Supreme Council for Culture, which came with an impressive monetary prize. Unusually, he had agreed to attend the awards ceremony and deliver a speech. Ibrahim began in a fairly conventional manner, condemning Israeli atrocities and repression of Palestinians. But in the course of his lecture he became more and more critical of the Egyptian state. 'We have no theatre, no cinema, no research, no education. We have only festivals and conferences and a television full of lies,' he stated, concluding with 'I publicly decline the prize because it is awarded by a government that, in my opinion, lacks the credibility to bestow it.' Then he and his wife left the building. The majority of the audience applauded rapturously and followed them out, leaving the embarrassed hosts and committee members on the stage in front of a handful of journalists.

Thus, in the final pages of *The Turban and the Hat*, when the narrator asks himself if he would have the courage to write the truth regardless of consequences, it is hard not to think of Sonallah Ibrahim himself. At the heart of the novel is a problem that plagues Egyptians still today: Who gets to tell their history, and who will maintain the archives and the documents necessary to tell that history? In the revolution of 2011 and its aftermath, Egyptian scholars and activists made valiant efforts to document events as they unfolded, so that there would be some reliable record of what had taken place, that the uprising not be consigned to the same Orwellian memory-hole as so much of the country's modern history. Ibrahim's fiction has always functioned as a kind of archive, and *The Turban and the Hat* is an excellent example. It is further testimony to the author's literary powers that he has created, from the words of an early-nineteenth-century chronicle, a gripping narrative that is also a moving account of a cross-cultural encounter and all it may bring of hate and love, war and peace.

*

The translation has benefitted immensely from the close and careful reading of Louisa Shea, to whom I am, as always, very grateful. I would also like to thank Zina Maleh, Giancarlo Casale, Yoav Di-Capua, Sayoni Ghosh, Abeer Khoury Roissard de Bellet, Margaret Litvin, Maurice Pomerantz and Rob Wisnovsky for their advice and assistance.

The Turban and the Hat

Chapter One

Sunday, 22 July 1798. Midday.

I plunged into the seething crowd. The sun's heat was stifling, and dust filled the air. I could feel the sweat streaming down my face and armpits. I stumbled on a mound of filth in the street, all sweeping and cleaning having ceased since the French appeared on the outskirts of Cairo. I would have fallen had someone not grabbed my arm and pulled me up. My turban fell to the ground and unravelled. I picked it up and wrapped it back around my head.

We passed by side streets and alleyways, the fish market, the caravanserais of the wheat and rice merchants, the Hanging Mosque. We passed the different caravanserais: where linen and oil are sold, that of seeds and spices and that of the clothmakers. The alley of the shearers. The alley of the Nubians. The donkey stand. The lane and mosque of Abu al-Alaa.

Yesterday we heard of Murad Bey's defeat across the river in Imbaba. Umar Makram, head of the shareefs, the descendants of the Prophet, had left the Citadel carrying an enormous standard, the one the common people call 'the Prophet's standard'. Thousands followed him bearing quarterstaffs and staves. Men from the Sufi orders came with drums and pipes, flags and cymbals. On their heels came the aged, the beggars, the paralytics, the blind and the leprous. Stores and markets shut their doors.

The whole group set out for Bulaq on the east bank of the Nile to join the forces of Ibrahim Bey, who had gathered his Mamluks in preparation to fight the French. Members of the different guilds divided themselves among the mosques and abandoned buildings. They set up camp and those who had means provided for those who did not. Merchants donated weapons and food to the bands of Maghribis and Syrians.

But it was all for naught. As soon as Ibrahim Bey met with defeat, he turned and fled, and they all started back to the city. I joined in the chant:

O God of unlimited mercies,
Save us from what we fear.

Look out! someone shouted behind me. I turned to see a young Mamluk on horseback. He wore large red trousers, a wide tunic with long sleeves and a turban wrapped around a tall tarboush. His clothes were stained with blood. He cut violently through the crowd; some were knocked down and trampled. I flattened myself against the wall. The Mamluk leant over, brandishing his sword, and snatched up a man's turban, revealing a shaved head with only a single wisp of hair. The Mamluk burst out laughing, then waved his sword again, this time in my direction. I threw myself to the ground, cursing him silently. I did not dare protest.

The Mamluk left. I got up and ran, the tail of my galabiya between my teeth so as not to trip on it. I passed by a granary. I passed by a shop with imported German linen, owned by the second wife of Sheikh al-Jabarti, and managed by his son, Khalil. I ran past the house facing the Mosque of Mirza Shurbagy, where the Sheikh usually spends the summer. This year he had not yet moved. Past the caravanserais where cotton, henna, sugar, saffron, coffee, gum Arabic and ivory are sold.

The lanes are narrow, not wide enough for two men to pass. The side streets tend to lead in circles, where newcomers quickly lose their way. Women wail in the houses. Men hurry along, loads balanced on their heads. Unveiled women with children on their shoulders.

Al-Maqs: the neighbourhood is a wasteland, empty of life. A woman carrying a bundle, headscarf tossed over her shoulder. Emaciated peasant women in black galabiyas, thin men, their blue shirts cinched round their waists with rough cords of hemp.

Ezbekieh: Houses of emirs and notables, their servants loading their possessions onto camels. People trotting along on donkeys.

At Lake Ezbekieh, I almost collided with an old sheikh and his mule. A group of Janissaries overtook him. They are soldiers of the Wali, the Turkish governor of Egypt, easily recognizable by the double-branched feather they wear on their tall hats. One of them went up to the old man, shoved him to the ground, took the animal by the reins and walked away with it.

I helped the old man to his feet and he began to wail about his stolen mule. I hurried on. The sun was setting; the light fading.

Muski: I pushed my way across the bridge; it seemed about to collapse from the weight of the crowd. I hurried to the end of Ashrafiyya Street, where Ghouriyya Street begins. Turning towards Sanadiqiyya, I rushed through the open gate of our enclosed quarter. There was the Sinaniyya Madrasa, where my teacher taught. Its doors were closed. Opposite stood the caravanserai of Sultan Inal, also locked up, and next to it, the house. Out of breath, I stopped below its shuttered mashrabiya windows.

The arched doorway leads into a short passage next to a stone bench; another door opens onto a small garden in the middle of a wide courtyard. Sheikh Abd al-Rahman al-Jabarti stood by the inner door, prayer beads in hand. He looked worried. At his side were his son Khalil, still only seventeen years old, two years younger than me, and his black slave Mansour, arms folded across his chest, eyes fixed on his master, anticipating his every wish.

The servant Jaafar brought me a jug of water. I told my teacher what had happened, how the Mamluks had fought valiantly, first firing their carbines, then slipping them under their thighs to grab their pistols. How they had then tossed the pistols over their shoulders for their servants to pick up while they let fly deadly palm arrows. Then they attacked with curved swords, sometimes even with two swords, the horse's reins clenched between their teeth. But they were forced to retreat, for the French had organized themselves in strange square formations that could not be penetrated.

—And Ibrahim Bey?

—He fled.

My teacher's dark face, whose features betrayed his Abyssinian origins, broke into a wry smile. He gave a dry laugh.

—So, in defeat, our two rival emirs finally come together.

I let my gaze wander around the partly covered courtyard. My teacher's mule was saddled, next to a large chest and a donkey laden with supplies. I assumed he was getting ready to visit one of the two houses he had inherited from his father, Sheikh Hasan. One was on the shores of the Nile by al-Abzariyya, the other towards Lake Ratli, among farms and gardens. He told me he was leaving the city to stay at his farm in Abyar until things settled down.

—Umar Makram and the rest of the notables and the scholars have already left the city, he added. Sheikh Sadat and Sheikh Sharqawi have fled to Matariyya.

He paused.

—There won't be any resistance now that the two emirs have been defeated. It's certain the French will enter the city in the morning.

—But the route isn't safe, I told him. The Bedouins and the fellahin will rob anybody they see leaving the city. They'll take everything! They'll take the clothes off your back!

—God is the best of guardians.

—At least take a pistol with you.

He sent Jaafar to buy powder for the firearm. He pulled off his turban and wiped the sweat from his brow with his sleeve. Forty-five years old, but his hair remained black as coal.

The sun was gone. A foul smell came from the pit where the toilets are emptied. It had been days since any of the waxers had come to clean it.

Ibrahim Bey has no luck, said my teacher. Just last week his wife caught him with a servant girl, and beat him.

—How can he allow that?

—There's nothing he can do with a woman of her status. People say she performs miracles and receives messages from the Prophet himself.

—Is there any news of your friend Sheikh Hasan al-Attar, I asked.

—He's gone to Upper Egypt. The well-to-do have all fled. Only the poor are left.

I told him that Emir Ayoub Bey had been martyred in the battle at Imbaba, as I knew he had been close to my teacher.

—Yes, he told me that he had seen this in a dream two months before the French arrived. When they gathered at Imbaba, he rushed into battle yelling, 'I give myself in the path of God!'

He thought for a while, then continued.

—May God have mercy on him. He was a crafty one. He pretended to defend what is true and right and to love the Prophet's descendants and the scholars. He would buy copies of the Quran and religious books and say his prayers, and he looked after beggars and travellers, but he was also debauched. He liked to listen to music, he even played himself!

Jaafar returned with the gunpowder and lead. They had become very expensive: one pound of powder was 60 *paras*, and a pound of lead 90 *paras*. Mansour brought the gun, wrapped in rags. A servant held a lamp while Mansour busied himself with cleaning and loading the weapon.

The sheikh mounted his mule and Khalil got on behind him. They did not own a horse because the Mamluks did not allow anyone but themselves to ride one.

He pulled up the lower edge of his kaftan to reveal a new pair of red shoes, the kind known as Constantinople shoes. Mansour carried the gun and pulled the donkey behind him. The groom led my teacher's mule up to the gate. Jaafar and I followed.

—Don't open the door for anyone, and don't go out, he warned us. You are in charge of them.

He meant his two wives. His father had married him to the first one thirty years ago, he was fifteen. He married the second one eighteen years ago, and she bore him a son, Khalil, and a daughter, Aman.

We went out into the alley. All the neighbouring houses were dark. The heavy door to the quarter creaked as the gatekeeper pushed it open for us. A dog barked. We waited until they were out in the road, then the gatekeeper closed the gate and reinforced it with a wooden bolt again. We returned to the house and Jaafar locked the outer door with the key and a sliding latch.

Sunday, 22 July. Evening.

We went through the inner door and I locked it. Across the courtyard, Jaafar headed to the servants' quarters while I made for my own room with its bright, lime-coated walls.

From the trunk that holds all my possessions, I took out a large mattress, two pillows and a sheet. In the hope of finding a bit of fresh air, I moved the black-and-yellow-checked palm mat to face the door and spread the bedding over the mat.

I chased away the flies and mosquitoes and, closing the door behind me, went to the toilet. It was in a nook, out of sight, and although there was a vent, it did nothing to lessen the smell. I urinated and washed my hands with the yellow, odourless root, *aysh al-nun*.

A servant had brought some food to my room. I lifted the cloth: moloukhiyya with bits of meat; radishes, onions, cucumbers and tomatoes; beets and cucumbers soaked in vinegar; two round pieces of bread. The loaves were smaller than usual. I could taste the dirt in them as I chewed, but I ate hungrily anyway. My stomach had been empty since morning.

I drank a cup of sherbet, belched, pushed the platter away and stood up. I went back to the toilet, scrubbed my teeth with the yellow roots, and did my ablutions. I returned to my room, dried my hands and prayed the evening prayer.

I went back out to the darkened courtyard. The air was hot and stifling. To the left were the stable, the granary and a large kitchen where the wood and coal were kept, piled in a corner. To the right were the servants' and slaves' chambers as well as the guest quarters. Low voices could be heard through the open doors. I went past the wide room reserved for students and lodgers, where the study circles were held. I looked around. There was no one. I pushed open the inner door and went up to the top floor. The smell of disinfectant, wormwood mixed with aloe, was overwhelming. A curving passageway overlooked the courtyard. Arches and pillars of coloured marble. Bright lamps of crystal and silver. Locked rooms. I passed the furnace heating the pipes that run to the baths.

I picked up one of the lamps, climbed two steps to a large room, and entered. The lamp lit up the ceiling and walls, revealing wood carvings rich in scent. Glazed tiles of many colours. A Venetian clock. Two cupboards of fine plates and dishes. Couches bedecked with silk cushions; rich carpets spread across the room. Treasures in every corner or hanging from the walls. The astrolabe my teacher had inherited from his father and with which he used to study the heavens. Candelabra and crystal chandeliers. The Sheikh Jabarti called this 'the private meeting room'. Verses of poetry sewn on pieces of silk hung from the walls, a gift from Sheikh Mustafa al-Sawi on the completion of the building. There were two doors adorned with mother-of-pearl and copper; one led to the library and to the women's and children's rooms, the second to a latrine and onto the large hall where important visitors would gather.

A leaf of paper lay on one of the couches. Leaving my shoes at the edge of the carpets I went over, set down the lamp and picked it up. It was a copy of the letter the French had sent from Alexandria; some Maltese infidels had served as couriers. Though I knew what it said, I held it to the light and scanned the lines again:

> In the name of God, the Compassionate, the Merciful: There is no God but He. He has neither son nor associate in His Dominion. On behalf of the French Republic, founded on the principles of freedom and equality . . . Bonaparte, Commander-in-Chief of the French armies, informs the people of Egypt that the Beys controlling the Egyptian lands have for a long time shown contempt and arrogance for the rights of the French community and have treated their merchants in an unjust manner . . .

I skipped over the lines I already knew by heart:

> O People of Egypt! You may have heard that I have come here only to abolish your religion. That is a blatant lie not to be believed. Say to those slanderers that I have come to you only to return to you what is rightfully yours from the hand of the oppressors. I, more than any of the Mamluks, am a servant of God, may he be glorified and exalted, and I respect His Prophet Muhammad and the Glorious Quran. Say to them also that all people are equal before God, and that they are distinguished from one another only by reason, virtue and knowledge. And what do the Mamluks have of reason, virtue and knowledge that should distinguish them from the others and allow them alone to possess all that is sweet in this earthly life? Wherever fertile land is found, it belongs to the Mamluks, along with the most beautiful slave girls, the most noble steeds and the most splendid properties . . .

I smiled as I read on:

> If the land of Egypt is a fief for the Mamluks, then let them produce the title deed in which God has deemed it so . . . Truly the French have at all times been the faithful friends of the Excellent Ottoman Sultan, and enemy to his enemies.

Still astonished at the deceit and falsehood of the letter, I put it back where I had found it. Through the window, the alley lay in darkness. Now no one left their house after the locking of the gates. Low voices rose from the other side of the wall.

Taking the lamp and treading lightly, I went to the door of the women's quarters. I opened it gently. In the low light of a hanging lamp a landing was visible. I put out my own lamp and laid it aside. In the corner a body lay outstretched on the floor. As I went towards it I tripped on a wooden clog and cursed myself. I bent over the black slave girl. Her eyes were open wide. She made no sound as I pulled off her ankle-length tunic.

I felt about for the waistband of her cotton garment and pulled it down. She did not resist. I grabbed her legs, bent them upward and I took her. It was hard to penetrate her so I had to use some of my own spit. I finished quickly. She never uttered a word, not even a moan. She just kept looking at me with an expression in her eyes that I could not fathom.

I got up, wiped my sweat with my tunic and pulled it on over my pants. Then I picked up my lamp and returned to my room.

Tuesday, 24 July.

I performed my ablutions, prayed and had breakfast, then went to the stable. Jaafar protested as I untied the donkey, reminding me of my teacher's instructions. He said the streets were full of riff-raff, that they looted and burnt the houses of Ibrahim Bey and Murad Bey near the Citadel. They also looted the houses of the emirs and took all the furnishings and brass and sold it all for a paltry price.

Jaafar is only a servant. He was already part of the house when Sheikh Jabarti took me in, having previously belonged to his father. Short and stocky, Jaafar oversaw the rest of the servants and slaves, and he continually tried to assert his control over me as well.

I stood in the courtyard, not sure what to do. The smell of frying food wafted from the iron grill in the kitchen. The door to the storehouse was open, revealing tall jars of oil and clarified butter and honey and wheat. A servant was busy crushing coffee beans. Next to her, chickens and ducks pecked their food from the ground. In a corner, another servant bent over a tub of washing. She had hiked her dress up and I could see her thighs. I kept my eyes on them hoping I would see more.

I become aware of the black slave girl cleaning a brass jug in a basin by the well, then filling a water jar. My teacher had bought her at the slave market several months ago, paying eighty Spanish piastres. Her hair was worn up in the slave girl fashion, and she had a simple linen headscarf. Our eyes met but she showed no emotion or expression.

I went upstairs to the private meeting room and, leaving my shoes at the entrance, crossed over to the library. I took out a medical text I was supposed to be copying for a chemist in order to help with my expenses. But then I did not feel like working so I put it back in its place and looked around at the other books: a copy of the Quran, estimated to be worth 120 *paras*; collections of Sufi readings and prayers; the encyclopaedic history of al-Maqrizi; the legal compendium of al-Shaarawi; the great history by al-Suyuti, in my teacher's own hand; two copies of the prayer collection, *Proofs of Goodness*, an inexpensive one the Sheikh bought for 10 *paras*, the other in elegant calligraphy, for which he had paid several hundred; the books of Galen, Socrates and Plato; a volume of short texts on medicine bought from a chemist for 50 *paras*; a manuscript of Imam al-Damanhouri's treatise on anatomy; the writings of his father, Sheikh Hasan; an incomparable copy of al-Jawhari's Arabic dictionary that stood out because it was not in manuscript form but had been printed as a lithograph in Turkey.

I looked for books of stories, wonders or proverbs. I could not find *The Affable Acquaintance* or al-Shirbini's *Brains Confounded by the Ode of Abu Shaduf Expounded*, or the jokes of Juha, not even *Kalila and Dimna* or the chronicles of al-Ishaqi, which were filled with all kinds of entertaining and scandalous anecdotes. The Sheikh must have taken them with him.

I took out the notebooks in which he was writing his biographies of famous men, at the request of the late Sheikh Murtada al-Zabidi. I leafed slowly through them, admiring his beautiful *ruq'a* script, then put them back. I found a blank sheet and, taking the reed pen and the oblong brass inkwell, sat cross-legged in my teacher's place on the couch. With the paper on my thigh, I began to set down what had happened to me since the clash at Bulaq and the rout of Ibrahim Bey. I hesitated whether to write down what happened with the black slave girl. When the Sheikh chronicled recent events, he focused on public affairs and avoided all personal matters. I resolved not to follow his example and recorded the encounter with the slave girl. I noted the date according the Islamic calendar, but then substituted the Christian date, as I had learnt from a French merchant. I multiplied the Islamic year by 131, divided the result by 135 and then added 621 to get the corresponding Christian year.

I sprinkled some sand on the paper, folded it, put it in my pocket. Back in my room, I pulled a blue linen shirt over the loose trousers and wrapped my turban around my head. Then I looked cautiously outside.

Jaafar was heading to his room; I stepped into the courtyard and took a drink from the water jar. I kept watch on his room, and when he didn't come back, I hurried to the gate. A servant returning from the market carried a palm leaf laden with round loaves of bread.

Outside in the alley, I hesitated, not knowing whether to head to the right, towards the caravanserai of the slave dealers, where slaves were put on display naked, or down the alley that gave onto the square of the Azhar Mosque. I chose the opposite direction, and made my way towards al-Ashrafiyya, past the caravanserai of Sultan Inal and past the caravanserai of the boxmakers, where the men worked with cedar and made thick paper. People were running in the direction of al-Gammaliyya, shouting that the French had crossed the Nile to the Cairo side and that their leader had entered the city at Bab al-Nasr. I followed.

The Palace Walk was much more crowded than usual: mules and donkeys, beggars and women draped in black. The men were trying to rub themselves up against the women. Amidst all the noise and shouting, the Ottoman governor's Janissaries just stood there, indifferent.

I caught up to the crowd before it reached the Palace Walk. After a few minutes I could see the distinctive dome of Sultan Barquq's mausoleum and, a little further, the madrasa and tomb of Sultan Nasir Muhammad bin Qalawun with its towering minaret. Then the Mansouri Hospital where Khalil studied medicine for a time but without success. I raised my eyes to the sobriquets of Sultan Qalawun engraved on the wall: Sultan of Basra and Kufa; King of the Land and the Two Seas; Master of the Two Qiblahs of Jerusalem and Mecca, Custodian of the Two Noble Sanctuaries.

I turned back towards the slow-moving crowd. A flag floated at the head of the procession—a large white square with blue and red in the four corners. That must be the French flag, I thought. The sheikhs and notables rode their mules ahead of me, clutching their prayer beads. As usual, a group of runners armed with cudgels went before them, clearing the way by randomly clubbing the passers-by. They were a dismal lot compared to the Mamluks.

When the Mamluks marched, it was with great pomp: weapons on full display, decorated turbans, flowing silk cloaks.

The procession turned towards Ezbekieh. We crossed the bridge facing the Frankish quarter, then slowed near Lake Ratli. I wormed my way to the front of the crowd and saw that they had stopped in front of the house of Muhammad Bey al-Alfi.

The house was deserted following the flight of its owner who did not lack for houses, having two more properties in Ezbekieh and another in Bab al-Nasr. He had also commissioned a moveable wood palace built from separate pieces that could be joined together by sturdy hooks. The pieces could be carried on the backs of camels, and when he wished to strike camp, his men would assemble it. It formed a room big enough for eight people, with windows on all sides.

Standing on tiptoe, I could make out the strangely shaped caps on the heads of the Frenchmen. They were led by a short, slight fellow. He wore three large feathers in his cap and the sword at his belt hung all the way down to the ground. His men followed him into Alfi's house, while the soldiers began unloading the trunks from a cart pulled by a donkey. It was the first time such a cart had ever been seen in these streets.

The leader, I understood, was going to live here. I shook my head and wondered how this could be God's wisdom. Alfi had built his palace the previous year, and it was the talk of the town. His men had fired bricks in several ovens and worked mills to grind the gypsum. They cut stones and carried them by boat from Tara and laid them in large slabs to form the palace floors. They brought different types of wood from Bulaq, from Alexandria, Rosetta and Damietta.

When the building was completed, Alfi held a large celebration, inviting his Mamluk friends as well as learned sheikhs like Jabarti. I had accompanied my teacher, and together we entered a great garden, brilliantly illuminated by a series of lamps. The garden had been adorned with pillars and a pergola for shade, and in a large marble fountain, a gift from the Franks, water spouted from the mouths of sculpted fish. Plate-glass windows, alabaster staircases and mosaic floors bejewelled the house.

We drank fruit juices from silver goblets and ate young chicken roasted over coals. We crumbled bread into a thick soup rich with fatty meat, oxtail, lamb marrow and the brains of birds. But Alfi did not get to enjoy his new residence for long. Sixteen days after taking up the place, his master Murad Bey was defeated by the French at Imbaba and he was forced to flee along with his women and children.

Now the sheikhs began to turn back and I followed them. Digging in my pockets, I came up with 5 *paras*, which was all that remained of the allowance from my teacher. I looked around for a donkey to hire, but found none. I thought of going to the donkey stand near the Kikhiyya Mosque but changed my mind. Circling around the lake until the Ruwaii house lay on my left, I crossed over the land endowed by Mustafa Katkhuda, near the Christian quarter. Some Janissaries and other people were gathered there. I headed directly for the house of Hanna.

He was about my age. I had come to know him through a French merchant who sold grain and medications. I used to work for him before Jabarti took me into his household. Hanna now worked as secretary in the house of Sheikh al-Bakri. We remained friends.

I knocked several times on the door. A pale face appeared; Hanna pulled me urgently inside. I followed him, repeating loudly 'O Protector!' to give the women warning I was coming. We sat down in a room near the entrance and he brought me a cup of water, which the Copts always take care to boil before drinking.

I reported all that I had seen, and proposed that we go out and take another look around. Hanna shook his head doubtfully. I persisted, and eventually he left the room to return wearing a black Coptic turban. Copts and Jews are not permitted to wear green, red or white turbans or to wear red or yellow shoes. They are also forbidden to ride horses or mules and must dismount from their donkeys when passing a mosque.

I asked him what was the matter, and he said he hadn't slept well because the children on the floor above had been running around all night in wooden clogs, banging pots and pans.

He asked me to wait at the door and opened it a crack. Outside we could hear shouts calling for the Jews and Christians to be killed. He turned pale and his big nose shook.

—Change your clothes, I told him.

—How?

—A different turban. Put on a white one and wear yellow shoes.

—But they'll find me out . . .

—Don't worry. It's the French who rule now and they're the same religion as you.

He went back in and returned wearing a white turban. We left the house. I saw that he headed, without thinking, to the left side of the street, as the Copts did, since they were required to cede the right side of the street to the Muslims. Taking his arm, I pulled him over to the right and we went out amidst the cries of the donkey drivers.

—Let's go see Bakri, he said. I'm worried about him.

—No harm will come to him, I replied. Nothing ever happens to those sheikhs.

—I'm afraid for Zaynab.

—Zaynab *who*? I was speechless.

He bowed his head.

—Bakri's daughter, he said.

—Oh no! Tell me what's happened.

—In the beginning I didn't see her or even hear her voice. I stayed and worked in the room assigned to me, just directly below the women's quarters. At first, the governess would give me Zaynab's orders, but then I was allowed to go to the room adjacent to hers, and she began to give me orders directly, through the open door between the two rooms. That's how I heard her voice.

—Did you see her?

—She hardly ever came out, but when she did she wore a wrap that covered her head and hung down to the ground. And a veil that showed only her eyes. One time she came out of her room all of a sudden, and her face was uncovered. I tell you, her face was like the full moon, framed by two braids of hair and a jewelled diadem. She was wearing a fine silk robe, open at the neck, and over it a long-sleeved velvet gown, pulled tight over her waist with an expensive Damascene belt of silk. She wore earrings, each with two large gems. I haven't been able to sleep since that moment.

—That's all?

—I kept seeing her uncovered. She would pass in front of my door without a headscarf.

—Do you know how old she is?

—Sixteen, I think.

He wanted me to accompany him all the way to Bakri's house in Ezbekieh, but I thought it better to return home.

Friday, 27 July.

I did my ablutions and prepared to go out. The stench from the latrine was unbearable, and no amount of incense made any difference. I saw the black slave girl filling jugs from the well, since the water carriers who usually brought it had disappeared. I followed her while she emptied cups of boiling mastic into the jugs to flavour the water. She seemed unaware that I was watching her. I had been going to her every night since my teacher left. She would lie still beneath me, and not a single word would pass between us. I learnt that she was called Sakita, 'the silent one', because she never spoke.

Jaafar appeared, on the heels of a servant carrying a dish of spiced and seasoned fish, yelling as he reached the door, Tell the oven-keeper to send it with his boy at the call of the afternoon prayer!

I left the house and headed to the right, passing the caravanserai of the slave merchants. Their voices could be heard from behind the partially open door. I emerged onto the square facing the Azhar Mosque and entered through the Muzayyinin Gate, above which stood three of the mosque's five minarets. The highest was the two-pointed minaret of Qansuh al-Ghouri.

I took off my shoes and walked on the carpets, each decorated with a prayer-niche design. I crossed the new portico with its gilded roof, inscribed with verses from the Quran in Kufic script. I paused to contemplate the sundial, a gift from a governor who had been the student of Jabarti's father.

I joined those praying in the courtyard of the mosque. Their faces showed they were anxious to hear what the imam would say in his sermon. But in fact the imam said nothing about the French; it was a Friday sermon like any other. It closed with an invocation on behalf of the Ottoman Sultan and a collective 'Amen' from the crowd.

I left and made my way to Khan al-Khalili, where a crowd had gathered around some French soldiers. They were unarmed. Hesitantly, I approached. Their trousers were extremely tight-fitting, and their hats looked like rice baskets. Their hair, which hung down over their brows, was tied in a knot at the back of their heads.

People found them quite amusing. One of the soldiers wanted to buy a chicken, so I volunteered to help him, since I had learnt some of his language from the French merchant. But there was no need for my help, since one of them just took the bird and gave the seller a French *riyal*, that is, 100 *paras*. The actual price was not more than 20 *paras*, and just 10 *paras* covers a day's worth of meat and vegetables for one household. And it's the same sum that my teacher receives in one day for his teaching. The soldier tossed me a silver piece worth 40 *paras* which I quickly hid in my clothing.

At home, the servant Salih was complaining about his eye, so I sent Jaafar to buy some Indian liquorice seeds. We would grind them for a poultice to put on the inflamed eye.

Saturday, 28 July.

Jaafar burst into my room.

—The French are breaking into the emirs' houses, he said. Some of them they will occupy and live in, and the rest they are just looting. People are taking precautions—they're getting an official paper to stick on their doors.

Then he asked me to run and get one of these papers. I was about to suggest that he leave it to the Sheikh to deal with when he returned, when I realized this was a good opportunity for me to take another tour of the city. I quickly donned a shirt and leather slippers and asked the groom to get the donkey ready. Jaafar objected, saying that I did not have far to go.

The French had appointed Barthélemy as Lieutenant of the Janissaries, responsible for order and security in the city, and his men had posts everywhere. This Barthélemy was one of the lowest of the Greek Christians living in Cairo. Formerly, he had been one of Muhammad Bey al-Alfi's artillerymen and he had a shop in Muski where he sold glass bottles.

I left for al-Ghouriyya, where I found one of the posts Jaafar had spoken of. When I explained what I wanted, the soldier told me gruffly that the proprietor had to come himself and bring proof of ownership.

Along then to al-Fahhamin, named for the coal merchants. I stopped to look at a group of Frenchmen riding donkeys. They were roaring with delight. Among them was a beautiful young blonde girl. I followed them until they halted in front of a house, where they left their mounts with the donkey drivers. They entered the house.

Through the open door I could see the Frenchmen seated on chairs around what looked like raised wooden benches. An attendant was serving them plates of food. I asked one of the donkey drivers whose house it was, and he told me it was a place for eating. One of the Franks living in Egypt had opened it; he prepared different types of food that French people liked. He would buy sheep, chickens, vegetables, fish, honey, sugar and whatever else he needed, and served his dishes to whomever, for a few dirhams.

I walked on, feeling hungry. I stopped before a shop selling cakes and pastries and fried cheese and roasted meats. For 1 *para*, I bought three boiled eggs. A week ago you could get five.

Tuesday, 31 July.

My teacher returned from Ibar bringing cases of fruits: grapes, figs, peaches. The whole household was excited: fruits were rare and expensive. To mark the occasion, dinner was a large pot of ragout and rice with saffron, raisins, peas and onions. We finished with chilled melon.

After the evening prayer, we gathered in the meeting room, joined by Khalil. My teacher first sent to the chemist for some electuary, then he explained to us that the French had set up a council, the Diwan, and invited him to attend their meetings. He asked me to tell him what had occurred during his absence.

I told him about the papers he had to obtain, and then I described Bonaparte's procession and how he moved into Alfi's house. My teacher shook his head sadly. He liked the Mamluk, whom he described as a great leader.

—Do you know his story? Some merchants from Anatolia brought him here twenty years ago and Murad Bey bought him for five thousand bushels of grain. That is why he named him Alfi: 'the Thousand'. He was handsome and Murad Bey was very fond of him, so he freed him and made him governor of Sharqiyya province. Alfi ruled like a tyrant, ruthless with the Bedouins, seizing whatever they had. Then he was four years in Upper Egypt, and came back after the plague, more level-headed, more sensible. He read books on history and the sciences. He kept buying Mamluks until he had about a thousand, and then started to marry them off to his slave girls. He gave them superb trousseaux, lodged them in spacious houses and gave them payments and positions of rank.

Something had changed in my teacher. Since his own teacher, Sheikh Murtada al-Zabidi, died of the plague four years ago, he had stopped writing his biographies of learned men. He clearly was losing motivation and interest. It sufficed him simply to record events and incidents on scattered pages. I had thought that his passion had left him, but now he seemed full of vigour again.

Khalil asked if he might be excused. My teacher inquired if he had read the book he'd been given, *The Correct Path in the Public Bath*, and when Khalil replied in the negative, he narrated this story: One wise man visited the house of another wise man who lived alone. How can you bear the solitude, asked the first man.

What solitude, answered the other. Many great scholars and writers keep me company; they speak to me and I speak to them. Putting his hand on a stack of books, he went on. This is Galen lecturing, and here is Hippocrates debating, Socrates preaching, and Plato listening, and here is Daoud of Antioch.

He sighed. It tortured him that Khalil did not like to read.

—Did you hear about Sheikh Yusuf al-Maghribi, he asked, who passed away more than a hundred years ago? He was a tradesman before he became a scholar. He used to make scabbards when he was young, but he would also recite the Noble Quran from dusk to night in the mosque of Ibn Tulun. One of his uncles forbade him from doing so, saying, we don't have any scholars in our family—whom are you going to follow? So he recited in secret till he left the scabbard business and a group of people helped him to devote himself to learning. They allowed him to sit in a cloth merchant's shop, and sell the wares, so that he could buy books and read them, and then join the classes at Azhar.

When Khalil departed, my teacher asked me what was going on amongst the people. I told him they were afraid. Every day the French would cut off the heads of five or six people in the street. Merchants of a certain type had opened shops right next to where they lived, and were selling different types of food. The Greek Christians opened taverns and coffee houses. There were also rumours, I told him, of battles between Mamluks and the French at al-Qubba, al-Matariyya, al-Khanka and Abu Zaabal.

He pushed the sleeves of his robe up almost to the armpits and asked for the inkwell, plume and paper. He sat cross-legged, bent over the paper resting on his thigh, and began to write. When he finished one page, he put it aside and took another.

Finding the inkwell dry, he sent a servant to the ink sellers in Husseiniyya to buy some. My curiosity got the better of me and I asked what he was writing. Brushing a mosquito from his face, he said, What you told me just now. I will write about the French in Egypt. I can feel that these are going to be momentous events.

We heard a knock at the outer door. He hurriedly gathered up the papers and hid them beneath a cushion. I stood up, also uneasy.

Jaafar appeared at the door. Behind him was Sheikh al-Mahdi, the one who rendered Bonaparte's proclamations into Arabic. He removed his sandals and left his cane by the door. My teacher greeted him and cleared a place for his guest. Mahdi wore a large turban wrapped around a tall felt cap that stuck out at the top. A sable fur was wrapped around his neck, its ends hanging down over his shoulders.

He removed the turban and the fur and tossed them on the sofa, complaining about the heat and wiping his head with the sleeve of his kaftan. A servant brought a cup of rosewater, then placed before him a tray of dried fruits from Turkey, sent before the arrival of the French.

Sheikh Mahdi had attended the meeting of the Diwan two days ago at the house of Qaid Agha the relative of al-Ruwaie. The French were present along with a number of sheikhs, among them Abdallah al-Sharqawi, Khalil al-Bakri, Suleiman al-Fayyoumi, al-Sawi and al-Sirsi.

—And what did they do?

—The French demanded a loan of 500,000 *riyals* from the merchants, but they've also set a number of conditions that are just ways of taking more money.

He counted on his fingers as he went on.

—All property owners must produce deeds or proof of ownership, whether purchased or inherited. But this is not enough. If they can show ownership, they must further prove it by finding a record of it in the archives of the property registers. And for this they pay a certain fee. If the landowner's title-deed is found in the register, then he has to provide legal 'confirmation'. Which means he has to pay again for someone to attest to the validity of the 'confirmation'. And when this confirmation is accepted, he receives an official document of possession. Then they assess the value of the property, and he has to pay two per cent. But if the owner cannot produce a title or if his has not been registered, or if its registration has not been confirmed, then his property is seized by the Diwan of the Republic.

—We get through one ordeal and fall into something worse, said Jabarti. Do you remember when the Turks imposed a tax for land protection? Ten *paras* for each acre, and everyone who owned something had to write an application and bring it to the Finance Registry, where they would sign it. Then you had to take it to the clerk for tax-exempt lands who verified it in the registry for the appropriate region and, for a few more dirhams, gave you another signature. Then back to the finance registry for yet another signature, which you took to the treasury clerk, who asked for the deeds and certificates confirming rights of usufruct to the land and how you came to possess them . . . And if all went smoothly, he would write something in Turkish confirming it all. And if not, he pestered and harassed you, and forced you to confirm every little thing in the deeds, and you would have to neglect your own work. It was impossible. It was exhausting. People would go into debt, or have to sell their clothes.

After Sheikh Mahdi left, I asked Jabarti if he was going to attend the meetings of the Diwan. He thought for a moment, stroking his beard.

—There's nothing to lose, he said. It will be a good opportunity to learn about things at the source.

Chapter Two

Friday, 17 August.

My teacher woke me at dawn for the celebration of the flooding of the Blessed Nile. We prayed and ate breakfast. He took his mule while I rode a donkey. At the Azhar Mosque, we met water carriers wearing their usual leather vests and high boots.

We headed south through lanes and alleys until we reached the street that runs along the canal, leading from Bab al-Shaariyya to Qanatir al-Sibaa.

We came across a procession of soldiers and pedestrians led by a giant man with bronze skin, bulging eyes and hollow cheeks. He wore boots, a large white turban and a black band wrapped around his forehead. A long dagger hung from the red belt over his brocaded tunic. His servants brandished their silver lances. It was Barthélemy; he had been put in charge of the police.

We slowed to let the procession pass, then joined the crowd all the way to where the canal empties into the Nile, just south of Qasr al-Aini.

Bonaparte was at the front, in the company of the rest of the leaders and members of the Diwan. To the rear were the soldiers with their drums and pipes. Crowds packed the water's edge where eucalyptus and willow trees afforded some shade. I noticed that most of those present were Syrian Christians, Copts, Greeks and some local Franks, accompanied by their wives. Normally, many more people would be out enjoying themselves, but today only a few idlers could be seen.

We could make out a platform with a canopy. The drums and cymbals began to beat and to great applause Bonaparte strode up to the dais, accompanied by generals and the Pasha's representative and the Agha, the chief of the Janissaries. When I saw what he was wearing, I could not believe my eyes: a Damascene kaftan and a turban with a goose feather planted in it.

He took his place on a gilded pavilion overhanging the swollen river. Someone was leaning over to measure the water level. All kept silent until he announced the level, then the crowd clapped and the signal was given for the barrier holding back the water to be smashed open. The pickaxes swung hard at work. When the barrier burst, the water gushed through the canal and began to fill the ponds and pools of Cairo and onwards to irrigate the Qalyubiyya and Sharqiyya districts to the north. Women's voices trilled with joy; artillery fire reverberated. Men and boys jumped in the canal while the women threw locks of hair and bits of clothing into the water.

Hundreds of boats were arriving from Bulaq; there was a prize for those who came first. Bonaparte himself awarded the prize to the winners. And began to hand out gifts even as the crowd fought over for them. He appeared to be sending out greetings with his palms, while leaning forward in a funny manner. He then presented the Sheikh Khalil al-Bakri a fur-lined cloak and made him head of the shareefs, the descendants of the Prophet Muhammad, in place of Umar Makram, who had fled the city. Finally, he gave the signal to depart.

My teacher turned his mule towards home. I sought permission to visit my friend Abd al-Zaher, who lives near Qanatir al-Sibaa and took off on my donkey, making my way between rows of dilapidated houses. Foul odours emanated from them. There were shops that looked more like stables, and men dressed in rags crowded the alleys or sat in front of their houses or shops smoking pipes. Blind beggars. A few hideous women concealed their emaciated faces behind evil-smelling rags, drooping breasts showing from beneath their filthy cloaks. Flies crawled on the faces of jaundiced children.

It was a neighbourhood of large courtyards, where peasants and their animals cram together in small shacks. I entered a courtyard where dirty children played around an open latrine. A youth was bent over, resting his head on the lap of the barber cutting his hair. I tied up the donkey at the entrance and went to the shack where Abd al-Zaher lives with his blind mother. They pay 10 *para*s a month in rent.

We had been in Quran-school together, and together we left Upper Egypt, fleeing the plague. He had to work in a fabric warehouse in order to support his mother. But we stayed friends and saw each other often in the company of Hanna.

He is my age, but darker and skinnier. He greeted me and we sat on a stone bench in the courtyard. His mother recognized my voice and called out a greeting from inside. She summoned him, and he returned with a plate of dates and a cup of curdled milk.

I asked him his news and he complained that they barely had enough to survive. The patron of the storehouse had reduced his wages on the pretext that he had to pay higher taxes now to the French. It had been months since they tasted meat.

All of a sudden, terrified screams rang out and the children disappeared into the shacks, shutting the doors behind them. The barber pushed his client away, waving his razor in the air.

A patrol of French soldiers appeared at the courtyard entrance. They moved on; the children rushed back out, the young man returned to the barber.

The French go up and down the lanes and alleys to harass the women, said Abd al-Zaher.

—But we're ready for them, he added with determination.

I recited a verse from the Quran: *and We never destroyed the cities, except those whose inhabitants were evildoers.*

—You forget the first part of the verse, he said. *Yet thy Lord never destroyed the cities without having sent in their midst a Messenger, to recite Our signs unto them.*

—But no one has come yet. Anyway, overall we're better off than we were under the Turks and the Mamluks.

—Are you mad? They were Muslims, not Christians.

—I heard from my teacher that the French aren't really Christians. They're materialists.

—O Master, he asked mockingly, and who are these materialists?

—They deny the Resurrection and the Hereafter and the Prophets, and they claim the world is eternal and that all cosmic events are caused by circular movements. They believe that reason is the best judge and that Muhammad, Jesus and Moses were all wise men and that the laws they brought were their own creations, only intended for the times they were living in.

—So they are unbelievers, and we must fight them.

—And how are we going to do that?

He didn't answer, but I had the feeling that there was something he wasn't telling me.

Our conversation turned to Hanna. Abd al-Zaher said that the Copts were benefitting from the presence of the French. Their Master Yacoub had gone as a guide with their army to Upper Egypt.

I defended Hanna, saying he had nothing to do with such things, and that Sheikh Bakri still trusted him. He invited me to eat with him, but I excused myself and left to join the Friday prayer.

Friday, 17 August. Evening.

My teacher lay on the low couch; I sat cross-legged at his feet. I read back to him the day's lesson, from Sheikh al-Nafrawi's *Responses to the Five Questions of Sheikh Ahmad al-Damanhouri*. I was moving my head right and left as I read, as usual, and he would interrupt me to ask about what I had understood, or to explain something I had not grasped. We finished with the first and second questions, concerning the refutation of atomism, and Avicenna's claim that God's essence is the same as absolute existence. We stopped at the third question, Abu Mansour al-Maturidi's claim that knowing God is a rational obligation, in spite of the fact that it is impossible to grasp what is in every respect unknowable.

—That is enough for today, said the Sheikh. Let us have our dinner here this evening.

It was his custom to have dinner in his bedroom on the upper floor. Khalil joined us, and the servant brought a tray with two plates of lentils and onions.

The Sheikh smiled.

—Do you know what Sheikh al-Anbuti al-Shafii said—may God have mercy on him?

Lentils and onions are not eaten late
Should you want to keep your thoughts straight.

Anbuti's verse did not stop us devouring the food with our wooden spoons. After we had washed, Jabarti took out his papers and began to write. I told him about the French patrol and what Abd al-Zaher had said about it, but I kept the rest of our conversation to myself. I set a leaf of paper on my thigh and dipped my pen in the inkwell. And set down the rest of the conversation and described the celebration of the flooding of the Nile.

He turned to me with a scowl.

—What are you doing?

—Writing down the details of the celebration.

—Why? I've already done so.

—I thought I'd follow your example.

He remained silent, but was clearly disturbed. After I finished writing, I returned the quill and inkwell to their place. Waving the paper to dry the ink, I withdrew to my room.

Lying on the bedding, I considered his reaction. I tossed and turned and longed to go to the black slave girl but with my teacher in the house, I did not dare.

Thursday, 23 August.

My days are spent between the bed and the latrine. I have dysentery—as I do every year when the flooding season arrives. As a remedy, I consume large quantities of broth of Indian roots, gum arabic and pomegranate.

Saturday, 1 September.

Jabarti returned from a meeting of the Diwan. He was angry. He and others had asked permission to continue managing the lands for which they held concessions. But the French said that they had to pay an extra fee. The sheikh held a concession to land in his village of Abyar, for which he paid a fixed sum and was entitled to take what profits he saw fit.

I followed him to the private meeting room where he took off his shoes and his fur cloak, sighing indignantly. He told me that Bonaparte had brought a shawl in the colours of the French flag and draped it over the shoulder of Sheikh Sharqawi, whose mood suddenly changed. He turned pale and angry, and threw it to the floor. Then Nicola Turk recited an ode in Arabic praising the French leader. Jabarti was quiet for a moment, then intoned in a mocking voice one of its verses, comparing Bonaparte to a noble lion of war who vanquished all the Mamluks and could accomplish anything.

—On our way out we ran into Sheikh Sadat, coming over to meet Bonaparte. I don't think *he* would refuse the French shawl, Jabarti added.

After the midday nap, I went to Fathi's coffee house, near the mausoleum of Hussein. Some protégé of the French owns it. There are wooden tables and chairs instead of stone benches and seats. People gather there to talk and tell stories, play games. Sometimes the French are there as well.

Hanna and Abd al-Zaher joined me. The French had taken Bani Suef in Upper Egypt, Hanna informed us. He was sad and gloomy. Abd al-Zaher asked him mockingly about Zaynab. He groused that the girl had lost all her virtue; she went out every day with her face uncovered. He fell silent for a moment, then told us what had happened.

—I spied on her one time in her room. Her face was uncovered, her waistcoat was open at the front and I could see her shirt. She had a cotton cap on her head with a string of pearls around it. Her hair was braided with silk tresses. She was holding a mirror and using a razor to trim her eyebrows and make them into two thin lines above the eyelid. Then, I realized that she was speaking to her father, and I saw her stretch out her foot towards him. She was wearing ankle bracelets. He bent forward and kissed it! She pushed him away with her foot and he fell!

We gaped at him in surprise. He said it wasn't so strange, the man was known for his shamelessness. Every night he drank the 'Burgundy' wine mixed with brandy. And he was the same with boys and girls.

Abd al-Zaher looked horrified.

—Infidels, both of them.

A French captain entered the coffee house in the company of a woman, a local degenerate. Abd al-Zaher glared at her.

—She and her kind deserve to be killed.

—Come with me to see Zaynab, said Hanna. She goes out about this time.

Heading towards Muski, we crossed the bridge and made our way past the shops dealing in European goods: baize, paper, rugs, handkerchiefs, tobacco, soap, dried figs, knives, razor blades, shawls, glass cups, sugar, wall clocks, gold watches and pins. Past the turn leading to the Jewish quarter, we arrived in Ataba, then towards Mushtahar Street and left by the Kikhiyya Mosque. A crowd of people blocked our way. Two donkeys had collided. The riders were French. This happened all the time because they always drove their donkeys much too fast

I noticed that many shops had put up signs in French. The tax collector sat in front of one of them. He was dressed like a Mamluk: billowing long pants tight above the heel, a turban atop his felt qawuq hat, a dagger in his belt. From his long outer robe hung the traditional curved sword. A French soldier was with him, carrying a notebook with the merchants' names and statements of the taxes demanded of them. There was a scribe, too, wearing a big turban and a copper inkwell in his belt.

A few more turns later, we entered the alley of Abd al-Haqq towards the house of Ali Bey Kabir which he had built on the Ezbekieh Lake for Khatun, his concubine, who later married Murad Bey. Bakri's house was next to it, overlooking the lake.

A large crowd had gathered: schoolchildren, jurists, the blind, muezzins, jurists and pensioners. They were protesting against the cuts to their salaries and bread rations since responsibility for the Muslim charitable endowments had passed into the hands of the Coptic and Syrian Christians who were treating it like their own private reserve.

Eventually a small delegation of protestors came out of the house and the crowd began to disperse.

We stood at a safe distance and waited. As the sun set, a grand carriage pulled by two horses entered the alley. Two soldiers with ostrich feathers in their hats sat in the front.

—That's the carriage of the Commander-in-chief, we all said at once. Only Bonaparte rides in it.

A girl came out of Bakri's house. She wore a long loose-fitting garment and a shawl over her head. A muslin veil covered all but her eyes. One of the soldiers stepped down to open the door for her. The coach turned around as it was a dead end, then passed right in front of us. Hanna hid behind us so as not to be seen. The carriage window was still open and I caught a glimpse of the girl taking off her face-veil, revealing a face of stunning beauty.

We followed the carriage for a distance and saw it come to a halt in front of Bonaparte's residence. Hanna was on the verge of tears, but Abd al-Zaher rebuked him.

—What's the point? You're a Copt and she's a Muslim.

—These things don't matter if you're in love, said Hanna defensively.

—She's an unbeliever and deserves to be stoned to death.

Thursday, 6 September.

Sheikh Sawi arrived in the early morning, in the company of another sheikh whom I did not know. They met with my teacher in the private room. I loitered by the door and could hear Sheikh Sawi saying that the French have given Muhammad Kurayyim until noon to pay 30,000 *riyals* or be executed.

Sheikh Kurayyim used to work as a qabbani, one who weighs goods for the public. He later became deputy to Murad Bey who put him in charge of the Diwan and the customs house of Alexandria. When the French fleet appeared, he began to reinforce the city's defences and formed an army of citizens to ward off the attackers. Eventually Kurayyim occupied the citadel of Qait Bey and fought the French until he realized it was futile and surrendered. Bonaparte treated him with respect and had him stay on as ruler of the city.

But he had continued to incite resistance, covertly, against the French and when they demanded a mandatory loan from the merchants of Alexandria, he made only the feeblest efforts to collect it. So they arrested him. When they brought him to Cairo, they found in Murad Bey's house a letter outlining Kurayyim's plans for opposing the French. He was imprisoned.

Sheikh Sawi recounted that in the morning Kurayyim had written to the sheikhs and to al-Mahrouqi, chief of the merchants. Some of them went to see him and he pleaded with them: 'O Muslims! Ransom my life!'

Jabarti was unmoved.

—Things are slow, as you know, he said. I can't even manage my own concession at Abyar, and I'm not able to collect from the farmers!

The two sheikhs gestured in agreement, and departed. Jabarti called for me to bring him papers, quill and inkwell. He was scowling, clearly disturbed. Wrote a little bit, then stood up and started pacing about the room, tugging at his beard. Towards midday, he asked me to go to Rumayla to find out what was going on.

I rode my donkey down the Palace Walk, south to Bab Zuweila and al-Darb al-Ahmar and on until the minaret of the Sultan Hasan Mosque came into view. I turned left and came to the mosque in Rumayla Square, below the Citadel.

At the square is the Souk al-Asr, known for livestock, grains and vegetables. I rode past the street vendors selling tobacco and sugar cane, past the monkey trainers. I stopped at the edge of the square by a small mosque on the corner of the street leading to Sayyida Zaynab. There I dismounted, tethered the donkey to a post and was sitting there when two men in traditional garb approached, looked at me suspiciously, then continued on their way. I followed them with my eyes. They were looking carefully at all the passers-by. I noticed that they never left the square, just kept circling around. They were Barthélemy's men.

The call for midday prayer sounded. I kept my eye on the Citadel Gate known as Bab al-Azab, fortified by two enormous towers decorated with white and red flags. The gate was closed; a number of French guards stood in front. I was feeling bored and had decided to leave when the Citadel Gate opened and out came a number of French soldiers with their swords drawn. A drummer followed behind them. Soon after appeared a bareheaded man on a donkey—it was Muhammad Kurayyim.

The soldiers marched towards the square to the beat of the drum. I followed on my donkey at a distance. They dragged Sheikh

Kurayyim down Saliba Street and bound his hands behind his back. The soldiers then shot him, cut off his head and, raising it high on a quarterstaff, paraded all through Rumayla, the crier calling out: This what happens to those who oppose the French!

I returned home, shaken. And narrated to my teacher all that I had witnessed. He didn't say a word.

Tuesday, 11 September.

Jabarti was giving his lesson at the Azhar Mosque, so I went up to the meeting room and shut the door behind me. The servants had finished cleaning the room. Khalil was at the caravanserai of his mother, and Jaafar had gone to the souk. I was in no danger of being disturbed.

I looked for the papers on which my teacher wrote his chronicles of the days' events. No trace of them below the couch, under the pillows or in their padding. I opened the bookcase and rummaged around, but it was futile. I searched the rest of the couches and cushions, underneath the carpets and behind the astrolabe.

He would not usually carry anything outside of the room, so his papers had to be here somewhere. Since he feared a surprise visit from the French, he must have hid them close by. I checked the bookcase again and noticed that one of its sides was thicker than the others. I removed the books on that side and inspected the case. When I pushed the edge, it moved a little. I managed to slide it upwards, revealing a space containing a bunch of papers.

I pulled out the leaves and flipped through them. They were arranged by date and began with a short introduction that concluded with the Quranic verse: *Yet thy Lord never destroyed the cities unjustly, as long as its people were righteous*. This was followed by an account of events since the arrival of the English at the port of

Alexandria just before the coming of the French. Then he recorded what happened after that.

I was about to put the papers back in their place when something caught my eye. I looked for the paper on which were recorded the events of 20 *Rabii al-Awwal* according to the Islamic calendar—which corresponded to the 1st of September. I looked at what followed and I saw that he had written nothing about the execution of Muhammad Kurayyim.

I was astonished. Did he forget? I flipped through the following pages, but there was no trace of the event. Sometimes, if something escaped him, he noted it in later pages. I was pleased with myself because I had recorded all the details in my account. I praised God and decided not to utter a word to him about it, so as not to reveal that I had been looking through his papers.

I placed the papers back in the space as I had found them, pulled down the wooden slat and closed the bookcase. I left the room giddy with the knowledge that I had recorded something my teacher had missed.

Friday, 14 September.

Khalil finished having his head shaved, and went to bathe. I took his place on the stone seat in the courtyard, the barber stood behind me. He began cutting my hair with his scissors. My eyes passed over the servants waiting their turn. It suddenly occurred to me that I had not seen the black slave girl for some days.

The barber wanted to leave the sprouting hair on my face so my beard could grow, but I said no, take it all off. It was Jaafar's turn next. Back in my room, I took out some clean clothes and wrapped them in paper.

I left the quarter and after a few steps ducked into an alley towards the Sanadiqiyya bathhouse. Inside, I handed the clothes to the servants who welcomed me. One of them handed me a towel that I wrapped around myself, and followed him down a corridor. I could feel the heat as I approached the second room.

Clouds of perfumed steam enveloped me as I entered and laid down on a piece of woollen cloth. A giant man, naked from the waist up, appeared and bent over me. He cracked my joints, and began to rub my body with a woollen glove. It felt like I was being skinned alive. Strips of dirt, grime and dead skin fell from my body.

Doused in sweat, I walked into the adjacent room, where he poured perfumed soapsuds over my head and left. There were two faucets in the room, one for warm water and the other for cold. I washed myself first and then entered a tub filled with steaming water. From there into the tub of cold water. I dried myself, put on a shirt and returned to the first room to sit on a mattress spread over the stone bed. A servant brought me a water pipe and a cup of coffee.

Next to me was a bald sheikh with a long beard. He was talking in a low voice to his grossly obese companion.

I eavesdropped on their conversation as the bald sheikh was enumerating the number of taxes imposed by the French: death taxes; inheritance taxes; income tax and property tax; taxes on gifts and on profits; taxes on lawsuits; civil actions and witnesses.

—You can't even travel without paying for a travel document. There's even a tax on being born—you have to pay for a 'birth certificate'! And on tenants and on rents and so on. Which is to say, on everything!

Another honourable sheikh chimed in with the news that the English and the Turks had reached Alexandria and destroyed the French fleet. The fat one looked me over, and I could hear him saying that the French would certainly cut off the tongue of anyone who repeated such news or even mentioned it.

—Have you heard the story of the Sultan's messenger, the third one asked, laughing. A Turkish commander was visiting Cairo, having come down from Alexandria, and was walking down the street towards the shrine of Hussein. The people were surprised by his appearance, said he must be an envoy sent by the Sultan to order the French out of Egypt. Meanwhile, Bonaparte hears that one of the sheikhs has a letter from the Sultan. So he rides out right away with his horses and his troops and goes to the house of Sheikh Sadat. And he passes by the Hussein Mosque and sees people crowding everywhere, inside and out. Seeing Bonaparte, they start reciting the Fatiha, the first sura of the Quran, all together, and of course by this they meant to call for the Turks to come and for the French to leave. Bonaparte is confused at this sight and wants to know what's going on. His dragomen of course don't know what's going on in the mosque and don't want to anger him, so they simply say: The people here are praying for you. Bonaparte believes them and goes on his way.

The men laughed, but then the sheikh noticed my presence and stopped talking, giving his companions a meaningful look. It wasn't long before they changed the topic of conversation and spoke of Sheikh Mahrouqi, chief of the merchants, who had amassed his wealth importing and exporting goods. Some Bedouins had accompanied him for protection on his return from the Hajj. They betrayed him midway, plundered his cargo and took possession of everything he was bringing back from the Hijaz and all he had with him. Mahrouqi lost about 300,000 French *riyals*.

—God's vengeance is terrible, said another. Mahrouqi worked in silks, and when the plague came he took over his partner's house, his wives, his business. Then he served Murad Bey and Ibrahim Bey and became even more rich.

I left the room and found my clothes had been scented with myrrh. The servant sprinkled perfumed foam over me. I paid 10 *paras*, consoled that Jabarti pays thirty at his bathhouse.

Wednesday, 26 September.

For the past four days the French have been having their celebration. They erected a large pole in the middle of Ezbekieh. The common people say it's a stake they're going to impale us on. They fire many cannons and gather around the pole. In the evening, they set off fireworks, flares and pinwheels, along with more cannon fire.

Today, in the morning, there was a violent knocking on the outer gate. I hurried out but Jaafar was already at the door. Before us stood a French soldier accompanied by two watchmen and a Syrian Christian woman, her head uncovered. Jaafar told them that Sheikh Jabarti was at the Azhar Mosque. They asked for the names of all the occupants as one of the watchmen listed them in a large account book. Then he ordered us not to house any foreigners, to put a lamp at the gate, and to commit to sweeping the street and spraying water to keep it clean. We were ordered not to bury the dead in graveyards near residential areas, like the cemeteries of Ezbekieh or Ruwaii. Only those further away in Bab al-Luq, Arab al-Yasar, Khalifa and elsewhere were permitted.

I told the watchman that that this was a lot of orders and it would be difficult to remember them all. He stared at me and said: I haven't finished. He ordered us not to ask or talk about matters of state which do not concern us. We should refrain from mocking or applauding wounded or vanquished French soldiers when we see them, as was the custom.

—Is that everything, I asked.

—You must spread all clothes, belongings and bedding on the roofs for fifteen days and fumigate all the rooms with incense. These are preventative measures against the plague.

—The bedding is already laid out in the sun, said Jaafar.

—We must make sure of that, said the watchman.

We protested that they couldn't possibly enter the women's quarters.

—That's why we've brought her along.

The woman entered and went up to the roof. When she returned, they noted everything down and posted a sheet of paper on the outer door.

Saturday, 6 October.

Jabarti returned from the meeting of the Diwan, saying *Non, non*!, sarcastically. Jaafar hurried to him with his coffee and water. The sheikh told me how the interpreter had asked them to choose someone as chief. Some we choose Sheikh Sharqawi. But the chief said, *Non, non*, you have to do it by ballot. So we wrote down names on ballots, and most of them were for Sharqawi anyway.

Jabarti was scowling.

— They chose well, I said. He's a brave man.

—What do you know about Sharqawi, he asked.

I told him I remembered how, about three years ago, some villagers of Bilbeis came to him to complain that Muhammad Bey Alfi's men were demanding exorbitant protection money. Sharqawi gathered the other sheikhs and had them tell the people to shut their shops and follow him first to Sheikh Sadat's house, then to the Azhar Mosque. It was a huge crowd. The next day, the Turkish governor brought the Mamluk emirs together, along with Sharqawi and others. Eventually, the emirs were forced to accept their demands and distribute the grains they had been withholding, and abolish the unjust taxes.

—He seems like a brave man to have done that, I added.

—Don't be so sure. He owns land in the village that was affected, he was just defending his own interests. I'll tell you the story of Sheikh Sharqawi.

And Jabarti told me how Sharqawi was born in that same village in Bilbeis. His family was poor. After he learnt the Quran at the village school, he went to Cairo to continue his education at the Azhar. He somehow eked out a living near the mosque, with all the other student boarders. He had to work as well as study. Under the guidance of Sheikh Kurdi, he joined a Sufi order. Living in poverty, he couldn't cook where he lived, but friends would send him food or invite him to eat with them. Slowly he gained in reputation. Syrian merchants and others would give him alms or gifts such that his situation improved and he began to wear better clothes. He had a group of students who were always with him. He began to attend funerals with them, reciting the Quran and chanting religious invocations, which earned him a few dirhams and the occasional invitations to dinner.

Jabarti drank the last of his coffee.

—After he was initiated into the Khalwatiyya Sufi order, something happened and he went mad. He spent days in the hospital for the insane. Once cured, he devoted himself to his lessons and to writing about theology and the histories of governors and sultans. With the help of some well-to-do friends, he managed to buy a house and became a property-owner. When he took up his position as a sheikh of Azhar, the first thing he wanted to do was to make up for his days of poverty by showing how powerful he was. In other words, he became even more swollen-headed. His turban got so big it became a joke. When the French arrived, he made sure to get close to them, and that is why they appointed him chief of the Diwan of Court Cases. He receives a salary, and he gets to keep all the belongings and deposits left by those who have died or fled. He even took over the Khan of Khound Tughay. He's built a mosque and a mausoleum there for himself, and right next to it a palace. His wife bought all sorts of properties and land and bathhouses and shops.

I was amazed.

—So how could he become a sheikh of Azhar, then?

—God has afflicted the Azhar with evil people who wear wide sleeves and big turbans so that people will think they are scholars. They carry a few religious books around wherever they go, hoping that someone will give them some money.

Sunday, 7 October.

The members of the Diwan asked Bonaparte to issue a decree allocating them 2,700 *paras* per month. The request was made in the name of all the thirty-three sheikhs.

Chapter Three

Monday, 15 October.

Decrees are posted at crossroads and on the doors of the mosques. New taxes are being levied on property and land, on caravanserais and bathhouses, on mills and tahina presses and on shops. They have cut the payments from charitable endowment to the poor who deserve them. People are saying: This is too much.

Sunday, 21 October.

Jaafar came home, clearly disturbed. My teacher came out to see him, as did the other servants and children. The people are rising up, he told us. Sayyid Badr al-Maqdisi had come with gangs from the Husseiniyya and some crooks from the outlying neighbourhoods. They attacked some of the French guard posts and killed the soldiers. Gathered at the Azhar Mosque, they shouted: O Allah, make Islam victorious!

•

My teacher told me to go out and see what was happening. He did not venture out because of the increasing hostility towards the members of the Diwan.

I stopped by the gate of the Inal caravanserai, looking for the gatekeeper. Above the storage spaces were the residences and the rooms for travelling merchants from faraway places. Merchants, agents, brokers, moneychangers and weighers crowded around. I spotted the Nubian gatekeeper and called out to him. He was speaking with one of the merchants and ignored me. He would earn only 40 *para*s a month, but made a lot more from the merchants and agents.

Finally, he came over to me. I asked him for the news and he said that General Dupuy, the governor of Cairo, had passed through the Sanadiqiyya district this morning with a troop of horsemen, heading towards the house of the Turkish judge, Ibrahim Adham Effendi. A crowd confronted him, pelting him with dirt and rocks. Frightened, he tried to escape down the Palace Walk. But the crowd caught up. They beat and killed the general. They killed many of his horsemen as well.

After that, the crowd attacked the Gawwaniyya neighbourhood, and looted the homes of the Syrian and Greek Christians, and even the nearby Muslim houses. Likewise the fabric market at the gate to the Greek quarter, where all kinds of goods and items were deposited for safekeeping.

I headed towards the Palace Walk. At the Manakhiliyya alleyway, people had smashed the stone benches in front of the shops and made them into barricades. Large groups of people stood behind them. I weaved my way between the barricades and arrived at a spot where Maghribis from the Fahhamin district had gathered. Just then a group of French soldiers appeared and opened fire. I rushed home.

I told my teacher what I had seen and he went on to write it all down. Jaafar came in, saying the French had mounted cannons on the hills of Barqiyya and the Citadel. At afternoon prayer, we heard cannon fire and bombardments. They were deliberately targeting the Azhar Mosque and its surroundings, the Ghawriyya souk, Fahhamin and Sanadiqiyya. Firing from the Citadel followed. We heard a noise very near: a shell had hit the neighbouring house, destroying the walls.

Then word came that some sheikhs had gone to Bonaparte to ask him to stop the fighting and bombardments, and the Muslims would put down their weapons. He ordered the ceasefire and the sheikhs declared peace. When the people heard this, they rushed to spread the news. Everyone was relieved.

That night we were awoken by dogs barking and a knock at the door. It was the owner of the neighbouring bathhouse, standing there naked as the day he was born. We took him inside and clothed him. He said the French had stormed the city, sweeping through the empty streets and alleys, destroying the barricades. He had been at the Azhar Mosque when they rode in. They tied up their horses at the qiblah wall, smashed lamps and the bookcases of the students, tenants and scribes, then looted everything they could find: plates, bowls, all that was hidden and kept safe in the closets and armoires. They tossed the books and copies of the Quran on the floor and trod over them. They defecated, urinated, blew their noses, drank wine, then broke the bottles and threw them in the courtyard. If they came across anybody passing by, they tore his clothes off and threw him out naked in the street.

Tuesday, 23 October.

In the morning I walked towards the Azhar Mosque to see what was going on. French soldiers were lined up before the gate of the mosque known as Bab al-Muzayyinin. Anyone who arrived for the prayer and saw them standing there beat a hasty retreat.

Retracing my steps and walking away from our neighbourhood, I saw them spread all over the souk, standing in rows. I saw them search a passer-by and take everything he had. I slipped thought the neighbouring alleys to the Ghouri Mosque. A group of them was removing the bodies of the dead, both Muslims and Franks. They pushed the stones of the barricades to the side to clear the thoroughfares.

I saw Barthélemy leading a procession, pulling behind him men bound with ropes. Barthélemy's men whipped them as they moved along the street.

Back home I learnt that Jabarti had gone along with a group of sheikhs to Bonaparte's residence. They had presented their excuses to the French leader and made offers of security. Bonaparte asked them to identify those men of religion who had instigated the uprising of the common people; they asked him to order the soldiers to leave the Azhar Mosque, which he did.

Jabarti told me they summoned the leader of the blind men's guild, Sheikh Suleiman al-Gawsaqi, along with Sheikh Abd al-Wahhab al-Shubrawi, Sheikh Yusuf al-Musaylihi and Sheikh Ismail al-Barrawi, and locked them up in the house of al-Bakri. They could not find Sayyid Badr al-Maqdisi.

Thursday, 24 October.

Umar Qulluqji visited us this evening. He is the chief of the Maghribis of Fahhamin. My teacher asked me to attend the meeting and take note of what was said so that he could write it down later.

The chief is white-skinned and has trouble pronouncing the letter *r*. He told my teacher that the Maghribi youth took part in the attack on the French and that everyone fears the consequences of these actions. He is thinking of asking for a meeting with Bonaparte to seek a pardon, just like the merchants of al-Ghouri, accepting responsibility for any future sedition against the French.

Jabarti seemed to welcome this idea, saying that those who rebelled had paid no heed to the possible consequences. They did not grasp that they were already captives of the invaders. He criticized those who attacked the properties of the notables and destroyed scientific instruments in the houses of the French.

Friday, 26 October.

I went with Abd al-Zaher to Bab al-Saada to verify the news about the Maghribis. People were saying that Umar al-Qulluqji had gathered a good number of his people, and gone to see the Commander-in-Chief. He chose the young and the strong and armed them, and just like that, they became part of the French army, with Umar at their head.

Through an opening in the gate before Qulluqji's house, we could see a row of Maghribis holding rifles. A French officer was instructing them in their language: *Garde à vous*!, and they would raise their weapons, holding the rifle butts in the palms of their hands. *Marche*!, in a line, and so on.

They exited, a Syrian drum leading them, as is the custom of the Maghribi soldiers. I asked one of them where they were going.

—North, he said, to put down the revolt.

Monday, 5 November.

Early morning, Hanna arrived, looking very worried. In the middle of the night, French soldiers showed up at the house of al-Bakri and demanded the handover of all the sheikhs being held there since the revolt. They stripped each of their clothes and took them to the Citadel. In the morning they brought them out, shot them and flung the bodies over the Citadel walls. They were eighty in number, some of them women. Among them were Sheikh Ismail al-Barrawi, the Imam Sheikh Abd al-Wahhab al-Shubrawi al-Shafii and Sheikh Suleiman al-Gawsaqi, head of the blind men's guild.

The latter was a well-known and powerful man. He had amassed enormous wealth by buying grain at the lowest prices from those who held land concessions and insisting they deliver the goods to him themselves and in full. If any of them held out, he would send an army of blind men to harass them. Then they would have to hand over the grain or pay the price right away, anything to get rid of the veritable invasion of the blind.

From his agents in Upper Egypt, he received shipments of grain as well as butter, honey, sugar and oil, which he sold in Cairo at a high price. He had much of it ground into flour: he sold the finely ground part in the Jewish quarter, and the bran he used to make bread for the blind, who subsisted on this and what they earned from begging. When one of them died, the sheikh inherited whatever possessions they owned.

So powerful was he that none dared oppose him, until one day Sheikh al-Hifni became enraged with him and had him dragged through the streets, bare-headed and in chains. He was beaten with sandals about the head and neck all the way to his house in Muski, for everyone to see.

I asked my teacher what made a man of such a position join the riff-raff in the revolt. He looked down.

—You're right. He had everything. He wore the right clothes, the furs, he rode a mule and his people all looked at him admiringly, he married many beautiful, wealthy women, he bought all kinds of concubines, white, black, Ethiopian . . .

Jabarti pulled on his beard.

—Pride and arrogance made him go against the French.

Sunday, 11 November.

In the cities of Qalyubiyya, Giza, Buhayra, Damietta and Mansoura, the attacks on the French continued. The French retaliated by burning the attackers' villages. Meanwhile in Cairo they smashed and tore out the gates to side streets and alleyways that had no other exit. They carried the wood away in carts to where they were setting up barricades in other parts of the city. Some of it they sold as firewood. They carried away all the iron, too.

French soldiers went to put down the uprising at Suez. They seized the camels of the watercarriers, and so water is now in short supply, the price has gone up to 10 *paras* for one waterskin.

Today they put up notices in the streets and the markets. It was in the name of the sheikhs of the Diwan, and this is some of what it said:

> Counsel from the Men of Islam in Cairo: We inform the inhabitants of the city that disturbances have occurred because of hooligans and evil people who have caused malice between the subjects and the French soldiers, where previously they had been friends and companions . . . However, the strife has been put down thanks to our intercession with General Bonaparte. The tribulation has passed because he, Bonaparte, is a man of perfect wisdom. He has compassion and concern for the Muslims, and love for the poor and downtrodden. Were it not for Bonaparte, the soldiers would have burnt the whole city . . . Allah, may He be glorified and exalted, *gives His kingdom to whom He pleases* and *He ordains what He wishes* . . . Our advice to you is this: Do not bring ruin upon yourselves. Occupy

yourselves with your livelihoods and with your religion, and pay the tax that is incumbent upon you. 'Religion is sincere and honest conduct.'

Thursday, 15 November.

I discovered that Jabarti had abridged his version of the account of the sheikhs killed at the Citadel. He did not mention their names.

Sunday, 18 November.

I came back to the house, shivering from the cold, only to find that I could not open the door to my room. The key would not work. I called for Jaafar but he could not open it either.

We brought the locksmith, who wet the key with his spittle then jiggled it in the lock to try to move the teeth inside, but it was no use. Taking a pair of pliers, he removed the entire wooden lock and put in a new one.

After he left, I entered and shut the door behind me. I always kept my papers under the pillow, arranged according to date. I took them out and found the pages were all mixed up. Was Jaafar searching through my belongings? He doesn't know how to read, but he might have taken some pages to the sheikh. Or it could have been Khalil or the sheikh himself.

I stood on tiptoe next to the wall and scraped out the dust from a crack between two stones. I stuck the folded papers into the crack. Jaafar would be too short to reach it, but not the sheikh. Anyway, there wasn't room for many more papers.

Looking around the room, I could not see anywhere else to hide them. There was the chest containing my things and the clothing that the Sheikh lets me wear. I turned it over. There was a space of about three inches between its bottom and the floor—enough for my papers. I was about to put them there when I remembered that the servants might move the chest or pour water on the floor to sweep and clean.

I went out in the courtyard. No sign of anyone. I rummaged in the corners of the stable and found four nails. Taking a rock from a corner of the courtyard, I went back to my room and closed the door. I put two nails in each side of the bottom of the upturned chest, about an inch from the ground. I could then place the papers in-between the nails and the bottom of the chest. I gave it a good shake to make sure they would stay hidden, then I put the chest back in its place.

That night as I got ready to sleep, I imagined that the stack of papers grew and grew until it became a proper book, with my name on it.

Friday, 30 November.

Following the afternoon prayer, I accompanied Jabarti to Ezbekieh, where many people, Franks included, were gathering. The French had announced the launch of a vessel that could fly in the air, by means of some special technique. Passengers could travel through the air to faraway lands, they said, to discover new things and send back messages.

A very large piece of cloth, red, white and blue, had been rigged to an upright pole and placed on what looked like the rim of a sieve. A bowl containing a wick covered in grease hung from iron wires connecting to the rim. Men on nearby rooftops held the contraption tight with ropes and pulleys.

They lit the wick and smoke rose into the cloth which began to inflate. It looked like a big sphere rising up from the ground. Then they cut the ropes and up it flew, carried by the wind. It went along for a moment; then the bowl with the wick fell, and the whole thing collapsed to the ground.

When this happened, the French were very embarrassed. All they had said about carrying passengers and travelling to distant lands did not appear to be true. My teacher said disparagingly that it was just like one of those kites that the servants fly at feasts and festivals.

Saturday, 1 December.

Jabarti sent me to inspect the changes the French are making to the streets of the city. I found they had created a new road between Bab al-Hadid and Bab al-Adawi, where the pottery workshops are located. They had cleared and levelled a long straight path extending all the way to the abattoir outside Husseiniyya. All buildings, trees and hills in between had been razed. A road now stretched from Ezbekieh in a straight line to Qubbat al-Nasr.

Work is still going on in some places, and I noticed how they worked with tools that were easy to handle. Instead of palm baskets, they use small carts with two long wooden handles extending to the rear. The worker fills the cart with dirt or clay or stones—and it can hold as much as five baskets—then he grasps the handles and pushes forward. The cart moves on a wheel and the worker does very little. To empty it, he simply tips it over, with no great effort.

The men told me that this was not forced labour but that they received their regular pay, which was disbursed just after noon.

At Ezbekieh, I found that they had flattened the buildings opposite the Commander-in-Chief's residence to make a wide-open space, now filled with dirt evenly spread out all the way to the Maghribi Bridge near Bab al-Shaariyya. From there a smooth embankment extends in a perfectly straight line right through to

Bulaq. All along the way, they have dug trenches on either side, and planted trees and sesban shrubs.

Noticing some Franks going on foot towards Ghayt al-Nouby, I followed them. They stopped in front of the palace of one of the Beys, and entered after showing special papers or paying a few coins. The palace had a large garden with orange and lemon trees and lamps hanging from the branches. I could hear music from a military band coming from the garden.

Then officers began to arrive, with them women: Circassian, Georgian, African. And a number of magicians, singers, dancers, all of them locals. There were also eminent men from the Christians: Copts, Syrians and Greeks.

I looked on for a long time, wishing I could join them. Then I left.

Chapter Four

Sunday, 2 December.

I rode with Jabarti to the Nasriyya quarter. Before reaching al-Kumi Street, we turned off at al-Darb al-Jadid, and dismounted in front of the palace the French had allotted to scientists, scribes and bookkeepers. It was formerly the house of Qasim Bey who is now fighting the French in Upper Egypt.

We tied up our mule and donkey alongside numerous other mounts. A number of sheikhs from among the members of the Diwan were already there. I noticed Sheikh Sharqawi, in his splendid attire, his large, parted white beard, long nose and imposing round turban. There was Sheikh Mahdi with his smaller turban and darker beard. And Sheikh Bakri who wore a round, black turban, and al-Fayyoumi, who had wrapped a white brocaded cashmere shawl around his head.

The French welcomed us and took us inside. The director, Fourier, told us that the Committee of Arts and Sciences had 151 members living and working in the palace and adjacent houses.

We entered a magnificent house and found ourselves in an enormous chamber with high ceilings and walls lined with wooden bookcases. Beyond, in the garden, the paths were lined with trellises and places where one could sit and admire the pond, the water wheels, the fountains, the greenery. There were even latrines for one's needs. The garden itself is terraced, and water pumped to the top terrace by means of special pipes. My teacher told me that Qasim Bey used to let people wander around what he called his 'Garden of Botanical Tranquillity for the Seeker of Fortune and Sociability'.

The French have designated one area for studying animals and another for birds. A portion of the ground is set aside for agricultural experiments and another for an observatory. They also have a print shop, a room for a collection of artefacts and a workshop for making surgical instruments, compasses, telescopic and microscopic lenses, instruments for drawing and measuring distance, as well as dyes for the printer, sword blades and hats.

In the observatory we met the astronomer Nouet and his pupils who showed us sophisticated Western astronomical instruments and expensive, wondrous instruments for measuring height and elevation.

They have lenses and tubes through which you can look at objects, and that fold up and fit into a small case. There are also lenses to see the stars, and things to mount them on, different types of valuable time-pieces that can measure minutes and seconds, and many other things.

Then we proceeded to the house of Hasan Kashif Jirkas, who was of Greek origin. He had had it built and decorated with the vast sums of the money he had taken unjustly from the people. The

French remodelled it as a place to study medicine and pharmacy. There were marvellous instruments for extraction and distillation of liquids, and salts extracted from herbs and plants. All along the walls, shelves held bottles of different shapes and sizes, containing various extractions and distillations.

They showed us some amazing things. One took a glass bottle containing some liquid, poured some of it into a cup, then added something from another bottle. The two liquids began to bubble and coloured smoke rose from the cup until all the liquid had evaporated and there was nothing in the bottle but a yellow stone. They did this again with two different liquids and produced a blue stone, and a third time to make a ruby-red one.

Then one of them took a very small amount of a white powder and placed it on an anvil. He struck it lightly with a hammer, and there was a great noise like the sound of a bomb. They laughed at us when we jumped, startled.

They turned a glass sphere, and sparks flew from it, with crackling sounds, and if someone touched it, his whole body would convulse and his arms would shake violently. And if anyone touched him or any part of his clothing, the same would happen to other person as well.

Jabarti shook his head.

—All these strange things, he said. Minds like ours can't grasp what any of this means.

—What did he say, asked Fourier.

I translated what my teacher had said. Fourier looked at me for a moment.

—You know some French, he asked.

—A little.

—We need some young people like you who know languages. How would you like to join us here every day and work with us in organizing the Arabic books in the library? We will pay you for it. We have someone named Ibrahim Sabbagh, but he's ill.

I asked Jabarti and he thought about it.

—It can't do any harm.

—You can begin tomorrow, then, said Fourier.

We then walked towards the house of Ibrahim Katkhuda al-Sinawi, a Nubian from Dongola who used to be a doorman in Mansoura. He joined Emir Mustafa Bey, learnt Turkish, then made his way to Murad Bey's clique, becoming close to him and eventually becoming one of Cairo's elite. Here they housed the artists and illustrators. One of them, Rigo, could draw a son of Adam such that if you saw it, you would think that it was about to leap off the page and come to life. He made a detailed portrait of each of the sheikhs in a round frame. We learnt that their chief, Denon, was now in Upper Egypt.

Another man was engrossed in drawing animals and insects, and a third drawing fishes and noting each species. They were catching all the animals or strange fish they did not have in their country, and immersing them in a kind of liquid that would preserve their dead bodies, without changing colour or rotting, for a very long time.

On the way home, I saw that Jabarti was clearly astonished by what we had seen. He told me that working at the library would be a good opportunity to improve my French.

—And, he added, looking at me carefully, to find out what they're doing.

—But what about my lessons with you?

—We can probably find some time in the evenings. In any case, we can wait until all of this is over.

Monday, 3 December.

My teacher permitted me to take a donkey to the Institute in Nasriyya. He gave me a cashmere shawl to wrap around my head and chest against the cold. Arriving at the palace of Qasim Bey, I tethered the donkey to the wall. They greeted me warmly and one of them led me to a room whose walls were lined with bookshelves. In the middle was a long, wide table surrounded by chairs. Around it sat people who seemed completely absorbed in their work. The ceiling was made of ornately decorated wood. It was warm, thanks to a fire in a stone hearth on one side of the room.

The man gave me a notebook and showed me how to keep a record of the Arabic books. I could sit wherever I wished. Pointing to a small open part of the room, slightly elevated from the rest, he indicated two facing worktables. I chose one and then went to inspect the contents of the bookshelves. Most were in French. Many of them contained pictures and maps of lands and seas. There were images of birds, animals, plants, ancient histories and civilizations, tales of the prophets (with pictures!), telling of their miracles and the fates of their peoples.

There was a large book on the life of the Prophet Muhammad, may God bless and keep him. There was a picture of him standing and looking up at the sky, a sword in his right hand, a book in his left. His Companions stand around him, swords in hand. On another page there is a picture of the Rightly Guided Caliphs, and on another an image of the Prophet's Night Journey and Ascension. The Prophet, may God bless and keep him, is riding his mount, al-Buraq, and taking off from the Dome of the Rock in Jerusalem. There were also images of Jerusalem, the Holy Places of Mecca and Medina, portraits of the Imams and the rest of the caliphs and sultans, and a picture of Istanbul and its great mosques—like the Aya Sofia and the mosque of Sultan Mehmet.

I recognized many Islamic books, translated into their language, like *Remedy* by the Maghribi scholar, the Qadi Iyad, and the *Mantle Ode* of al-Busiri. They had whole books on different languages, on their morphology and etymology, in order to help with translating from one language to another. Books on medicine, anatomy, geometry and mechanics.

There were not that many people working in the library. But I noticed many visitors who came in and sat around the table. They request whatever book they would like, and someone fetches it from the bookcase. Then they flip through it, read some pages and write something down. There were soldiers, some local Syrian Christians who knew languages. One of the soldiers was busy memorizing verses from the Quran.

Tuesday, 4 December.

I went early to the Institute. Sitting down at my desk, I found a beautiful young woman seated across from me. Milky skin, perfect lips and shiny teeth. Blue eyes, long lashes and golden hair. She wore a grey dress and a woollen scarf around her neck, covering her chest. She smiled at me and I recognized her. She was the blonde girl I'd seen in the street, joking with her friends on the donkey.

In the name of God, the Compassionate, the Merciful, I wrote at the top of the page in my notebook. I determined which bookcase I would start with, when a young man—though older than me—approached.

—What are you doing here, he asked sharply in their language.

I didn't answer, so he indicated with his hands that I should leave my seat. I took my notebook and looked around. I didn't know what to do. But then the young girl motioned to the place next to hers.

—Come over here, she said.

I sat where she indicated, as the man took my place. A quill, inkwell and reed pen lay on the desk. There was less than a foot between us. She asked me if I was researching something, and I answered in her language that I work in the Institute. She praised my French, and I explained that I had learnt it from a French merchant and practised with books from time to time, but I needed more practise. I told her my name and she hers—'Citizen Pauline'. They now called each other *citizen*, unlike when I worked with the French merchant. I had to call him *monsieur*. I told her how I had learnt to read and write, and memorize the Quran at my village school. And how my family all died in the plague, so I left Upper Egypt and boarded in the neighbourhood by the Azhar Mosque. I explained how it worked: we were fed thanks to the daily distribution of two hundred pounds of bread, and we also received the necessary fuel for the lamps and a stipend each month. I tried to draw her a picture of what the teaching was like, with all the noise and chaos created by the Syrians, Persians, Kurds and Nubians as they debated legal rulings, algebra, exegesis and philosophy, but my tongue betrayed me. I said that I had frequented the lessons of Jabarti before joining his household and becoming his pupil.

She asked me how these studies progress, and I told her that a student becomes a scholar after ten years and then takes up teaching, but most abandon their lessons after two or three years.

She looked contemplative for a moment, then resumed her work. I went over to the Arabic bookcase and brought back some books and began to leaf through them. One treated the syntax and alphabet of Arabic and French. Another dealt with the fall of Constantinople. There was a pamphlet containing the Arabic names of the administrative districts of Egypt. A book on smallpox and one on ophthalmia in Arabic and Italian, and a third containing Quranic verses in their language.

The young man who had taken my seat was still watching me, and he still had a scowl on his face. Without moving her eyes from the pages she was reading, the girl whispered to me.

—Don't mind Gaston. He's always like that.

I went back to work, but I could see that he hardly took his eyes off of her.

Wednesday, 5 December.

A fitful sleep. Visions of the blonde girl haunted my dreams. I heard the dawn call to prayer: *Glory to God who guides His servants, Glory to the One and Only, Glory to the King whom we worship, Praise to you, Everlasting One*. I ignored it for a while but eventually got up and did the prayer. And rushed to the Institute.

The two of them were already sitting at their places. I wished them a good morning in their language. Gaston mumbled something incomprehensible. But Pauline looked up at me smiling.

—*Bonjour*!

I sat at the desk next to hers. A man in his fifties entered the room, greeted her and said something to Gaston before leaving.

—Do you know who that is, she asked me. It's Monge. He's a genius. He was in charge of the balloon.

—The balloon that fell down?

She frowned.

—He's a genius in mathematics. He was assistant to Lavoisier. Have you heard of him?

I shook my head.

—He is a great scholar of chemistry and physics. He discovered, with the help of Monge, that water is made up of two gases: oxygen and hydrogen.

Her tone indicated that this was an important discovery.

A man in shabby clothes appeared at the door of the room. He had a round head and dishevelled hair. In a loud voice he asked after Monge. She answered him. That man, she told me, is Berthollet.

—Another genius, I asked.

—He's a physician and a chemist, she said, ignoring my sarcasm. He has written books about colours and pigments. He and Monge are inseparable, people call them Mongéberthollet.

Pauline also introduced me to Venture, chief of the interpreters, and the oldest member of the expedition. He congratulated me on my French and said I could become a very good interpreter if I studied diligently. I replied that it was difficult to learn his language, especially the conjugation of the verbs. She added that she could help me, in exchange for teaching her Arabic. I was delighted to hear this.

Once Venture left, she asked me, Are you a Mamluk, a Turk or a fellah?

I didn't know what to say. The question had never occurred to me. I thought for a moment.

—Egyptian, I said.

—Then I'll call you the Egyptian.

She asked me where I lived and I told her. Then she pointed to the upper floor and said she lives there with her husband. I felt uncomfortable. Her husband is an army officer, she said, adding that she herself was the daughter of a countess executed six years ago during their revolution. She had been obliged to earn a living and worked selling hats. Then she met the officer, they fell in love and were soon married. She looked on dreamily as she spoke.

—I wore a translucent veil, and we rode in a carriage covered in white roses.

Laughing, she told me how she had come to Egypt. When her husband joined the expedition, she wanted to accompany him. But Bonaparte forbade all wives and lovers from travelling, so she dressed as a man: army boots, loose baggy trousers, waistcoat, overcoat. She hid her hair under a three-pointed military hat and took the ship from Toulon with her husband.

—I'll never forget how Bonaparte stood there, with his braid and the hair hanging down to his shoulders. He promised the troops heading to Egypt that each one of them would have three hectares of land. The gleam in his eyes had some kind of magical effect on them.

I asked her about Bonaparte. With some pride, she explained that he was an artillery officer who achieved the rank of general when he was only twenty-four years old, for having seized the city of Toulon from the English. Three years later, he saved the Republic when he put down the mob revolt. He showed no mercy. So the government put him in charge of the French troops in Italy. He is a national hero.

I was able to follow what she was saying. My eyes did not leave her lips.

—Have you met him in person?

Her eyes brightened.

—Not yet.

—It seems he's another genius.

—You don't know what kind of questions he asks the scientists, she said excitedly, again ignoring my sarcasm. Is it possible to grow grapes in Egypt? How much wheat can be produced here compared to France? Is it possible to dig wells in the desert? Is there life on other planets? How old is the earth? Can we really interpret our dreams?

She related how she was taken aback by the sight of Alexandria.

—Filthy streets, no trees anywhere, so many barbers, so many stray dogs. And Cairo is the same.

She must have noticed that I was not happy to hear any of this. She added quickly, You know the most beautiful thing I saw in Alexandria? Pompeii's pillar and Cleopatra's obelisk. You know how her beauty made Anthony fall in love with her. He married her and she sat on a throne of gold.

All this talk about Cleopatra did nothing to make me less angry about how she described Egypt. I busied myself with my work. After a while she got up and went out. She returned with a cup of chocolate and offered it to me.

I took it and thanked her. It was delicious. She really wanted to talk, and was soon telling me about the troops' journey from Alexandria to Cairo.

—Dry biscuits were the only rations available. We were thirsty and the sand burnt our feet. Hundreds went mad and killed themselves. Some died of thirst, begging for water. And thirty soldiers died suffocated or trampled when they rushed towards a well. But things got better when we approached Cairo because we found melons. But then many people got diarrhoea from eating them. And when one village refused to give us any food, we slaughtered them. Killed nine hundred of them—men, women and children. We burnt the village to teach the miserable savages a lesson.

This time she realized her mistake right away, and put her hand on mine apologetically.

—The Mamluk warriors at Imbaba were a magnificent sight, she said. So splendidly dressed, and all the weapons and everything they had with them! My husband found five hundred gold pieces in a dead Mamluk's turban!

She told me that some fell prisoner to the Bedouin, and upon their release told horrifying stories of cruel treatment and attacks on their honour. She laughed, saying that finally the men accepted such attacks on their honour as one of the dangers faced by soldiers in the Orient. But some said they would rather die than be subjected to that humiliation.

Bonaparte, she said, was highly critical of this excessive virtue, saying to one weeping soldier who had been violated by the Bedouin—What are you crying about? All this fuss for nothing! Imbecile!

I asked her how she felt about life in Cairo, and she told me she suffered from the flies and the mosquitoes and the sweat; she itched and scratched all night, then would get up in the morning weak and depressed, unable to move.

At noon, I saw her husband for the first time. He came in and accompanied her to the apartment upstairs. He is tall and handsome. She did not come back down.

Thursday, 6 December.

She gave me a wooden stick from which protruded a thin piece of lead. She said it was an invention of Conté, one of the expedition's scientists.

—Another genius?

—He can make any instrument from the most basic materials.

It is true. Writing with this new kind of pen is easy. I don't have to use the inkwell or sand to help it dry. At midday she brought me a book entitled *Exercises in Literary Arabic: Selections from the Quran for the Benefit of those Studying Arabic*. She moved her seat close to mine so we could both read. A strong odour of perspiration hit me, and I realized that her clothes had not been washed for a long time. We began to read and translate the verses together. She was surprised at how I shifted left and right while reading, like we do at the Azhar. She convinced me to sit still while reading, but it is difficult for me. Then she brought the newspaper the French distributed each week, *Le Courrier de l'Égypte*.

I leafed through the first issue which had come out four months ago. There was an article devoted to the Prophet's birthday celebration; news of the troops; events in Cairo and the most important local news like festivals, celebrations, parties of music and dancing in the house of Ghayt al-Nouby, which they now called the Tivoli, after a place in Paris. There was also news of the Diwan, and calls for people to remain calm. We read together a funny account of a Nubian who had his portrait painted by Rigo. When the painter began to colour in the head and chest, the Nubian jumped up terrified and asked Rigo to give back his head. Another refused to sit for a portrait, convinced that if a part of the body was painted, it would soon seize up and the person would die.

Friday, 7 December.

I was surprised to find that she had moved her writing desk right next to mine. As it was warm, she had removed her shawl. Her low-cut blouse revealed the beginnings of her breasts. I caught the scent of some perfume.

I had prepared for her a list of useful Arabic expressions and their French equivalents. We studied them together, then we read the headlines of *Le Courrier de l'Égypte*. When she leant over the paper, I could see her small, round breasts. I was so aroused that I had to ask God to protect me from temptation.

I copied down the translation of the headlines as follows:

• At the end of the rue Phénicie, the house of the good citizen Wolmar produces all kinds of beverages including methylated spirits, as found in Europe.

• Citizens Faure and Naseau and their associates manufacture all kinds of beverages. At the Square of Birkat al-Fil, near the hospital. Reasonable prices.

• French bathhouses behind Square of Birkat al-Fil.

• French tobacco, all varieties, manufactured at the house of Hasan Kashif on the rue du Petit-Thouars, in from of the Milano Restaurant.

• French Milliners' Boutique informs the citizens that they are making hats. Located behind the Post Office.

• Playing cards for sale at the Army Printing House.

She left at midday, but I stayed on until evening in order to attend one of the unofficial gatherings at which the scientists discussed their work.

We sat in a large reception hall in the former harem of the palace. Some of the scientists wore jackets with high collars that obscured half the face. The rest dressed casually. I saw Cafferelli, whom they call Abu Khashaba because of his wooden leg. He is tall and dignified, with grey hair.

Pauline came over and sat next to me, wearing a brocaded dress. I expressed my surprise at the dress, but she told me that Parisian women now prefer gossamer muslin.

—They don't wear heavy brocade any more. With all the gold threads it's very resistant. Of course, muslin doesn't last long.

She leant over, whispering.

—Imagine the wife of Citizen Tallien, and she was a marquess, is wearing translucent clothes, with no shirt underneath! You can see everything—Do you like that?

She did not wait for my answer.

—She also wears skin-coloured socks. Her husband and Bonaparte have something in common: their wives were both lovers of Barras, the leader of the Directory.

I don't think I fully understood what she was saying.

Monge opened the meeting with the results of the Cairo census. There are 300,000 inhabitants, he declared. It would be possible to settle a few thousand Frenchmen here in order to till the soil and manage trade and commerce. This country would come to be not just our most beautiful colony but also the best situated. It is the responsibility of the scientific committee, he put forth, to see that this plan succeeds.

I noticed that many of the members of the committee did not seem to share their leader's enthusiasm. He also talked of digging a canal to connect the Red Sea with the Mediterranean.

Another said that the wheat mills were weak. The flour they produced was not fine enough; they did not even manage to separate all the bran, so it was it impossible to eat bread here—it wasn't anything like the bread they have in Paris.

I left before the meeting was over. On my way home, I passed by the market where they sell old clothes.

Saturday, 8 December.

Ibrahim Sabbagh has returned to work after his illness. He is about my age, thin and pale. Pauline introduced us. He looked at my desk, and I understood that I was sitting in his place.

—Let him sit next to me, said Pauline. We are studying language together.

She then pointed to a spot next to Gaston's and Ibrahim Sabbagh went and sat there.

We agreed to divide the work between us. I learnt that he is a Greek Catholic and the grandson of the previous vizier of Dahir al-Umar, the former governor in Palestine. Caffarelli had taken him under his wing and was teaching him French, geography and drawing.

I went to the evening debates of the Committee in the hope of seeing her there, but she did not come. Caffarelli of the wooden leg was there, accompanied by Ibrahim Sabbagh.

One of the scholars gave an exposition on agricultural land. He said that cleaning the irrigation canals and planting more trees for shade would make Egypt once again the bread basket of Europe, as it was during the Roman Empire.

Somebody asked him about tax farms. He explained that the concession-holders own the land, and the farmers have to purchase a plot of land to cultivate. In the case of death, the plot is put up for sale again. The farmers also pay to the concession-holders an annual fee of around thirty million francs per year. From this, the concession-holders pay out six million in local taxes, the same amount to the Sultan and to the village chiefs who act as their agents, and eight million to the Coptic tax collectors. An additional four million is collected by the regional governors in kind such as camels and horses. The farmers also pay nine million to the Bedouin tribes to avoid being attacked by them. In the end, the farmer is left with nothing.

Caffarelli argued that a general reform of agricultural land ownership was needed to make the farmers true owners of the land and improve the conditions of the two-and-a-half million farmers, out of a total of three million Egyptians. They would then acknowledge the generosity of France.

Many of those present were opposed to this plan. One of them said that granting the land to the Egyptian farmers would make it impossible to distribute it among the French army officers and their patrons. Conversation turned to the eccentric ideas held by Caffarelli. Apparently he thinks that labour should be the sole source of ownership, and that the codes that sanctify ownership also sanctify theft and pillage. He proposed dividing society into present landowners and future landowners. The latter would rent the land from the former for a period of twenty years and work it for the benefit of the owners. Then they, in turn, would assume ownership and the former owners would rent the land from them.

Sunday, 9 December.

Today is my day off from the Institute, and I spent it studying French. I cannot stand not seeing her even for a day.

In the afternoon, I prayed at the Sayyida Zaynab Mosque, walked past the turner's workshop at the beginning of Ashrafiyya Street. I used to always stand there watching him skilfully move the piece of wood with his toe, while shaping it as he wished with the aid of a bow in his right hand.

Today I was surprised to find him standing behind a counter on which were various types of food.

He saw that I was puzzled.

—Business is not so good for many artisans these days, he told me. Less and less demand. The only thing that sells is food.

I asked him about his son who helps him. He said his son had bought a donkey and was working as a driver.

—He earns a good living, since many of the French will pay a large fare, and they spend the whole day on the donkey, doing nothing but riding around too fast. Of course, my son has to run behind them so he comes home exhausted every evening.

I thought of buying a gift for Pauline, so I went to the Agatiyya caravanserai where they sell coral necklaces. Then I thought about a shawl imported from Europe I'd seen at Khan al-Khalili, but decided it would be better to buy something locally made (and less expensive, too). So, on I went from the Palace Walk to the market of Amir al-Guyush, at the edge of the Bargawan quarter, where one finds the weavers and darners. I bought a shawl in the style of al-Mahalla al-Kubra. Then I went to our usual coffee house by the Muski bridge.

It was full of the usual customers: scoundrels, pedlars, donkey drivers. The poet sat in his usual place. Abd al-Zaher was waiting for me. We talked about the lack of demand for most goods and how prices have risen, the absence of news from abroad, the presence of the English fleet and the strength of their blockade on imports and exports, such that prices of everything imported from the Mediterranean had risen.

Hanna joined us. He had with him a French booklet that claimed to be the declaration of the rights of man that they had made at the start of their revolution. He translated for us, astonished, the parts about the rights to freedom and property and security and resistance to oppression. I told them about my new job. Hanna asked me to see if I could find him a job as well. I told him I would, but I didn't mean it. I imagined him talking freely with Pauline, since he knows the language better than I do.

We asked him about Zaynab; he said he hardly sees her, that she goes out every day in the company of a Frenchwoman, sometimes with one of their officers.

After a while he left, and Abd al-Zaher spoke.

—The lowest of the Copts and the Greek and Syrian Christians and the Jews are riding horses and carrying swords. They are speaking shamelessly and humiliating the Muslims.

Monday, 10 December.

I gave her the silk shawl. She thanked me and put it around her neck. She gave me a French sweet, a cherry covered in chocolate. Gaston did not take his eyes off us.

She had with her the new issue of the journal *La Décade égyptienne* which the Institute published in the form of a copybook. Together we read Monge's explanation of the phenomenon of the mirage. On the march from Alexandria, the soldiers would see, shimmering in the distance, islands reflected in pools of water. But as they approached, these pools remained always at the same distance.

Monge explained that in the heat of the day, the sunlight raises the temperature of the sand. The air closest to the earth expands due to the heat and becomes less dense than the layers of air above. There is turbulence where warmer air meets cooler air, and when light rays from the lower part of the sky reach this area, they are reflected back up, like in a mirror. The result is that an image of the sky appears on the ground, and looks like a pool of water. Any object reflected in the pool will seem closer than it really is.

I didn't really follow all of this but I noted it down to show to my teacher. Perhaps he will understand it.

Tuesday, 11 December.

My master went to the house of Sheikh Nabulsi, where important merchants and scholars meet to read books and debate what they read. He said that Bonaparte complained to Master Gergis al-Gawhari about the lack of support from the Copts, as compared to the Muslim notables who visit every day and tell him where the Mamluks had hidden their wealth and treasures.

Wednesday, 12 December.

I could not keep my eyes off the door. Finally, she arrived and sat down beside me. An aroma of soap came from her body. I kept working, writing down all the details of the books, but I could not think of anything but her. Then I heard Gaston humming a tune that was lively and very pleasing. She told me it was the anthem of the revolution, known as the Marseillaise. In a low voice, she repeated the words:

Arise, children of the Fatherland
The day of glory has arrived
To arms, citizens, to arms!

She had me repeat the words until I had memorized them.

Gaston collected his papers and left the room without a single word to us. She told me that Citizen Fourier was very pleased with my work and decided to keep me on even though Ibrahim Sabbagh had resumed his duties.

I read some of the proverbs from the book of al-Damanhouri with her. She laughed at the one that says 'Marriage is one month in bed, a lifetime of dread, and then you're dead.'

—Exactly, she said.

After a while she suggested that we go up to her room and she would play the anthem on a musical instrument. Leaving our seats, we headed to the door that led upstairs. She glanced behind her at the room. Then she went up the stairs. I followed her, trying to avert my gaze from her slender behind.

We entered a small residence of two connecting rooms. A large piano stood in one. She removed its covering and ran her fingers over the keys. She got it from one of the local Franks, she said. Then she sat on the stool before it and I stood to one side. She played the music of the anthem. Then she took a notebook from on top of the piano and opened it to a page written in a strange language. She began to read from it while playing some pieces that I didn't much like.

I asked about the notebook, and she explained that it is a tune in written form. The notes and tones become signs and markings.

—How can you write music on a page? I asked. I couldn't understand.

—I'll show you. Sing something from your kind of music.

So I sang:

O you of white jasmine,
O you with the look that romances,
I swear by the whites of your eyes,
I am the prisoner of your glances.

When I translated it for her, she blushed. She had me sing the lines several times while she listened carefully and made some notes on a piece of paper. Then to my astonishment, she repeated the tune.

—Give me another song, she said.

I obeyed:

In your cheeks the red rose
And the wine dance a minuet
In ecstasy I cry out:
Your eyes have trapped me in their net!

She made her notes on the paper.

—I can't stand your music, she said. It's nothing but these high-pitched, grating notes. It's just noise.

This made me angry, but she came over and said, I'm sorry, I was just teasing you. Her hands touched my face, she ran her fingers over my cheek and looked straight into my eyes.

I froze. We stayed like that for a long moment, then she turned and said, Let's go back.

We returned to our desks and immersed ourselves in work, studiously ignoring each other.

Thursday, 13 December.

Today I found that my desk had returned to its original place, away from hers. A mountain of French books was piled before her. I asked her about today's lesson, but she said she was busy.

She and Gaston talked about the fierce battles with the French in Girga. He said that a North African in Mecca had called for a jihad against the French. They crossed the Red Sea to Quseir and a great many people from Upper Egypt joined them, along with some Turks and Maghribis.

I relayed this news to my teacher. I stayed in my room but had no desire to study French. At sunset, Jabarti went to see Sheikh Sadat who had invited Bonaparte to a meal in celebration of the birthday of Sayyida Zaynab. When he returned, he told me mockingly all that he had heard. Bonaparte claimed that the Arabs had cultivated science and culture in the time of the caliphs, but today live in deep ignorance, knowing nothing of the accomplishments of their ancestors. Sheikh Sadat answered that they possessed the Quran, in which all knowledge is contained. The Commander-in-chief asked if the Quran explained how to make cannons, and the sheikhs all declared boldly: Yes!

Cannot sleep. I keep thinking about what happened between Pauline and me. How can she be so cold?

Friday, 14 December.

I told Hanna about Pauline. He was surprised and looked at me enviously. I told him what happened in her room and then how her mood changed. What did he think of her behaviour? We talked about it for a long time, and finally he said: She's depraved. He advised me to ask her to teach me to play the piano, then when once we go up to her room, I should then grab her and kiss her. He says that French girls, in general, love kissing and it has a kind of magical effect on them.

In the street, we watched a dancer, a local woman. There were two men and another woman with her, playing musical instruments. She moved her feet and the upper part of her body in quick movements, but the expression on her face and her physical bearing soon betrayed tension and anxiety. Then a shudder of pleasure flowed through her body. A kind of languor mixed with shame seized us, then little by little disappeared.

Saturday, 15 December.

I spent some time perusing a beautiful Coptic manuscript, with colours and gold illuminations. Pauline told me her husband was staying at the army encampment. This encouraged me to ask her to teach me to play the piano. She glanced at Ibrahim and Gaston.

—Not today, she said.

At noon the two of them went out, and she suddenly asked me to come upstairs. My heart was beating violently as I thought of what Hanna told me to do. But she didn't give me any chance to apply his advice. As soon as we entered her flat, she put her arms around me and pressed her lips to mine. Then she did something very strange: she put her tongue in my mouth.

I am not sure what happened after that. We found ourselves on the couch, I was on top of her and inside her. She held me tight, and suddenly I came, as she panted: Not yet, wait. Then she pulled away and wiped away my semen with the edge of her dress. I could sense that she was dissatisfied for some reason.

She undid my turban and looked at my head.

—Your hair is soft and beautiful. Why do you have to shave it? If you let it grow, you'd be even more handsome.

—Protect me from Satan! Do you want me to look like a woman?

She undid her braids and I ran my fingers through her long hair and inhaled the fresh scent of soap coming from her body. She said she has difficulty keeping her hair properly curled so she had to use pieces of paper, and she is thinking of cutting it short according to the latest fashion with a fringe of hair covering the forehead.

She got up and led me by the hand to the inner room. There was a sort of bedding in the middle of the room, consisting of a carpet spread over wooden pieces, with four big pillows and a covering of silk or muslin. I looked away.

She took a small box from a stand next to the bed and opened it. I could see some red powder inside.

—It's rouge, to give your cheeks colour. I don't use it. Do you know that the ladies of the royal court in France use rouge to beautify their faces? Thirteen different shades, one on top of the other. All I use is a cream called 'Dew of the Lily'. I just put a little of it on my face before I go to sleep. And when I go out I just wet my little finger and run it over my eyebrows and lashes so that they shine.

She was speaking like a child. I put my arms around her and she buried her head in my neck. She is a little bit shorter than me. When I kissed her neck she raised her head and put her tongue in my mouth again.

I sang to her:

My gazelle said, Here I am, come and see
Take me, do anything you want to me,
Breasts like pomegranates to be felt,
While you untie the alfiya belt

I explained the lines to her, and that an alfiya is a belt worn on the waist, embroidered with a thousand colours.

Then I pulled her to the bed, and this time I took all my clothes off, so that I was completely naked. I helped her remove her inner shirt and petticoat. She is very thin. I was stunned, looking at her ivory naked body. I touched her breasts.

—They're small, she said. When I was twelve, I used to put four handkerchiefs under my clothes for each one.

I advised her to do what our girls do—put pieces of hot bread between the breasts to help them develop.

—But I'm not young any more.

—I have another solution, I said. I took one of her breasts in my mouth and began to suck on it, pulling it outwards. Then I did the same with the other one. Her nipple swelled and she began to moan. I wanted to bend her legs back but she refused and spread them apart instead. I entered her, gently.

—Do you know what to do so I don't get pregnant?

I nodded.

—Don't rush, she whispered.

I clenched my teeth, trying to control myself. When I did lose control, I pulled out of her and ejaculated on her belly. I heard her scream and it seemed to me that she had lost consciousness. She looked at me in a kind of stupefied way, and I looked around for some water. Then suddenly she was smiling, taking my hand and kissing it.

She stretched out and gave a contented sigh. Then she put her hand on her stomach and wet her fingers with my semen. She rubbed it over her breasts with a wicked smile.

—This is the best way to make them larger.

I lay next to her and tried to embrace her, but she slipped away.

—We need to go back downstairs, before anybody comes.

I asked her why Gaston had been giving her angry looks. She laughed.

—He tried to seduce me but I wasn't interested. He's insufferable.

—Tomorrow is Sunday, I told her, and I couldn't stand the thought of not seeing her all day.

Saturday, 15 December. Evening.

I went to Hanna's house and told her what happened and how she lost consciousness.

—She climaxed, he said. The woman only ever does that if she loves the man. French men are effeminate. Their women prefer the strong men of the Orient.

Sunday, 16 December.

Busy with my language lessons. I tried to keep warm by drinking cardamom and cinnamon infusions.

Monday, 17 December.

Today she was smiling and full of energy. I thought that she must have been happy because of what happened between us; I felt very pleased with myself. Then she excitedly told me how she had been to the Tivoli with her husband. Bonaparte was present, and was eyeing her the whole time. He even asked her for a dance. While they were dancing, he asked her about what she was reading. Then he mentioned the story by an unknown German writer that he was reading with great interest. The story is called *The Sorrows of Werther*. It is about a young man who kills himself because the woman he loves marries one of his closest friends.

I pretended to be busy with the papers on which I had written some common Arabic expressions for her to learn. But she kept talking. When it came time to leave, she said, Bonaparte had summoned her husband. Citizen, he said, your country needs you. Tomorrow you will depart for Alexandria. You must sail to France and remain ten days in Paris. I will entrust you with secret papers for the Directory and instructions that you must not look at until you are at sea. You will receive a payment of 3,000 francs for your expenses.

—Did he leave?

—He goes tomorrow. He takes the first postal boat to Rosetta.

The French have set up a system of boats that deliver messages and passengers to and from Cairo.

I thought of the opportunities this would give me to meet with her. Then, for some strange reason, I felt uneasy.

Tuesday, 18 December.

She did not come to the library today. According to Gaston, she was busy with preparations for her husband's departure.

Wednesday, 19 December.

I found her in the library when I arrived. She was clearly tense and unable to concentrate. We did not continue our lesson. When I suggested we go upstairs, she made an excuse saying she had to prepare for a dinner that evening and Bonaparte would be present.

Ibrahim said that the French were building a quarantine at Bulaq. They had constructed a building to keep all arriving travellers for a fixed number of days, to be certain they were not carrying diseases. He also said they were talking about the spread of venereal and skin diseases among them. Louis, the brother of Bonaparte, was sent back to France because he had syphilis.

Thursday, 20 December.

She came down from her quarters around noon, saying she had gone to bed at a very late hour last night. I asked her about the dinner party but she answered brusquely and pretended to work. I waited for her to invite me upstairs but she never did.

Friday, 21 December.

She did not appear today.

Jabarti told me that they had rearranged the Diwan. They appointed sixty members, each of whom received a monthly salary, and this they called the Permanent Diwan. They had also elected fourteen members to what they called the Special Diwan, and these had to be present at every meeting.

I followed as he counted on his fingers. The fourteen are: the sheikhs Sharqawi, al-Mahdi, Sawi, al-Bakri, al-Fayyoumi; the merchants, al-Mahrouqi and Ahmed Muharram; from the Copts, Lutfallah al-Misri; from the Syrian Christians, Yusuf Farhat and Mikhail Kuhayl; and the Englishman Rawaha, and from the French, Badeuf and Musa Caffe. As well as their various agents, and the assistants and translators.

I counted again: there were only thirteen. I asked him who is the fourteenth? He kept reading and did not respond. Was it him? Why didn't he answer? Was he ashamed at being part of the Diwan?

He showed me a proclamation from Bonaparte. It was full of falsehoods such as: 'The rational person knows that our acts are due to the strength, will, and decree of God . . . the Mighty Quran in many verses explains events that have occurred, and in other verses indicates events that will take place in the future. The word of God in his Book is true and truthful . . . Everything I have done and decreed is divine judgement that cannot be gainsaid . . .'

Saturday, 22 December.

She did not appear today.

I waited a long time until my patience ran out. I asked Gaston about her and he gave a strange smile.

—I don't think she'll be coming here any more.

When I enquired further, he said she had moved to a house in Ezbekieh. Ibrahim Sabbagh confirmed this, and added that the French have strange habits when it comes to women. I did not understand what he meant.

Sunday, 23 December.

I strolled through Ezbekieh in the hopes of meeting her. I stood in vain for a while in the square by the Commander-in-chief's palace until some of Barthélemy's men started to get suspicious. Then their chief told me to leave.

Now I keep going back and forth between my room and the courtyard, unable to do anything.

Monday, 24 December.

She did not come. Gaston said she had quit working with us.

Ibrahim Sabbagh did not come, either. I learnt from Gaston that he was travelling to Suez with Caffarelli, who was accompanying Bonaparte. I mentioned this to my master in the evening and he told me whom they had taken along with them: Sayyid Ahmed al-Mahrouqi and the Secretary of Spices, Ibrahim Effendi, together with administrators, engineers and draughtsmen and others.

Tuesday, 25 December.

My eyes are constantly moving between her empty desk and the library entryway. I can still smell her scent.

Wednesday, 26 December.

I was surprised to find her this morning sitting at her desk, talking with Gaston. He was saying that scientists have confirmed that the water of the Nile is healthy to drink, rich in nutrients, and helps with urination and perspiration. She said she heard that it made the animal population increase at a high rate. Gaston laughed and said maybe that's the reason for the high birth rate of these people.

I asked her if she was going to come to work with us. She said, no, she had just come to collect some of her things.

She went up to her former quarters. When she came down I helped her carry things to a carriage with two horses waiting outside. Just before boarding, she spoke to me.

—Maybe you can come visit me in my new house tomorrow. It's next to where Bonaparte lives. There's just a two-storey house between them.

Back in the library, Gaston was speaking to a friend of his. They were laughing, and I understood that they were talking about Pauline. He looked at me.

—She never dreamt she'd be living in a palace and riding in carriages.

I was angry.

—What do you mean? She was born in a palace.

—Was she the one who told you that?

—Yes. Her father was one of those who perished by the guillotine.

The two of them seemed to think this was very funny.

—She lied to you. Her mother was a cook and she never knew who her father was.

I don't believe him.

Thursday, 27 December.

As I went to Ezbekieh around sunset, I came across a group of their soldiers surrounding a miller's place. I came to understand that they were taking a horse from every mill. The miller told me they were preparing to travel to Syria.

I rode around the square on my donkey. There was a large garden next to the Commander-in-chief's house. Before it was a two-storey house and next to that a small palace with a French soldier standing out front. I rode up to him and dismounted. After I explained why I was there, he let me pass.

I knocked on the door and a black servant opened it. He seemed to be expecting me because he took my donkey's halter without a word. I walked along a garden path towards the inner door and knocked again. A Syrian Christian woman, head uncovered, answered. She was clearly a local, with wide black eyes, white skin and a long, hooked nose. She led me inside to a salon on the ground floor. I left my shoes at the door, and walked across the carpet to the sofa.

Presently Pauline came in, dressed in a sheer oriental gown that reached to the floor; a hood covered her head. I leapt and rushed to kiss her. She kissed me on the cheek and gestured for me to sit. My eyes devoured her. I couldn't believe she was finally here in front of me.

When she pulled off the hood, I saw that she had cut her hair to just below the neck.

—What do you think of my hair?

My annoyance must have been clear.

— Napoleon likes it like this way.

It was the first time she mentioned the Commander-in-chief by his first name.

—And how do you know?

—Remember the day my husband left? I was invited to a dinner party at Bonaparte's house, with some other French ladies and officers' wives. It was a brilliant party. He spoke about his projects. He said that offensive warfare is good for the economy. And that it is our sacred duty to plant the seeds of freedom, brotherhood and equality in all corners of the world. And if necessary, we will do so by force.

She stopped, seemed as if she were trying to recall something, then went on talking.

—You should have heard him when he spoke. He said that he is of the kind who can build states and lead them. One of the men who make history.

Her words were torturing me. But she went on.

—He was looking at me the whole time. His eyes had the same effect on me as his words. It was bewitching. He said he would prefer me with shorter hair.

She stopped talking and smiled maliciously.

—And you don't want to hear the rest of the story.

I did not feel well. But she didn't wait for me to answer.

—When the coffee was served, the officer sitting next to me spilt some on my dress. He took me to a room next to the hammam so I could clean it. I was still scrubbing away when Napoleon came in. And we stayed in the room for several hours before going back to the guests.

—And what happened during those hours?

She looked quite amused.

—What do you think happened?

Some expression on my face must have told her she should not wait for my response.

—He told me about a story he wrote when he was nineteen years old. It was about a prophet named Hakim who was blinded in a battle with the caliph's men. So he covered his face with a veil to hide his disfigurement. People claimed that if he were to lift the veil, a brilliant light would blind anyone who looked at him. He made his followers dig a deep well for his enemies to fall into, should they attack him. When the pit was ready, he invited them to a banquet where he secretly poisoned them all. Then he dragged their corpses to the well, lit a huge fire, and threw himself into the flames.

—That's all that happened in those few hours?

She did not respond.

—What will your husband say?

—Don't you know he is travelling?

—And when he comes back?

—He loves me. And I love him, she added, after thinking for a moment.

I got up, saying: You're a worthless whore.

She slapped my face, hard.

I felt my cheek where she had hit me. I quickly moved towards the door, started putting on my shoes but she followed me and put her arms around me, pulled me back to the couch and kissed me on the mouth. Then she ran back to lock the door and threw off her gown. She was naked. I had no control; I was rubbing and touching her like a madman.

I entered her violently and moved on top of her angrily.

I heard a faint voice. Why are you hurting me? She had said it in Arabic, in Syrian dialect. I told her I loved her and I didn't want any other man to touch her.

—Even my husband?

After we came together, she kissed me all over. We stayed locked in an embrace for a while.

I felt her hand on my thigh. She raised her head and leaned over me, contemplating my member.

—I didn't know that when circumcised it could be so beautiful, she said as she fondled it.

Her caresses aroused me again, so I mounted her once more.

—When can I see you next, I asked.

She said that setting up the house and the furniture was going to keep her busy, so she would come to the Institute when she had time to spare.

Wednesday, 2 January 1799.

All day I thought about what happened between us, what she said, and how I could not resist her. I do feel some pride that Bonaparte was interested in the woman I love and who loves me. I try to draw up excuses for her—after all, her husband is not here, and who could refuse the wishes of the Commander-in-chief?

Friday, 4 January.

A strange event today. Gaston was complaining about losing one of his notebooks. He looked for it in his desk then asked me if I had seen it. He didn't believe me when I said no, and insisted on searching my desk and the bookcase behind me. Then he rummaged Pauline's desk, but couldn't find the notebook.

Sunday, 6 January.

I found myself heading towards her place at sunset. Slipping into a corner between two shops on the other side of the street, I kept an eye on the entrance to the house. I stood there for a long time, not daring to move, shivering in the cold. Then, there was Gaston, coming from the direction of Bonaparte's place. The guard stepped aside and Gaston entered. Time passed. I was torn up inside imagining that he was going to spend the night with her. But after a while he left, and the lights inside went out. When it was completely dark, I left—in tears.

Monday, 7 January.

In the morning Gaston was giving me strange looks. In the afternoon I went on foot to Ezbekieh. I saw her leaving the house and getting into one of the Commander-in-chief's grand carriages. I retraced my steps and stopped at the coffee house, but neither Abd al-Zaher nor Hanna was there. I sat on a long bench covered with a mat, next to a man in a turban smoking a water pipe with a translucent marble mouthpiece. I drank coffee from a porcelain cup imported from Germany, set on a small copper tray, and listened to the musicians' singing:

Why, my beloved, must this be your choice
To leave me to suffer as my enemies rejoice?
Why, my timid gazelle, why this insistence
On testing the limits of my heart's resistance?
My heart is weakened, and yet you persist;
All for your sake, I no longer exist.

I paid one-and-a-half *paras* for the coffee and left, fighting tears.

Tuesday, 8 January.

We were about to leave the Institute when, to our surprise, Pauline's husband burst in. We gathered around him and he told us that he never left for France. He had been taken prisoner by the English as soon as he departed, and they returned him to Alexandria. The French governor tried to keep him in the city on some feeble pretences, but he insisted on travelling to Cairo to be with his wife. He asked about her and we didn't know what to say. We didn't answer. Gaston told him she had moved to a house next to the Commander-in-chief's residence in Ezbekieh. He looked surprised. Then he mounted his horse and rode off.

Heavy rain.

Wednesday, 9 January.

The day before yesterday, Ibrahim Sabbagh returned with the Commander-in-chief. He told me that while in Suez, Bonaparte spent the whole time riding, surveying the whole area, both coast and inland, night and day. All he had for food was three roasted chickens wrapped in paper: no cook, no servant, no bedding and no tent. Each one of his soldiers ate from a large piece of bread stuck on the end of his lance, and drank from a tin container around his neck.

He said that the French are talking of building a canal between the two seas in order to help commerce and make Egypt a depot for goods coming from Europe and Asia. French ships would not have to pass through the Straits of Gibraltar or take the long voyage around the Cape of Good Hope.

Thursday, 10 January.

Sabbagh heard from Caffarelli that Pauline complained to Bonaparte about her husband, saying that he had treated her savagely since hearing the rumours about her. She asked for a divorce, which Bonaparte immediately granted in his capacity as judge.

Friday, 11 January.

Trying not to think about her. I will not go to Ezbekieh. I'll wait for her to come.

Intense cold, the ground covered in a light layer of white frost.

Saturday, 12 January.

According to Sabbagh, Bonaparte hosted a dinner party last night, presided over by Pauline. While the guests were eating, news of the plague arrived. He dismissed it, but told of a physician in Alexandria who, having refused to treat the wounded who were mingled with the sick, was dressed in women's clothing and paraded through the streets on a donkey, as punishment. Pauline retorted that she did not see why women's clothing should be associated with cowardice and that she was ready to debate the matter with Bonaparte.

In the afternoon, the French captain who lives at the shrine of Hussein called for the opening of shops and markets for the Moulid of Hussein. Anyone whose shop remained closed would have their doors nailed shut and would have to pay a fine of 10 French *riyals*.

I knew from my teacher that this moulid had been invented by the man responsible for the shrine's charitable foundation. Afflicted with syphilis, he vowed that if God cured him, he would initiate the celebration. When he recovered, he hung lamps and lit candles in the mosque and on its dome, and paid people to come and recite the Quran during the day and al-Jazuli's *Proofs of Goodness* at night. He attracted all kinds of dubious religious types: some gathered in a circle and recited the names of God, others recited religious odes and poems, especially, al-Busiri's *Mantle Ode*.

I went with Abd al-Zaher to the mosque of Hussein in the evening. There was a huge crowd, the street full of people. Some were eating and some were reciting the Quran. We took off our shoes, entered the mosque and stood beneath the dome, in front of the noble tomb. A brass enclosure separates us from the tomb and the ebony sarcophagus, inlaid with silver and mother-of-pearl, covered with red embroidered silk.

The Issawiyya order of Sufis, a group of Maghribis, stood facing each other in two rows, speaking strangely but melodiously in their language while beating hard on drums and tambourines. Then they turned and, shoulder to shoulder, began to bend and stand up repeatedly, pounding the ground violently with their feet, all in one movement.

All this, plus the crowds, made an awful din, not to mention the mobs of unskilled tradesmen, men gathering to talk, laugh, gossip and chase the handsome boys. People selling food made the rounds, behind them came water carriers; the whole mosque floor was covered in nut shells and bits of food.

Leaving, we stopped to watch a man giving a marionette show. From where we stood, we could see him on a small wooden stage, peering through small holes in a curtain, from which he could see his audience but they could not see him. Through another set of openings he made the marionettes move by strings attached to them. His voice changed by means of a device he put in his mouth that made it sound exaggeratedly high-pitched. He made the marionettes quarrel and insult one another and the whole crowd was laughing at them.

Sunday, 13 January.

Sheikh Hasan al-Attar visited us this evening. He is a close friend of my teacher, though younger than him by ten years. According to Sheikh Hasan, people are talking about troops going to El-Arish, in preparation for Bonaparte's journey to Syria. They say that this campaign will be the end of him. He also recited for us the latest of his odes. It had these two verses:

Cairo's taverns and her donkey drivers
Have left the Frenchmen poor.
What will they find in Syria?
How dear the price of war!

They spoke of the coming of the plague. Sheikh Hasan said it begins with fever and headaches. Then comes swelling the size of an egg in the armpit or groin. And at that point there is no hope.

—The plague appeared among the soldiers a month ago, my master said. But in the Diwan they were told not to mention it, to say it was just a fever that passed quickly from one person to another.

Sheikh Hasan al-Attar heard from some of the French that Bonaparte had ordered the soldiers to wash their hands feet and face on a daily basis.

Jabarti asked how he came to be talking with the soldiers.

—I teach them Arabic. And I learn from them, because they are brilliant when it comes to research and investigation, in all things. If you look at our learned men of previous generations, you find that they were learned in various sciences. And they wrote it down, even if it went against other beliefs. As for us today, we don't measure up. All we do is transmit from the ancient scholars. We don't create anything ourselves. If we are presented with a theological question that we don't find in our books, then we just say 'that's philosophers' talk'. We don't even know the value of books in the natural sciences or principles of geometry.

Tuesday, 15 January.

I try to banish her from my thoughts but I find myself desperately hoping she comes to the Institute.

They have posted papers announcing that they are going to fly another device like the one they tried to fly earlier but failed.

Wednesday, 16 January.

We left the Institute at noon and went to Ezbekieh where crowds had gathered. We followed the balloon as it ascended until it reached the hills surrounding Bab al-Barqiyya, where it came down.

I came directly home and told my teacher what I had seen. He said had the wind carried it away till it disappeared from view, the French would have tried to deceive us and say that it was travelling to faraway lands.

Thursday, 17 January.

I notice that my master goes early every morning to the Diwan. I asked him what they are doing. He said they go to Bonaparte's palace and are welcomed with respect, and served coffee and drinks. Then the Commander-in-chief sits among them on the couch, and discusses the Quran with them, asking their interpretations of certain significant verses. He seems to be very interested in the Messenger of God. He complains to the sheikhs about the aggressive sermons the imams were preaching in the mosques.

—Once he even asked the Azhar to issue a fatwa saying that the people should swear obedience to him.

—Did the sheikhs agree to that? I asked.

—Sharqawi asked him to embrace Islam. He said that there were two obstacles to him and his soldiers becoming Muslim:

circumcision and the prohibition of wine. The sheikhs discussed this for a long time and eventually they asked for more time to consider the matter.

Friday, 18 January.

In the mosque I heard that the Prophet, may God bless and keep him, appeared to Bonaparte asking him to proclaim his faith in the pillars of the religion, since it is the religion of God. Bonaparte responded that he needed a year to prepare his soldiers for this transition. The Prophet granted him the deferral.

Saturday, 19 January.

They have made a request for many riding camels and demanded from the civilians a large number of donkeys and mules. So most donkey owners have gone into hiding, and everybody is afraid of losing their animals. The water carriers use camels to transport the water, so they are nowhere to be found, and the same goes for those who transport the clover for the livestock.

Saturday, 26 January.

They executed about ninety people at the Citadel, mostly Mamluks. Some had fled and were caught, others had hidden in homes in the city and been caught by the wicked Barthélemy and his men.

Jabarti returned from a meeting of the Diwan.

—They are preparing to travel to Syria to fight the governor of Acre, he said. Why don't you go with them?

I was stupefied.

—What would I do? I don't know anything about war.

—You wouldn't be waging war. You'd just be helping them with translating and interpreting. And you could send me news of what they're doing.

I thought of Pauline. Would she be going?

—Anyway, he said firmly, I've already given them your name.

Friday, 1 February.

Jabarti summoned me to his salon. I found him busy with his papers. He looked up at me.

—Sakita is pregnant.

The news hit me hard. It hadn't occurred to me that she could get pregnant. Then I thought that it must have been from somebody else. Maybe even from Jabarti himself. Who knows?

—Do you know who had relations with her?

I shook my head but didn't utter a sound.

—Think hard, because it's serious. And she's not saying anything.

I know how serious this is. If my master cannot determine who the father is, then it falls on him. He will be considered the father and since she will have produced his child, Sakita could never be sold. The child will be born free and entitled to a share in the inheritance. The funny thing in this is that Jabarti's own mother was one of his father's concubines.

I swore to him that I knew nothing about the matter. He sighed uncomfortably and let me leave.

Saturday, 2 February.

I made up my mind and went to say goodbye to her before I travel. The guard let me in when I told him in French that I had a letter for her from the Institute. The Syrian servant opened for me, recognized me and led me into the reception hall on the ground floor. Then she disappeared, closing the door behind her. Soon after the door opened again and in came a French soldier wearing a suit with gold stripes, tight trousers and feathered cap. It took me a moment to recognize that it was she.

I embraced her. Her fingers touched my cheek. Then she gently pushed me away, turning to look towards the door. Her brilliant blue eyes looked up at me.

I told her I missed her and never stopped thinking about her. She laughed, revealing her shiny white teeth. She led me to the couch and sat down next to me. Her legs were open and she rested her arms between them.

I gestured at what she was wearing.

—Are you going to Syria as well, then?

—No. It's just that . . . Napoleon likes to see me in these clothes.

I felt as if I had just been stabbed with a knife.

—I happened to be passing by here one day, I said, and I saw Gaston entering.

—He was asking me about a notebook he'd lost.

—When I returned two hours later, I saw him leaving. Did his question take up that much time?

She frowned.

—What are you getting at?

—Nothing, I replied, feebly.

—You have to leave now, she said as she stood up. It's time for me to go to Napoleon.

—What if I asked you not to go to him?

She just laughed.

—If you go, I said, it's all over between us.

—You're free. You can do as you like.

She stepped towards the door but I rose and approached her. I wanted to embrace her but she pushed me away. I put my arms around her and grabbed the waistband of her trousers. I pulled it such that the fabric almost tore. This seemed to frighten her, for she suddenly said, *Bien* . . . Then she angrily pulled off the pants and stretched out on the couch. I threw myself on her and without any enthusiasm, she submitted. When I finished, she said: You're still very young. And she put the pants back on.

On the way out, I found that there were even more French guards waiting at the door.

Sunday, 3 February.

Hasan Agha Muharram, the market-inspector, rode out with great pomp for the sighting of the crescent moon signalling the beginning of Ramadan. The chiefs of various trades went before him with their drums and their pipes. They cut the regular path through the city of Cairo, passing before the governor, the pilgrimage leader and the Commander-in-chief Bonaparte, then returning to the house of the Qadi at the Palace Walk where the people were gathered. I was among them.

They confirmed the sighting of the Ramadan crescent moon, then the procession continued, lit by torches, and accompanied by drums and pipes and the proclamation of the fast. Behind rode a number of Frenchmen, bareheaded, their hair hanging down to their necks in a disgusting manner.

Monday, 4 February.

The first day of the noble month of Ramadan.

Last night I took the suhur, the meal before the fast begins, with my teacher and Khalil. I slept late and did not go to the Institute. I prayed the Zuhr prayer and spent the rest of the day studying the manual for learning French. Since Ramadan fell in winter this year, the day passed quickly. At dusk, I broke the fast with my master, then he left for a meeting of the Diwan. After the night prayer, I left the house. Shops were open and people carrying Ramadan lanterns filled the streets, heading to mosques or to visit their loved ones, eating sweets or crowding in the coffee houses listening to the storytellers. Outside the mosques, the lanterns cast their bright lights.

Hanna and Abd al-Zaher met me at the coffee house. Hanna wore a black turban.

—What happened, I asked.

—Didn't you hear? The French ordered us to stop wearing coloured shawls and white turbans. For the whole of Ramadan, we have to go back to the old ways. No eating or drinking openly in the markets, no smoking. None of it within sight of the Muslims.

—They're trying to distract people while they go to Syria, I said.

Abd al-Zaher said he saw a procession heading to al-Adiliyya. In it were the Qadi, Mustafa Katkhuda Basha and four sheikhs—al-Fayyoumi, al-Sawi, al-Arishi and al-Dawakhili.

—They didn't take Sheikh al-Bakri along, then, I asked.

—He excused himself because he is not able to leave the city, answered Hanna. Do you know why? Because of 'Hélène'.

We already knew the story of the bloody struggle between al-Bakri and the Agha of the Janissaries over the beautiful young Mamluk, whom the French are calling '*la belle Hélène*'.

—Poussielgue, the French administrator-general for finances, found that al-Bakri can keep the boy if he gives the Agha land of equal value.

We listened to the storyteller recount the exploits of Antara ibn Shaddad, accompanying his tale on a rebab. Hanna and I played a game of chess, then all three of us played draughts on a piece of chequered cloth. We stayed until it was nearly time for the suhur.

Back home, I ate with Jabarti and he told me about the meeting of the Diwan.

—Bonaparte attended. He announced that he was going to Syria and would be back in a month.

He was silent for a long while.

—I think he will return very soon, defeated. He'll never defeat al-Jazzar. His army is not in the best shape. They had to mortgage the crops of Upper Egypt, before they are even harvested, in order to pay the soldier's back wages.

I asked him about al-Jazzar.

—He's sixty or seventy years old. Born in Bosnia, joined the Turkish navy, then sold himself to a slave trader in the Astana market who took him to Cairo where Ali Bey al-Kabir bought him. He helped Ali Bey get rid of his enemies among the Mamluks, and earned the name 'Butcher' for his savagery. Some years later they quarrelled, and he went to Syria where he sought refuge with the Emir of the Druze. Then he turned against the Emir, stole from him. The story ends with the Ottoman Sultan naming him the Governor of Acre!

Tuesday, 5 February.

Sheikh al-Tuwalibi visited Jabarti. He used to own a workshop in Bab Zuweila. It produced molasses, raw sugar, refined sugar in big cones and candy as well. He wanted to strike a deal with my master. Jabarti would plant sugar cane this month and he would buy the crop after the harvest next November.

My master showed no enthusiasm for this plan, owing to current circumstances and the fact that the French had already granted various concessions to their own merchants.

—The English are blockading the sea, he answered, and so there is no export. What will you do with it all?

—That's exactly what guarantees the plan. Here all they want is unrefined sugar. So there'll be no need to refine it.

Jabarti asked for some time to consider it.

Wednesday, 6 February.

In the morning, we discovered that Sakita was gone. We spent the whole day looking for her, but to no avail.

Chapter Five

Thursday, 7 February.

Instead of going to the Institute, I spent the day preparing for travel. Jabarti advised me to take warm clothes because it would be cold. He also told me I could take a donkey. I packed clothes in a cloth sack, along with some bread. The servants prepared for me a package of cheese from Upper Egypt. I took my inkwell and two reed pens.

When I asked my teacher about fasting, he said that I should do so only if it was possible; if not, then conditions for travel and war applied—and it is permitted to break the fast in those cases.

No news of Sakita.

Sunday, 10 February.

Early in the morning, on a donkey laden with my cloth sack and bedding, I rode towards the Palace Walk. Al-Azm Street was unusually crowded with soldiers and all kinds of tradesmen, like blacksmiths and carpenters.

I headed to Adliyya where the French soldiers had assembled. The Commander-in-chief joined us, as well as a great many officers. There were also civilians: interpreters, servants, camel drivers, a group of merchants, local Janissaries and Syrian and Coptic Christians.

Guiding my donkey through the crowds, I noticed a group of the French scholars, among them Monge and Berthollet and the great interpreter, Venture de Paradis. Camels were laden with supplies: flour, biscuits, water and fodder for the animals.

The French soldiers wore light clothing that would be no help against the cold and the rain. Their matching pants, shirts and tunics were made of linen. Piles of bedding, mattresses and mats were loaded and ready to go, along with litters for the commanders' women and the slave girls—white, black, Abyssinian—they had taken from the emirs' homes. Most of them were dressed like Frankish women.

There were Frenchmen wearing Arab galabiyas and turbans, leading a train of camels. I asked one of the soldiers about them.

—You haven't heard? Bonaparte is going to be circumcised and put on a turban. He'll follow the religion of Muhammad!

Then he laughed, and I realized he must be joking.

The commanders gave the order to start moving towards Salhiyya. I was in the vanguard, while the Commander-in-chief stayed further back.

Monday, 11 February.

We did not stop in Salhiyya. We kept going until Qurayn and Bilbeis. The day's ration was half a pound of bread and half an ounce of olive oil per person. I was determined to fast, so I saved my ration for iftar.

Near Qatiyya, Bedouins attacked and killed three men and took control of one of the food caravans.

We travelled toward El-Arish, about nine hours away. The sand was hot, and it was not long before we needed water. They distributed the remaining waterskins equally, and each person got a few drops. I swallowed my share, breaking the fast. One soldier threw himself on the last waterskin, trying to get to it before anyone else.

After a few hours the soldiers began to collapse from exhaustion. They lay there not moving until it grew dark and we began to crawl forward again. Before long we were lucky to come across a water reservoir. Once we had emptied it, we dug further and managed to find a bit more water.

At daybreak, we could look down on El-Arish, and could make out a forest of palms next to the sea. It was clear that the place was just a bunch of old huts guarded by a small number of Turkish soldiers. We fired a few cannon balls at them, then approached. This was what they had been waiting for; just as we moved forward, a heavy rain of fire came upon us.

We were able to enter the city even after heavy fighting that lasted the whole day. For the first time, I witnessed the ugliness of war. The French had killed the inhabitants with their bayonets.

There was nothing to eat. We became desperately hungry. The soldiers slaughtered camels and horses and ate them. I ate with them and spoilt my fast for the second time.

They gave me a place in the interpreters' tent. Worried that someone would steal my donkey, I tied it to my bedding. With me were a Copt, a Maltese, an Iraqi and two Syrians. There was not enough light to write.

Tuesday, 12 February.

In the morning, I wrote down the events of the previous days. A captain summoned me.

—My name is Captain Hauet. And you are . . . and he read my name from a page in front of him.

—Yes, I said.

—You will assist me in preparing my reports. I will show you how.

I sat down on a wooden chest next to him and he showed me his papers. They were reports containing the names of the officers, the arms of each regiment, number of troops and cannon. My task was to review the names and positions of the Egyptians and Syrians.

Around noon more troops joined us, under the command of General Kléber. The French blockaded the fort of El-Arish—an imposing square stone structure with octagonal towers on each side, surrounded by high walls. In front of the fort was a large encampment of Ibrahim Bey's Mamluks, Bedouins, Turks, Maghribis and Albanians sent by al-Jazzar.

Wednesday, 13 February.

I left my donkey tethered to a tent pole and went to the Captain's tent. He was outside, screaming at some soldiers. It appeared that his horse had disappeared, and he was demanding to know where it was. The soldiers eventually confessed that they had eaten it. In their defence, they claimed it had been a wicked beast. When I returned to my tent, my donkey was also missing. I searched all day but could not find it.

On my way back, I noticed a black woman laughing with a French soldier. She looked familiar, and it took a moment to realize that it was Sakita. I think she recognized me, but she said nothing, wrapping her arms around the Frenchman.

Friday, 15 February.

Last night the French launched a surprise attack on the Turkish camp. The Turks, as a rule, do not fight between sunset and sunrise. The French entered their camp unnoticed after midnight and killed the sleeping men with their bayonets. Hauet wrote his report on the dead and wounded and the causes of death. Three Frenchman against 500 dead and 900 prisoners among the enemy. I expressed horror at the numbers. Hauet said that Egyptians and Bedouins were savage brutes, and that God had sent Bonaparte to punish them.

Monday, 18 February.

Bonaparte arrived yesterday with a number of officers, among them Caffarelli, the 'Man of Wood', accompanied by Ibrahim Sabbagh. Another regiment arrived today, having crossed the desert. Many soldiers had died by suicide on their way, some shot themselves in the head. Negotiations began with Ibrahim Agha, the Turkish commander of the citadel, but without success.

Sabbagh did not stay with the other interpreters. He spent the night in Caffarelli's tent.

Tuesday, 19 February.

The Commander-in-chief ordered curtain fire from the cannons circling the fort. But many cannon balls went right over and landed among the French troops on the other side, killing three men. By the evening, there was a small gap in the wall and some men managed to get through to one of the towers—380 French casualties.

Sabbagh told me that if Bonaparte captured Acre, he would put on a turban, and the soldiers would start wearing billowing Turkish sarwals instead of trousers. He would proclaim himself Emperor of the Orient. He also said that Bonaparte talked about creating a state for Jews in Palestine.

Wednesday, 20 February.

The cannons fired all morning. Around noon a messenger went to the fort carrying a flag signalling truce and calling on its commander to surrender. They reached an agreement that the people of the garrison could keep their arms and their possession with the exception of horses, and that they would set out in the desert towards Baghdad. The garrison numbered about 900 men. But as soon as they left the fort, they were surrounded by the French and pressganged into serving with them.

Joy spread over the camp. Inside the citadel the provisions were abundant. A room had been designated for those dying of the plague. All the Turkish flags captured by the French were sent to Cairo to be displayed at the Azhar.

Sunday, 24 February.

This day we looked down upon Gaza. Surrounded by olive trees, it was a splendid sight to behold. They took the city with no resistance. We found storage depots full of rusks, barley, a huge quantity of gunpowder, twelve cannons and a depot full of tents and another with shells.

The soldiers looted and pillaged the city. Everybody received 500 grams of rusks and a piece of horse meat.

Thursday, 28 February.

We left Gaza. Pouring rain and we sunk to our knees in the mud and the water. Camels perished from the cold.

Friday, 1 March.

We entered Ramla and found that its Muslims had fled. Only the Christians remained to welcome us. All the women had taken refuge in two convents. They were white-skinned, but the whiteness was tainted by yellow. They were not concerned to cover their faces.

We came across provisions left behind by Ibrahim Bey's men.

The Captain said, No doubt the bones of our ancestors buried in the Holy Land are feeling happy that we've arrived. I realized he was speaking of the Crusaders.

Sunday, 3 March.

In the morning we marched on. Before midday we reached Jaffa, on the coast. It sits on a hill covered with trees, orange, lemon and almond. At its centre is a surrounding wall with towers on each side.

The Captain called us to his tent.

—You must tell me what you hear from the Syrians and the Egyptians. What are they saying?

—Nothing important, I said. They are telling each other Ramadan tales and war stories.

I mentioned what the French soldier had said about Bonaparte's circumcision and conversion to Islam. The Captain frowned.

—The soldiers also say that the French scholars are donkeys, and that the mules are half-scholars, I added.

—The General and the French do not concern you. What I want from you is news of the Egyptians and Syrians.

Thursday, 7 March.

Preparations for the offensive were completed. After the garrison refused to surrender and took the messenger hostage, the attack began in mid-afternoon. The sappers made a hole in the city walls, and after a few hours the city fell and the garrison surrendered. Still, the French killed around 2,000 of them.

The French were slaughtering like men possessed, all through the evening and into the night, making no distinction between Muslims and Christians, men or women. I stayed in the camp, afraid of what might happen if one of them noticed me. Towards the end of the night I heard Sabbagh calling my name. I went out to see him and he told me he could not sleep because of what he had witnessed in the city. The French were transformed into wild beasts: stabbing old men and young girls; violating the honour of young girls still in their mothers' arms. The screams pleading for mercy only made them more crazed.

Friday, 8 March.

Today is the Eid al-Fitr, it marks the end of the holy month of Ramadan. The Muslims gathered to pray outdoors. I wonder if I will ever be able to see Pauline again?

I returned to the Captain's tent after the prayer to find he counted 441 dead last night. He must have noticed something in my face.

—*C'est la guerre, mon petit.*

Midday. Bonaparte sends two of his aides-de-camp—both young men, one of them his wife's son—to the citadel of Jaffa. The

Turks called to them from the fort's windows that they were prepared to surrender if the French promised them amnesty, and that they would not face the same fate as the rest of the people of Jaffa. The aides assured them they would not be killed. The Turks came out and gave up their arms.

Ibrahim Sabbagh told me this evening that when Bonaparte heard what his envoys had promised, he was furious.

—And what am I supposed to do with them?

Then he gave the order for their execution.

Saturday, 9 March.

This morning the French sorted the Maghribis from the rest of the prisoners. These latter were assembled in front of Bonaparte's tent and not allowed any food. The Maghribis were led to the seashore. I followed at a distance and saw them being lined up at the water's edge. Then two battalions came up and began shooting them.

Some of them started to run, trying to flee, but the French called them back, saying it was all right, that Bonaparte had pardoned them. But as soon as they returned, the soldiers began shooting again. Some threw themselves into the sea and tried to swim away, but the soldiers took their time firing at them, until the sea was red with blood and the corpses floated on the surface.

Sunday, 10 March.

Towards midday, having registered the quantity of dry biscuits we had captured (400,000 daily rations) and rice (200,000 pounds), the Captain dispatched me to where the rest of the prisoners were gathered—in front of the Commander-in-chief's tent. They called for the Egyptians among them and made them stand aside.

The Turkish prisoners were led to the waters' edge and spread out in a row. I counted 120 Turks, among them were children clinging to their fathers. They began to recite the Quran and the profession of faith—*There is no God but Allah, and Muhammad is His Messenger*. Then the shooting started.

All of a sudden, an officer came running and gave the order to cease fire. I thought the prisoners had been pardoned, but the officer was simply telling his men to save their ammunition. So they bayoneted the prisoners instead.

I saw the living among the prisoners pile the dead corpses in front of them to serve as shields against the relentless stabbing, but their efforts were in vain.

Came back to my tent. Vomited.

I went to Caffarelli's tent in the evening. Sabbagh was sitting in front. I joined him and asked about the Egyptian prisoners. He said that Bonaparte had rebuked them for having fled Egypt. He ordered that they be given back their clothes and that they be sent to Damietta by boat. Among them was Sayyid Umar Makram, former head of the shareefs, along with a bunch of administrators who had taken flight.

Monday, 11 March.

Hauet recorded 21 cases of fever at the hospital of the Greek Orthodox monastery. I asked him if this was due to the plague. He said no, the physicians said it was not the plague. But he did stress to me the importance of washing daily and maintaining standards of cleanliness. He further added that Bonaparte had visited the hospital with his officers and spoken with some of the sick soldiers. In a crowded ward, he had helped carry the foul corpse of a soldier whose tattered tunic was filthy from the bursting of huge purulent boils.

—If it were truly the plague, he added, the General would have fallen sick as well.

I could hear him whisper to himself, shaking his head.

—What a great man!

Tuesday, 12 March.

I noticed that the Maltese interpreter was listless and unsteady. He started raving, saying he was feverish and had a violent headache. Taking off his shirt, he revealed dark spots all over his body. And a swelling on his neck. I ran my hand over it and he screamed in horrible pain.

Wednesday, 13 March.

We transferred the Maltese to the hospital, but they refused to let us visit him. I learnt that the abscesses had appeared all over his body.

Thursday, 14 March.

Marching orders. The French have taken Haifa, Jazzar having withdrawn and left the city.

I looked for Caffarelli's tent and found the entrance open, but he was not there. Sabbagh was asleep in the corner. It appeared that there was only one bed in the tent. I left but came back in the evening. This time I called for him and he came out. We sat next to the tent and he lit a fire, placed some cinnamon in a coffee pot and held it over the flame. We talked about the plague. He said that many had died of it and some had even killed themselves, but the French were concealing this so that panic would not spread among the soldiers. I knew he was getting his news from the French officer. And I told him that I believed God sent the plague to the French in return for what they had done in Jaffa. He didn't answer, just busied himself pouring the cinnamon drink into two cups.

I changed the subject and asked him about the Institute, about Gaston and the nature of his relationship with Pauline. He said that Gaston tried to court her but she rejected his advances. Caffarelli praised her, saying she was very serious about her work. Then he told me she had become Bonaparte's 'official companion' following her divorce. He had heard the soldiers calling her 'Cleopatra' and sometimes 'Madame Général'.

—People always tell lies about women, I said.

Sunday, 17 March.

Two English warships off Acre. According to Sabbagh, six vessels of the French flotilla had been captured. They had been coming from Damietta, carrying siege cannons.

Monday, 18 March.

We took up positions in front of Acre. Its fortifications looked dilapidated to me, but a large section faced the sea where the English warships waited. As for the part facing inland, the walls had battlements at each corner and towers along the sides. Next to the wall was a square structure—this was the citadel of al-Jazzar.

Soldiers and engineers were busy building fortifications and digging trenches from the camp to the walls in order to protect the attackers from enemy fire. Caffarelli was directing them, walking on his wooden leg without assistance, riding his horse and galloping with ease.

Tuesday, 19 March.

I could not sleep last night. Intense fever. I lay awake all night, terrified, hearing the Bedouins imitate the screams of foxes. This morning an abscess appeared in my right armpit. I called for a doctor, but they told me he was taken ill. The pharmacist advised me to vomit and sweat it out as much as possible and keep warm.

Wednesday, 20 March.

Feeling a bit better.

Thursday, 21 March.

Today I felt strong enough to walk around the tent for a short while. The camp now resembles an outdoor market, with the locals on the outskirts selling wine and figs and wheat cakes and grapes and butter, all of it at exorbitant prices. There were many idle women as well.

I watched a number of soldiers crawling in the trenches, carefully getting closer to the walls and towers to lay mines; the cannons from the citadel bombarded them constantly.

Sabbagh tells me that Kléber mocked the trenches, saying they were suitable for someone of Bonaparte's stature, but not for him—giant that he is, they wouldn't even come up to his waist.

Friday, 22 March.

The French were prepared for the attack. First they fired their cannons intensely at one point in the wall to create a breach. Then the real assault began. They distributed wine, in quantities much larger than their regular rations. The grenadiers charged first, attempting to scale the debris and enter the breach. As for the enemy, they countered with all they had—bullets, shells and stones. Anyone who made it to the breach was met with swords.

Many lives were lost. The French repeated the attack, but without success.

I saw Sakita bent over a fallen French soldier. She was crying. I don't know if the soldier was wounded or struck by the plague. I preferred to slip away.

Monday, 25 March.

A postal boat arrived from Cairo. Sabbagh and I sat with one of the pilots, an old Maltese. We asked him about the situation in Cairo. He said the plague was spreading. The French had posted notices in the markets ordering quarantine for anyone suspected of being infected. Each new case had to be reported to the French by the sheikh of each market or quarter.

The sheikh of each market or quarter was obliged to inform the French official about those infected in their neighbourhood. Anyone not obeying would be punished by death. And they warned against mingling with women of ill repute.

The Maltese said that a large number of young Mamluks were living in secret at the sheikhs' houses in Cairo. They were plotting to sow discord and cause trouble in the city. The Diwan ordered that all Mamluks and foreigners must carry papers establishing their identity.

Tuesday, 26 March.

Sabbagh showed me the text of a letter he translated to be sent to the Diwan in Cairo. We were both astonished at the misrepresentation it contained. It read, in part:

> We also inform you that General Junot has triumphed over 4,000 warriors, on foot and on horseback, who had arrived

> from Syria. He met them with just 300 infantrymen from our camp (. . .) They suffered around 600 dead or wounded, and we took from them five flags. This was an astonishing achievement—never in the history of warfare have 300 men defeated 4,000. We know that victory comes from God, not from troop numbers!

Wednesday, 27 March.

Sabbagh called for me this morning. I sought Hauet's permission and went to see him. He said that among the letters he had translated so far he came across one that had clearly been misplaced. It was a letter from Bonaparte to Pauline. He read it to me, translating from the French:

> Not a minute passes I do not think of you . . . A thousand kisses on your eyes, on your lips, on your tongue and on the small golden forest . . .

There was no longer, then, any doubt.

Thursday, 28 March.

At dawn, the bombardment of the citadel began. After a couple of hours, forty French artillerymen had been killed or wounded by Turkish fire. But they had managed to make breach high in the wall, so Bonaparte ordered that it be scaled with ladders. The Turks massacred the attackers, and they were forced to retreat again.

I put aside all thoughts of Pauline.

Sunday, 31 March.

The French succeeded in placing a mine underneath the big tower, despite the cannon fire raining down from the citadel.

Monday, 1 April.

Another offensive. Most of the French attackers were killed or wounded.

They continue digging trenches and laying mines. The rains stopped and the khamsin winds are blowing. The plague is getting worse.

The wife of General Verdier has been to Kléber's tent several times. Is she his mistress? It made me think of Pauline. I wonder if she might feel differently, now that I am away.

Tuesday, 9 April.

Caffarelli's arm was shattered by Turkish cannon fire; it had to be amputated. Soon after, he developed an intense fever. Sabbagh is inconsolable.

Monday, 15 April.

Hauet has recorded 421 cases of the plague, of which 57 died and 137 recovered.

Tuesday, 16 April.

Bonaparte has decided to go to the south and assist Kléber. Sabbagh shall accompany him.

Wednesday, 17 April.

Bonaparte and company returned this evening.

Caffarelli still unwell and feverish.

Monge has dysentery and is raving. Bonaparte ordered him to be transferred to his tent.

Sabbagh described to me the events of their short journey. They received a great welcome from the Christians in Nazareth, and his forces succeeded in saving Kléber. The following day the church bells tolled. Sabbagh attended Mass in the church with Bonaparte and the French soldiers. He said it was the first time in six years that the French had been to Mass—because their revolution had closed down the churches and now they follow the religion of reason. After the Mass there was an amusing incident: The head of the monastery told them that the chapel of this church was the bedroom of the Virgin, and when the Angel Gabriel came to deliver the good news that she would bear a son, he had struck his heel against a column of black marble next to the altar and it has remained broken ever since. The French began to laugh on hearing this, until Bonaparte gave them a sharp look.

All this while the French were burning the city of Jenin near Nablus.

Saturday, 20 April.

New heavy siege guns arrived today, and with them green-palm baskets of biscuits, rice and barley, and more than 2,000 large waterskins.

Wednesday, 24 April.

At nine in the morning, the French began a new attack with the detonation of mines under the tower. The grenadiers went courageously at the breach but the defenders pushed them back. Two barrels of gunpowder rained down on them—the men choked from the explosions. Some managed to flee, at least half of them suffered burns.

Thursday, 25 April.

Another round of attack meets with the same fate.

Among the wounded is a youth, sixteen years old. It seems that Citizen Favier, civil engineer and member of the Scientific Committee, loves this boy. Favier carried him out of the ditch on his shoulders, laid him down and closed his eyelids. Then he seemed to go into a frenzy. He exploded at Bonaparte, who listened to him in silence, then withdrew without saying a word.

Friday, 26 April.

Caffarelli was in agony. He died in the night. Sabbagh was by his side.

Sabbagh left the tent wailing. I took him aside and tried to console him. He said before he died, Caffarelli asked him to read to him Voltaire's Introduction to Montesquieu's *L'esprit des lois*. Caffarelli had promised to take him back to France.

Sabbagh now took a bed in the tent with the other interpreters.

Sunday, 28 April.

Sabbagh saw me writing this morning, and asked what I was doing. I told him I was recording the day's events. He asked me to look at what I had written, so I showed him some pages. He studied them carefully. Once he left, I wrapped my papers in some cloth, dug a hole in a corner of the tent, placed the bundle inside and covered it with sand.

Tuesday, 30 April.

Some of the siege artillery arrived. We learnt from a camel driver that a Maghribi in Damanhour has proclaimed himself the Mahdi, and says that he is a messenger from God. He claims he can turn any substance into gold; and if attacked, he can deflect shells lobbed at him or his supporters, and even keep the shells suspended in mid-air. Thousands of fellahin joined him, besieging the garrison of Damanhour for five days.

Another camel driver told us that Muhammad Bey al-Alfi and his Mamluks had managed to skirt Cairo, and had now reached East Delta.

Wednesday, 1 May.

Another failed French offensive.

Thursday, 2 May.

Today it was the captain who asked me what I was writing each morning and asked to see my papers. I went to my tent to retrieve them, but could not find them where I had buried them. I overturned everything inside the tent; I rummaged through Sabbagh's bedding.

I didn't care so much about losing the papers, since I have an excellent memory and I could rewrite the journal easily word for word. But I was worried about who might have taken them.

Friday, 3 May.

Another French attack; another defeat.

Tuesday, 7 May.

They launched another attack yesterday to no avail. But around nine o'clock this morning, they managed to set foot on the tower.

Hunger suddenly hit me. I craved a plate of broad beans cooked in oil, green pepper and lettuce. It wouldn't cost more than a *para* in Cairo, but how far away that is.

I did not ask Hauet about my papers. Did he find them?

Wednesday, 8 May.

The fighting resumed in the morning, along the walls and the coast where the English sailors had come ashore. By the time darkness fell, the tower was in the hands of the French. A small number of them had managed to break through and get inside the city, but the rest were held off by the Turks with the help of the English.

The French called off the attack only after twenty-five hours of continuous fighting.

Friday, 10 May.

Bonaparte wanted to lead a new assault, but his officers refused. The men threw themselves into the breach like they were possessed, over the corpses of their comrades. Half the combatants perished.

The postal boat arrived in the evening. We learnt from the captain that the French had launched a terrible attack on Damanhour. They had allowed looting and killing, and they had impaled 1,500 of its inhabitants.

Saturday, 11 May.

They finally admit defeat. I came to know from Hauet that Bonaparte had decided to retreat now that a third of his army had perished.

I saw him, Bonaparte, pacing slowly, head bowed, hands clasped behind his back. His officers behind him. I felt malicious joy at the sight, and wished that that a shell would come and hit him right then and there.

Monday, 13 May.

The day of Eid al-Adha, the Feast of the Sacrifice. It passed as if it never was.

Wednesday, 15 May.

On Bonaparte's orders, Hauet divided the sick and the wounded, a total of 2,300 men, into three separate groups: those who were able to walk, those able to ride and those who needed to be carried on a stretcher. They would all be taken to Jaffa, from where the most afflicted would be sent by ship to Damietta.

Thursday, 16 May.

I was with Hauet in his tent when we heard the news that Venture, the great translator, had died. It is a great loss, Hauet said sadly. Venture knew Arabic, Turkish, Italian and Greek.

He had shown symptoms of the plague but Hauet—as he was ordered to—recorded the cause of death as dysentery.

Venture was replaced by his former pupil, the young Jaubert.

Sabbagh tells me that a soldier stricken with the plague asked his comrade to end his life, and the comrade complied.

Friday, 17 May.

Sabbagh translated Bonaparte's letter to the Diwan in Cairo:

> At last I must inform you that I leave Syria for Cairo with utmost haste.

We will depart in three days' time from the date of this letter, and arrive in Cairo in fifteen days. I shall bring along many prisoners and many enemy flags. I have destroyed Jazzar's palace and the walls of Acre, and bombarded the city such that there is not left one stone upon another. The inhabitants fled by sea.

Jazzar himself is wounded. He has withdrawn with some of his people to a fort on the coast. His injuries are severe.

I am most eager to reach Cairo and see you, all the more so as I have learnt that, despite your zealous efforts, a band of miscreants is threatening to disturb public order. All of this will be dispersed with my arrival, as the morning sun disperses the clouds. Venture has died of an illness. His death is a great loss that affects me deeply.

—*Bonaparte*

Saturday, 18 May.

The soldiers lined up in formation and an officer read them a letter from Bonaparte:

You have traversed the desert that divides Africa from Asia, and you have done it faster than any Arab army has done. The army that was marching ahead to invade Egypt has been vanquished.

. . . With a handful of men, you have waged a three-month-long war in Syria, you have valiantly captured 40 pieces of cannon, 50 flags, 6,000 prisoners and razed the fortresses of Gaza, Jaffa, Haifa and Acre, and so we will return to Egypt. I am forced to return now because we expect enemy forces to land there in the coming months

> . . . Indeed, we will face more trials and more danger, and you will find new opportunity for glory.

I noticed that the men to whom this message was addressed were sneering. They knew full well that Acre had not been razed, that the Turkish army had not been thwarted, that the siege was lifted because they were defeated and half of them got killed in this futile adventure.

Monday, 20 May.

The enemy launched a counterattack that lasted all day. The Turks kept throwing themselves into our trenches. When darkness fell, the journey began.

The captured enemy flags had pride of place. When we reached the first village, the flags were unfurled and the soldiers burst into song. I followed directly behind them on foot along with the other interpreters.

We had barely any means of transport. It fell to the soldiers to carry the sick and wounded—Hauet estimated them to be 1,200—as well as forty pieces of artillery.

Bonaparte travelled on foot, leaving his carriage to the convalescing Monge, Berthollet and the mathematician Costaz, and they took with them two men suffering from the plague and an officer's wife who was nursing a child. No one else was infected.

Near midnight we reached Haifa. About a hundred sick and wounded lay in the middle of a square. The air was filled with their screams. Some were tearing at their bandages and writhing in the dirt. We just stood there, immobilized by the horrible scene.

A few men in each brigade were designated to carry the sick and wounded up to Tantura. Then the march resumed.

At Tantura, on the coast, we found 700 wounded and plague-stricken men and not a single ship to take them.

The order came to bury cannons and burn the ammunition, in order to free up horses for the sick and wounded. While this was being done, a case of artillery shells exploded, killing and maiming a number of bystanders. I saw men with missing limbs being thrown off the stretchers by the men who were supposed to be carrying them. Some wounded and sick were abandoned in the fields.

Our path was lit by the torches the French used to burn towns and villages and crops. On either side of us lay the dead. I heard one of them screaming: I'm only wounded! it's not the plague! But nobody believed him.

Friday, 24 May.

We arrived at Jaffa in the afternoon.

Word spread that Bonaparte refused an English offer to transport soldiers to Alexandria. The soldiers were livid. I heard one of them asking sarcastically about the six acres that Bonaparte promised each of them in Toulon.

Tuesday, 28 May.

The French ended their occupation of Jaffa with fireworks, then resumed the march. I travelled with Sabbagh. He said that Bonaparte had written to his government in Paris telling them of his triumphs and how the plague had struck Acre. Had his soldiers entered its citadel, Bonaparte wrote, they would have brought the horrible disease back to camp. Thus, he made the decision to withdraw.

Sabbagh looked around and said to me in a low voice that there was an order to poison those left in the hospital at Jaffa. There were about fifty of them. The physician Desgenettes refused to carry out the order. Bonaparte procured the drug from the Turkish physician Hajj Mustafa and the pharmacist Royer administered it to the patients.

Wednesday, 29 May.

They fell dead on the road from exhaustion or minor wounds. I saw a soldier bend over a fallen comrade and cut off his money belt. The fallen one begged him to keep the 12 francs in the belt so he might be able to give them to the Bedouin in exchange for his life. But the soldier took the belt and went on his way.

Thursday, 30 May.

The army arrived at Gaza yesterday. This morning, we marched on.

Saturday, 1 June.

After two days' march, dawn to dusk, through the desert, we reached El-Arish. Hauet is busy counting the remaining men. I think that less than half of the troops are left.

Monday, 3 June. Evening.

After nine hours, we arrived in Qatiya, whence the Syrian expedition had started. The soldiers looked delighted. With some exceptions.

At Salihiyya, Bonaparte gave strict orders concerning agitators in the army. He asked the leader of each brigade to keep a list of names, and if any were found guilty of agitation, they would face execution by firing squad, without trial.

He also ordered that some of the sick should be left behind.

Wednesday, 5 June.

We took a short break before sunset. When Kléber ordered us to resume, no one moved. He repeated the order but still no movement. Instead, a torrent of insults rained on the officers' heads. An aide-de-camp hurried to confront them, but he was faced with a row of soldiers' bayonets. He scuttled back to Kléber's side.

—Leave them be, said Kléber. Let them release some of their pent-up rage. We'll continue on our way and they will follow us.

And that is what happened.

I noticed a group break away from the procession and walk off with the injured on the camels towards an unknown destination.

Saturday, 15 June.

A terrible sandstorm and dreadful heat. We arrived at Cairo in a disgraceful state, without uniforms or provisions, struck by dysentery and the plague.

At Adliyya, they left a large number of sick and wounded behind as we continued onwards. Pauline began to intrude on my thoughts.

We entered the city through Bab al-Nasr, the 'Gate of Victory'. The way was lined with palm leaves, and each soldier carried a leaf in his hat. Bonaparte went forth high on his horse, hand on his side. Members of the Diwan and the French garrison accompanied us to Ezbekieh; music played.

All the officials and officers attended, with corteges, drums and pipes, Turkish musicians and Syrian percussion. Captured enemy flags were on display; the streets crammed with people.

I was walking alongside Hauet, who told me bitterly that the people would be eager to learn just how many of us returned alive.

It took five hours to reach Ezbekieh.

I headed directly for home. Jaafar and the rest of the servants welcomed me warmly. I didn't see the Sheikh Jabarti, who was with a group welcoming Bonaparte. I washed and then ate. They had prepared for me a meal with meat, okra, aubergine and afterwards melon. I learnt that the price of one melon was now 5 *paras*. It used to be 3.

My teacher retuned home shortly after. He welcomed me with tears in his eyes. We took our places in the meeting room. Khalil, back from the business in Bulaq, joined us.

I told them all that had happened. The Sheikh took out pen, ink and paper but I noticed that he wrote down very little of what I was saying. It was clear to me that he was extraordinarily preoccupied, as he brushed away flies with a horse-tail fly-swatter.

When I was finally alone, I checked that my papers were still safely hidden in the chest.

Sunday, 16 June.

For the first time in a long while, I slept well. I could not believe that I had returned safely. Woke up around noon and spent the afternoon talking with my teacher, who had not gone to his lesson at the Azhar Mosque. He showed me a paper printed by the French while we were in Syria.

We both laughed at the expression:

> We oblige our flocks from the people of Egypt and its countryside to strive for politeness and fairness and to refrain from spreading lies and fables for the speech of hashish-smokers is harmful to those who would take heed.

He told me that Muhammad Bey Alfi had gone to join the Bedouins in the Jazira. Around a hundred men joined him, mostly fugitive Mamluks of those parts and various Bedouin. The French sent a number of troops to deal with him. The same with Murad Bey in Upper Egypt, who is said to have killed about 300 Frenchmen.

We were joined by Khalil who asked if it was true that the officer Menou had embraced Islam, and had he done it out of faith or just in order to marry the daughter of the bathhouse-keeper in Rosetta.

—Apparently he's performing all the rituals of his new religion with great care, my teacher said.

—No doubt she's a young temptress, playing with the mind of an old man, said Khalil.

Jabarti said he thought it was politically astute.

He gave me permission to look at his own papers so that I could learn what had happened in my absence. I read what he had written on 4 June, the end of the Islamic calendar year, of events he had not noted when they occurred. This was his custom at the end of each year. I found that he had documented the execution of Kurayyim nine months after the event, with the words: The distinguished Muhammad Kurayyim died at the hands of the French.

I also read that the sheikhs of the Azhar issued a fatwa stating that circumcision was a supererogatory act, not required for one who converts to Islam. As for wine: the Muslim might drink it, but then he will not enjoy the delights of Paradise. The French could then drink wine and still enter Paradise as long as they paid a fifth of their income as alms.

Once back in my room, I set to chronicling the events of the Syrian campaign.

Monday, 17 June.

My feet led me to Ezbekieh, where I found that musicians and acrobats, snake charmers and monkey trainers, jesters and clowns and dancing girls had gathered in the square. Swings and see-saws were set up, like at the time of the Eid or the festivals. After dark, there were cannons, rockets and fireworks.

I stood there for a while, looking at the snakes dancing to the flute, raising their heads and their bodies.

Pauline's house was in darkness, while Bonaparte's palace was a blaze of light. When I returned home, Abd al-Zaher was waiting for me. We went to Hanna's place.

We learnt from him that Sheikh Bakri had presented Bonaparte an Arabian stallion, with a saddle of gold, precious stones and pearls, and a slave named Rostam to look after it. The gift was all the more valuable because Bakri was infatuated with Rostam, in an unnatural way. Master Gergis al-Gawhari, the tax collector, had given Bonaparte two camels, each adorned with very expensive fabrics.

I asked about Zaynab. He shook his head sadly.

—I don't think about her any more.

Chapter Six

Tuesday, 18 June.

Gaston greeted me with unusual warmth and peppered me with questions about the campaign. When I told him about the victims of the plague, the wounded and the killed, he did not seem to believe me. He asked about Jazzar, and was it true that we killed him and razed his citadel? I told him the truth. He turned pale. When I told him with disgust about giving opium to the wounded and plague victims in Jaffa, he said, should they have left them there for the Bedouins and the Turks to slaughter them?

I asked him about Pauline. He told me with some distaste that she had come to the Institute some days ago, but rarely left the house now for fear of the plague.

Sabbagh joined us and inquired about Menou's marriage and his conversion to Islam. Gaston confirmed it was true: the wife was a relative of al-Mahrouqi, the chief of the merchants, and his brother Ali now flaunted the French insignia everywhere he went. People called him 'Official Ali'.

—Did they circumcise him? asked Sabbagh.

Gaston laughed.

—He got an exemption for that.

Wednesday, 19 June.

General Desaix was having trouble fighting Murad Bey in Upper Egypt, Gaston said. Ophthalmia was widespread among his troops.

I visited the strange workshop of Conté to get a new pencil.

When I returned, Gaston asked if I knew anything about raising baby chicks. I knew nothing about it. He'd heard it was easy and very profitable in these times.

Thursday, 20 June.

Yesterday evening Gaston visited an incubator for chicks near Sayyida Zaynab.

—Nothing could be simpler to build than one of these. Each one is made of small cells, spread out on two levels, and between them a wooden board, covered with baked bricks. The lower part is for the eggs, and you make a fire on the bricks above. You have a place to live for the main worker and his helper who watch over the whole process. And there's another room for burning camel dung and straw. There's a third room where the chicks are to be kept a few hours after they hatch.

I tried not to laugh and busied myself in my work.

Friday, 21 June.

Gaston is still talking about the chickens. He says the whole project wouldn't take much time.

—You start in March. You work for just two months, time for three incubation periods, each one with three to four thousand eggs. The main worker goes into the lower rooms to turn the eggs over, move them around, keep them away from places that are too hot. That's the main work. It's a miracle. And the Egyptians don't even know what a 'thermometer' is. Eggs need a stable temperature of 23°C. You need a thermometer for that, but here they just depend on some special sensitivity they pretend to have inherited from ancient Egyptian priests.

I was a bit surprised by this information.

—But how do you get the eggs? I asked.

He smiled, taking pride in his knowledge of chicken rearing.

—As soon as an incubator is opened, all the people in neighbouring areas bring all the eggs they've got. You record their names, and after the hatching, you give them fifty chicks for every hundred eggs they brought. Then you sell a hundred new-born chicks for, on average, 89 *paras*. A little bit less than 3 French francs. The profit is huge.

—Don't you have incubators like this in France?

—Unfortunately, no. They've tried, but all attempts have failed. I'm thinking of building one here in Egypt.

Saturday, 22 June.

A new Frenchman arrived at the library. Thin, wild hair. Gaston introduced him to us as Parseval-Grandmaison. His craft is writing poetry. He mentioned that Bonaparte got angry with him for refusing take charge of *Le Courrier*.

—The real reason, the young man claimed, is that I didn't write a single ode in praise of him. I tried, but I just wasn't able.

—Did your poetic muse leave you, asked Gaston in jest.

—Never! I am now composing an epic about Richard the Lionhearted's capture of Acre.

Sabbagh broke in, He'll be twice as angry with you, then, for drawing attention to his failure at Acre.

Parseval shrugged, unperturbed.

They talked about Egyptian glass. Gaston advised him to buy Austrian crystal in Muski. Then their conversation turned to harems and slave girls.

—Women in our country don't cover their faces, said Gaston. And they manage their own affairs.

—You forget, replied Parseval-Grandmaison, it wasn't so long ago that they had to wear chastity belts and the feudal lord had the first rights with any girl on her wedding night. And this *droit du seigneur* was sanctified by the Church!

Monday, 24 June.

Members of the Special Diwan composed, printed and posted papers in the markets. My teacher showed me one of them, and I copied it here:

> The Leader of the French Armies, Bonaparte, Beloved of the Muhammadan People, has returned to blessed and protected Egypt . . . because he promised us that he would after four months, and a free man's promise is an obligation . . . He has informed all the members of the Diwan that he loves the religion of Islam. He glorifies the Prophet, eternal peace and blessings upon Him; and he respects the Quran, which he recites masterfully every day. We know that it is his intention to build a great mosque in Egypt, one that will have no equal in all the lands, and that he will enter into the religion of the Prophet, the Chosen One,

the greatest of blessings and the most complete eternal peace upon him.

Wednesday, 26 June.

Pauline came to the Institute, unexpectedly. She was wearing a new coloured dress made of smooth and light fabric. It revealed a large part of her chest. Her hair was concealed in a kind of headdress.

I was very upset, and pretended to be busy with my work while she sat down at her usual place next to mine.

Gaston greeted her and asked if she was going to join us again.

She shook her head.

—I was just on a walk in Roda Island, and wanted to congratulate our heroes on their safe return.

She looked at me as she spoke.

I pulled myself together, and told her that none of us even touched a weapon.

—Nevertheless, you were part of the battle.

Then she changed the subject.

—Have you heard about Menou's marriage?

—No doubt she's just a young temptress, playing with the mind of an old man, said Gaston.

—On the contrary. He was with us two days ago, and he told us that he didn't even lay eyes on her before the wedding, when it became apparent that she wasn't as young or as beautiful or as rich as she had been described.

There was a moment of silence, and I thought of those words: *He was with us two days ago.*

She stood up and walked around the library, picking out Rousseau's *Confessions* and two other books. Pauline asked Gaston to record what she had taken and promised to return them soon. As she was leaving, I couldn't hold my tongue.

—Do you still play the piano?

—Sometimes, she said, turning and looking directly into my eyes.

Gaston walked her to the door.

Monday, 8 July.

Sayyid Umar Makram Efendi, former chief of the shareefs, arrived from Damietta. He and Sheikh al-Mahdi went to meet Bonaparte, who received him warmly and returned some of what had been confiscated from him earlier. Umar Efendi was allowed to go back to his house, and people began to visit him again, streaming in and out just as they used to do.

Thursday, 11 July.

I stayed at the Institute until sunset so as to listen to the illustrator Denon who'd just returned from Upper Egypt. He was a charming, energetic middle-aged man. He carried a number of large, rolled-up papers, like maps.

I sat near him with paper and pencil, ready to take notes. He had volunteered to join the army of General Desaix nine months ago on the expedition to Upper Egypt. People called this the 'army of Master Yacoub' because Desaix had taken the Coptic notable with him as guide and intermediary.

—I spent most of my time with General Belliard, and that was the most difficult part of the adventure.

Everyone laughed. He went on:

—Despite that, my energy was not diminished. I had paper and pencils, from our friend Conté, and began to sketch. People, temples, everything. When the pencils were gone, we made more by melting the lead from the rifles. Before we reached Girga, I suffered from ophthalmia and my eyelids were stuck. But I still managed to draw.

He paused to take a drink of water.

—Thus I found myself one morning standing in awe before the temples of Thebes. And I was not the only one. The soldiers stood in formation and gave the military salute, to the accompaniment of drums and musical instruments, as if the occupation of these ruins was the goal of the Egyptian expedition. I sketched everything, and I believe I am the first to do this.

He took some of the rolls, then looked around and beckoned me. I got up and helped him spread one out. Each of us held one side.

—This is an image of the temple at Dendera. And the sight inside was simply astonishing. I said to myself, Whatever happens to me after this is of no importance. What I have seen here is enough for me.

He coughed, then resumed.

—My feelings were contradictory. When I saw the Pyramids for the first time I felt fear. And wondered what kind of tyrannical, despotic regime could have produced such a thing? What kind of miserable, oppressed masses must have built these? In the Valley of the Kings and Dendera, something else struck me. I discovered that the Egyptians did not borrow anything, they did not add any interior ornamentation, nothing superficial or unnecessary. The temple structures are characterized by a captivating simplicity and order, which they brought to the highest level.

He rolled up the paper and opened another one. It showed an island in the Nile.

—The occupation of Aswan began as a pleasant excursion. Within two days of our arrival, all sorts of businesses were set up —French tailors, shoemakers, barbers. And restaurants. I visited Elephantine Island with Belliard, but when we wished to advance further to Philae the inhabitants yelled and shouted and the women began to wail. Belliard finally took the island by force and I saw women drowning the children they couldn't carry with them. I saw them mutilate their daughters so that they wouldn't be raped. I saw one girl, about seven years old, in a state of convulsions. We discovered that she had been sewed up such that she was unable to urinate.

There was some shuffling in the seats, and I sensed that not everyone was comfortable with such talk. Denon may have sensed it, too, for he changed the subject.

—On New Year's Eve, the annual caravan from the south arrived. Two thousand camels carrying elephant tusks and gold and tamarind and black slaves. Do you know the price of a black slave? One rifle for a woman, two for a man. This was also the opportunity to ask if there really was such a place as the city of Timbuktu, but this question was met with silence. In any case, the experience made me think that there is a huge market for our goods in Africa.

One of those seated asked about the booty and how it should be distributed.

—When we attacked the caravan from Darfur, we captured 897 camels. We distributed the loot as follows—a share of 12 for the attack leader, and 6 for his assistant and one share for each officer and cavalryman. Some of the soldiers got the equivalent of 15,000 or 20,000 gold francs.

When everyone was about to leave I asked Denon if I could see the rest of his drawings. He invited me to visit him the next day at the house of the illustrators.

Monday, 15 July.

A strange rumour is spreading, but Jabarti tells me it is true: Murad Bey is communicating with his wife Nafisa by signalling with lamps from the top of one of the pyramids to the roof of her palace in Cairo. This means he must be very close to us.

Tuesday, 16 July.

Some people have received news from Alexandria that boats carrying Ottoman troops have arrived at Aboukir.

Wednesday, 17 July.

I visited Denon in his studio. He showed me pencil drawings of people and temples. He knows a lot about ancient history.

Once I returned to my teacher's house, I went up to the sitting room to look for the book *Delightful Descriptions of the Kings and Sultans of the Egyptians* by Sheikh Sharqawi., which I had read with my teacher. I flipped through the first pages and read that the pharaohs lived extraordinarily long lives. The shortest lifespan of a pharaoh was 200 years, and the longest 600. The Pharaoh of Moses was short in height, only a few handspans tall, while his beard was seven spans. Others said that he was one cubit tall and that he sat on the throne in Egypt for five centuries.

Saturday, 20 July.

Gaston told me that the members of the Institute listened to a speech by Citizen Lancret describing the discovery of inscriptions chiselled into a slab of basalt in Rosetta. The writing was in Greek letters, hieroglyphics and a third unknown script. I did not understand why Gaston was so excited.

Sunday, 21 July.

Word spread that the Turks had attacked the fort at Aboukir, fought the remaining French and taken possession of the fort. People were in an uproar; they announced the good news and openly cursed the Christians.

In the evening, Jabarti sent me to Koum Sheikh Salama, next to Ezbekieh. There has been some unrest in the area, and he asked me to find out what happened. I went to Hanna's place in the Christian quarter and together we made our way to the site of the battle. The inhabitants told us that a Muslim from the Barabira quarter quarrelled with a Syrian Christian. The Muslim cursed the Christian: God willing, in four days we'll be rid of all of you. The Christian went with a gang of his own kind and reported the incident to the French. They rounded up the sheikhs of these areas and put them in jail.

All the while Hanna remained silent and nervous. Before we parted, he asked a question.

—Do you think the Turks are coming back?

—I have no idea.

Monday, 22 July.

My teacher showed me a letter from Bonaparte to the Diwan regarding his plan to combat the Turks at Aboukir. It claimed that the Turkish boats also carried a large number of Russians:

> . . . with their manifest hatred for all those who claim that God is One, their clear enmity for those who worship the One True God. They detest Islam; they do not respect the Quran. In view of their unbelief they make the divine into three, and God is but the third of those three. May God be exalted above these polytheists! But it will soon be clear to them that three will not give them strength, that a

plurality of divinities is of no use, for God, may He be exalted, is the One who gives victory to those who declare Him to be One. He is the Compassionate, the Merciful . . . In His eternal knowledge and His mighty judgement, He has granted me this territory, and it is He who is responsible for my presence here in Egypt, in order that I eliminate this corruption and these kinds of oppression, and bring in their stead justice and tranquillity.

Tuesday, 23 July.

When I returned from the Institute I heard from the Nubian doorman at the Inal caravanserai that the Muslims, the Turkish troops and those accompanying them had captured Alexandria at three o'clock last Saturday. I told Jabarti and he asked me to confirm this from the source.

I went back to the caravanserai, where I learnt that the purported source was a letter received by a textile merchant in the Souk of the Copiers. I went to see the merchant but he denied having such a letter, saying that he heard that it had come from a letter addressed to a merchant in the Herbalists' Souk near Khan al-Khalili. I went to see that merchant and it was the same story again. I spent the whole evening talking to different merchants but no one had ever actually seen the letter.

When I returned, I found my teacher had gone up to the terrace overlooking the courtyard to get some fresh air. I informed him of the results of my excursion.

—There's nothing to it, then, he said. It's a joke, it's not true.

Then he muttered: God be exalted, He who is Knower of all the unknowns.

Wednesday, 24 July.

Yesterday the word spread that the French had clashed with the troops who had come ashore at Aboukir, killing most of them and taking back the citadel. They had even taken Mustafa Pasha prisoner, along with Osman Khoja and others.

This news was confirmed in the morning when they fired cannons from the mountain citadel as well as the surrounding fortifications. After sunset, they set off fireworks in Ezbekieh using naphtha, gunpowder and rockets. I passed in front of Pauline's house. It was dark. Did she go with Bonaparte to Alexandria?

Thursday, 25 July.

Rumour has it that the French have made Master Yacoub the Commander-in-chief of the Copts, and that he has assembled a group of Coptic youths, bringing some of them from Upper Egypt and creating his own army. They flattened the buildings surrounding the Christian quarter where he himself used to live, behind the Red Mosque, so as to build his own citadel with defensive walls.

Friday, 26 July.

Denon asked me about the Syrian campaign and I told him of my experiences. He could not believe what happened in Jaffa but I swore to God it was the whole truth. He looked grave.

—We pride ourselves on being more just than the Mamluks, yet we commit many injustices. Did you know that I participated in the crushing of the Cairo revolt? I used to believe that we were bringing civilization to this country, but we just made of it a new colony, to compensate for the losses we suffered at the hands of the English in the New World. All we've done here so far is shed blood and collect taxes. Do you know who the true victims are? The fellahin, the peasants. In Asyut, Murad Bey used them as a barrier between us and them. Then he fled into the desert to hide while we slaughtered about a thousand of them. In Bani Suef, we killed 2,000 armed fellahin. The Mamluks before us taxed them just like we did. And Desaix had to take their livestock and their camels and horses so he could go after Murad Bey.

He began to fiddle with a pencil. His fingers were long and elegant.

—We came to Egypt for the welfare of its people. But we burn the roofs of their houses and their tools and their ploughs to cook our food. Their pots are broken, their wheat is taken and their chickens and their pigeons are devoured. On top of that, we double their taxes. And when they obey us and come to make the payment, sometimes our men make a mistake: because there are so many of them, carrying sticks, they think they're some kind of armed group and they open fire.

He smiled sadly.

—It's true that if they had remained in their villages and paid the tax, they would have been spared the hardship of going to the desert, and they could have had the pleasure of seeing their food consumed in an orderly manner, and even received a share of it as well. They would have been able to keep some of their riding animals. They could have even sold eggs to our soldiers. And fewer of them would have been raped. But the Mamluks consider any sort of cooperation with us to be a crime, so when we are gone and they return, they will take revenge. And they won't leave anything for the fellahin.

Sunday, 28 July.

The mathematician Fourier gave a lecture this evening on the Syrian campaign. I found it hard to concentrate, as I kept reliving the events of those days. But I sat up when I heard him say that the detailed history of the campaign would give many examples of French honour and values, the likes of which had never been seen before.

Sunday, 4 August.

Khalil said that they have arrested Hajj Mustafa al-Bashtili, a respected oil merchant in Bulaq. He is imprisoned at the house of the governor of Cairo because a group of his neighbours denounced him, saying he had a number of pots filled with gunpowder in one of his warehouses. In the ensuing raid, they found all that they were looking for.

The markets are brimming with saffron, henna and dates as always at this time of year.

Sunday, 11 August.

Word spread yesterday that the Bonaparte had returned triumphant from Aboukir. Upon leaving the Institute, I went to Ezbekieh to see if this was true. The French had returned with a large group of Turkish prisoners, and I saw them standing there in the middle of the place.

I walked past Pauline's house. Guards were walking in and out of the gates.

At sunset, my teacher left the house to join the sheikhs and the notables going to greet Bonaparte. On his return he told me that General Kléber was going to take over from Bonaparte. Allow me to kiss you, General, for you are great like the world! Bonaparte had said, loud enough for all to hear

After that, Bonaparte spoke to the sheikhs through an interpreter.

—The Commander-in-chief informs you, that when he travelled to Syria, your situation was good in his absence. This time, it will not be thus, because you used to believe that the French would not return, that they would die, down to the last of them. So you were happy—you rejoiced. You opposed the rulings of the Agha, and the sheikhs Mahdi and Sawi did not act in a correct manner.

Tuesday, 13 August.

It was the celebration of the Prophet's birthday and the festival was held at Ezbekieh. Shiekh Khalil al-Bakri invited the Commander-in-chief and a group of their notables to dine with him. There were fireworks and cannon fire. They called for the streets to be decorated, markets and shops to be open through the night and lamps to be lit. Dervishes gathered in the square, sitting cross-legged, murmuring invocations and tilting their heads right and left in a continuous movement that shook the little bells hanging from their garments.

Thursday, 15 August.

People are saying that Bonaparte is travelling north. Gaston says he knows nothing about it. My teacher says they inquired about this rumour at the Diwan, and were told that the Commander-in-chief is in Menoufia, staying as a guest of the governor.

Their soldiers are wearing new uniforms—a short tunic without pleats, trousers turned up at the bottom and goatskin hats with earflaps, visor and a wool tassel at the top.

Friday, 16 August.

I went to Ezbekieh at sunset. I could see some light inside Pauline's house and some movement within. There were guards out front. So she did not go along with the Commander-in-chief.

Tuesday, 20 August.

They searched the house of Ramadan Kashif's wife, one of the few of the Mamluks' women to remain in Cairo. They found weapons and clothes belonging to the Mamluks.

No one knows the whereabouts of Bonaparte. Should I try and visit her, I wonder. But what if the Commander-in chief suddenly returns and surprises us?

Monday, 26 August.

The annual flooding of the Nile is announced as usual. All the Christians, Copts, Syrians and Greek Orthodox went out to Bulaq or Roda or Old Cairo, and gathered in boats, with musical instruments and singing. Their behaviour tonight was immodest.

Friday, 30 August.

Jabarti was invited to meet the governor, General Dugua, with the rest of the sheikhs of the Diwan. He read to them a message that Bonaparte had sent from Alexandria. He had travelled to the land of the French last Friday—it read—in order to give some relief to the people of Egypt and to end the maritime blockade, and that he would be absent for three months, during which General Kléber, governor of Damietta, would have command over the people of Egypt and the French army.

My teacher was puzzled at how Bonaparte would travel by sea, given the presence of the English fleet. I pretended to listen, but I was thinking only of Pauline and wondering if she gone with him?

Later in the evening, her house in Ezbekieh was dark and quiet. But there was a guard in front.

Saturday, 31 August.

Upon his return from Bulaq, Khalil told us the new Commander-in-chief had arrived from Damietta this morning. All the French turned out to meet him and cannon fire celebrated his the event. The new Commander-in-chief proceeded to Ezbekieh across the new bridge the French have built from Bulaq.

Around 500 guardsmen preceded him. With quarterstaffs in their hands, they were ordering people to remain standing while the procession passed by. In his company were a great number of Frankish cavalry, swords drawn. The Wali was there and the Agha and Barthélemy, each with his entourage. There were security guards and local Janissaries, and members of the Diwan.

Khalil said he followed them to Alfi's house, where Bonaparte used to live.

In the evening, my teacher went with the notables and other prominent locals to meet the new Commander-in-chief. He did not come out to greet them and the meeting was put off until the next day.

Sunday, 1 September.

I decided to visit her. In the herbalists' quarter I bought her a paste for fattening up—consisting of chufa and colchicum root. There were no mounts in the stable. I thought about going on foot, but I was afraid I would arrive all covered in dust and sweat, so I hired a donkey to take me as far as the square, arriving at sunset. I paid 9 *paras* to the donkey driver who had run along behind me, a small stick with a bell in his hand.

There was only one guard at the house. He paid me no attention and let me in. I crossed the garden quickly. My heart was pounding as I knocked on the inner door.

The Syrian woman who opened the door recognized me, but she asked me to wait until she had informed her mistress. She closed the door and I waited for what seemed an eternity. Finally, the door opened again and the woman led me in silence to a sitting room on the ground floor. I sat on a couch next to the piano. Presently, Pauline burst into the room, wearing a long, oriental robe that reached to the floor. Her hair was wrapped in a towel.

I almost rushed towards her, but I stood frozen. She motioned for me to sit.

—I was expecting you.

She sat down at the other end of the couch. She had just bathed.

—In France, I would bathe only once a month. Most people only wash a few times per year. But I'm not used to the summer sweat in Egypt. Anyway, I still wonder if washing is worthwhile, since I sweat constantly.

The Syrian woman brought me a tamarind drink and a narghile for Pauline.

She looked desolate as she exhaled smoke nervously. I presented her the herbal paste and she laughed, saying how happy she really was with her body and that the women of the court dreamt of being her size.

—You Egyptians like a lot of flesh, she added.

—I thought you were leaving with Bonaparte.

—I only learnt about it at the last minute.

She looked at the floor, plucking at the fabric of her robe.

—I should have expected it when they came for Monge, Berthollet and Parseval in the middle of the night. They joined him in the garden where he was walking with Denon. I was at the other end. Then he called me over, patted my cheek and said he was travelling now but would be back in two or three months. Then he rode to Bulaq and took a boat to Rosetta.

Suddenly she laughed.

—Do you know what Kléber said to his comrades when he heard about Bonaparte's leaving?—He said, That bugger has left us with breeches full of shit. When we get back to Europe, we'll rub his face in it.

I mentioned that my teacher said Kléber praised Bonaparte in front of the Diwan. She shook her head.

—Bonaparte says Kléber is just an opportunist, incapable of organizing anything, that he's a hothead, that he is going to need a monthly supply of at least ten thousand soldiers.

She leant forward to adjust the coals of the narghile. Her robe hung down, and I could see the sides of her small breasts. I felt the fire spread throughout my body, and she raised her eyes to meet mine, smiling deviously. I stood up. Her eyes were fixed below my waist. I knelt before her and wrapped my arms around her legs, looking up at her with imploring eyes.

For a moment she looked back at me, then gently pushed me away with her foot. I toppled onto my back. As she reached out to touch my cheek, she whispered, Shut the door.

Not caring if she could see what state I was in, I quickly bolted the door. I kneeled again in front of her. She kicked off a slipper and put her foot before me. It was a brilliant white.

—The servant scrubbed my foot with a smooth stone, she said.

The foot rotated in the light. I took both her feet in my hands and I kissed them. She lifted up her robe to reveal her bare legs. I leant over them and kissed them all over. I felt crazed. The narghile pipe dropped to the floor. Eyes shut, she leant backwards.

I could feel her hands pulling off my turban, her fingers running through my hair. She pulled my head up to her knees, and I could see she was not wearing anything under her tunic. She pushed my head between her thighs. I didn't know what she was trying to do. Her smell was so strong that I had to pull my head away and stand up.

I pulled off the robe and mounted her. She was panting.

—I missed you a lot, she whispered.

We both came quickly but I stayed on top of her and before long we came again.

She sat up, sighing, and spread out her arms as if she were stretching. Then she kissed me several times on the mouth. I tried to get her to lie back.

—That's enough for tonight, she laughed.

—So when can I see you, then?

—Next Sunday.

I couldn't believe it.

—A whole week from now?

She said she had many things to so, as she was looking after wounded French soldiers.

Monday, 2 September.

Hanna is angry. The new Commander-in-chief wants 150,000 French *riyals* from the Copts. They have asked his family to contribute.

Sunday, 8 September.

I found her looking pale. She said she was unwell. It was the monthly sickness, she explained.

She played some music from a German named Hayden, and when she sensed that I didn't like it, she switched to a nice piece by an Austrian called Mozart.

She asked me about Jabarti's house, and was interested when I told her he writes down all the events that take place and that I was doing the same. She wanted to know what we wrote about the French. I believe she is seeing me in a new light.

In turn I asked her if she had loved Bonaparte. She was evasive.

—Did he love you?

—He believes that love is bad for the individual and bad for society.

She drew on the narghile pipe.

—He admitted to me that all his life he was shy in front of women. He had earlier plans to marry, always with women much older than he. He wanted someone of wealth. Finally, he married Josephine who was only six years older. He told me I'm the only woman younger than him he has loved.

—Is he . . .

I couldn't complete the sentence. I wanted to ask her about Bonaparte's sexual prowess, but I did not know how to formulate the question. But she seemed to understand, and laughed.

—He was always in a hurry. His work kept him very busy, and so he didn't have enough time for other things.

—Did he get circumcised, like people were saying?

—Definitely not.

Another question was on my mind, but I hesitated. Still, she smiled at me with her blue eyes.

—You're much bigger.

Sunday, 15 September.

I went to see her today as we had planned, but I could not find her.

Monday, 16 September.

It is impossible to sleep.

Tuesday, 17 September.

When I returned from the Institute, I learnt that the sheikh of the quarter, a French soldier and a Syrian woman had entered the house, to inspect the clothing and check that everything had been laid out in the sun. Neither my teacher nor Jaafar were at home, so my teacher's wife refused to let them in, thinking they wanted to look at the house and all the possessions. Eventually she relented. Jabarti confirmed that they were concerned only with taking precautions against disease and epidemic.

Wednesday, 18 September.

Today I found her. And the same thing happened as before.

Jaafar was not at home when I returned. I realized that I hadn't seen him for two days. They said perhaps he had gone to buy sugar at Sukkariya.

Thursday, 19 September.

Something strange occurred today. I was in bed after the night prayer when I heard movement in the courtyard. Jaafar was at the outer door, holding a lamp. The door was open, and there appeared in it a large man draped in a black cloak that almost covered his eyes. Jaafar locked the door and the two of them walked across the courtyard to the house. Jaafar gave a special knock and my teacher Abd al-Rahman Jabarti answered the door himself. He embraced the visitor and they disappeared inside.

I sensed they did not want anyone to see them, so I retreated inside to sit in the darkness, the door ajar. The stranger's clothes looked expensive; I would have guessed he was somebody important.

For most of the night, I did not leave my place. Then I heard a squeaking. Moving to the partially open door, I could see Jaafar holding a lamp for the visitor. He was about to stumble, and he pulled the abaya from his face. I had to stifle an exclamation when I saw who the mysterious visitor was. It was Muhammad Bey al-Alfi!

Back in my bed, I could only think of how daring he was, to be moving around while wanted by the French. Was it Jaafar who was behind this visit, and what did it mean? Is my teacher working with the Mamluks? Are they planning something?

Friday, 20 September.

The moulid of Sayyid Ali, who is buried in the Sharaibi Mosque, is announced. To prepare for the festival, they ordered the lighting of lanterns in the alleys leading to the mosque. People are allowed to come and go without any hassle.

I learnt about the story of Sayyid Ali from my teacher. He had been one of the imbeciles that walked around the markets stark naked, head and private parts exposed. He had a brother, a crafty fellow, and when he saw how people inclined towards his mad brother, and how they believed in him, as Egyptians do with people like that, he forbade him from leaving the house and made him wear clothes, so people would think he was a Sufi saint who could do miracles and who knew people's thoughts and had knowledge of the unknown, who could utter what was in men's souls. Men and women would come to visit him and seek his blessings and listen to his utterances and ravings and then interpret them as they wished. They came with gifts and votive offerings of all kinds, and presents from the wives of the emirs and the notables.

The brother was profiting handsomely from all this, while the sheikh himself was getting so fat from all the food and idleness that he started to look like great stuffed camel. And so it continued until his death six years later. His brother buried him next to this mosque, and they built a tomb with an enclosure. They regularly bring Quran-readers and chanters and praise-poets to speak of his miracles. At the moulid, the people shouted and called to each other and rubbed their faces with dust from the bars and steps of the shrine and tried to capture the 'blessed' air with their hands and put it in their pockets.

Monday, 7 October.

The level of the Nile has been low since the Feast of the Cross—and the flooding this year was already lower than usual. People are panicking—there's a clamour to buy wheat. The wheat merchants are raising their prices.

Tuesday, 8 October.

The French gathered all those dealing in grain and rebuked and threatened them. They said: The wheat that is available now is from last year's crop. This year's crop will not be sold until next year. And the merchants restrained themselves and sold at the current price. There would have been a terrible rise in price had it not been for the benevolence of God.

Thursday, 10 October.

Today she played for me a short piece by somebody called Beethoven. She tried to teach me but I couldn't concentrate. My eyes stayed fixed on her chest. Finally, what had to happen, happened.

Thursday, 17 October.

The word was out that there had been communication between the French and Murad Bey at his camp in Fayyoum. They had agreed to a truce, and Murad Bey agreed to conditions among which he was to be recognized as the Emir of Upper Egypt under French authority.

That evening I asked my teacher about it. He did not consider it unlikely.

Saturday, 26 October.

Ibrahim Sabbagh danced with joy at the Institute. Commander-in-chief Kléber has agreed to send him to France to complete his education. This was on the recommendation of Fourier, Monge and Berthollet.

Sunday, 3 November.

She surprised me today when she came in wearing the dress of an Egyptian dancer. Her shoulders, arms and chest were visible through the red garment, and the open robe revealed her neck. Her hair was braided with ribbons and she had a turban on her head. Around her hips was a wide belt, and a sheer cloth was woven around her belly. The lower part of the garment had long slits on the sides, revealing her legs all the way up to her thighs.

I had the impression of a sorceress from among the jinn. She began to shake her middle and wave her hands like the Egyptian dancers do. When she raised her arms up high, I could see the yellow fuzz in her armpits. The belt fell from her hips and she tried to tie it back, turning around me several times before kneeling in front of me.

—What do you think? Would I make a good dancer?

I pulled her towards me and put my lips on hers, but she pushed me away, then lifted up my galabiya and buried her face between my legs.

I pulled away. This had never happened to me before. But she wrapped her arms around me, under my hips, and pulled me towards her.

Perplexed, I looked down at her head bobbing up and down. Then she raised her eyes to mine when she sensed I was losing control.

I pushed her away and laid her on the couch. I went into her, and when I was about to come I pulled out but she said, no, no, stay. When it was over, I asked her why.

—It seems I can't get pregnant. I tried with my husband and with Napoleon, with whom I wanted to have a baby, but it was no use.

Friday, 8 November.

Abd al-Zaher was waiting for me at the entrance to the quarter when I returned from the Institute. He said he wanted me for something important. I invited him inside but he refused, saying he'd rather talk outside.

Silently, he led me through a number of streets and alleyways. The ground was still muddy from the rains the day before yesterday. He was taking a strange route and looking back over his shoulder from time to time, as if anxious that we were being followed. Then, he asked me to swear on a copy of the Quran not to repeat to anyone what he was about to tell me. I was surprised, but I obeyed. He said that the French soldiers were fed-up; they were complaining, and one of them even wanted to return to his country. People were willing to help the soldier, in order to rid Egypt of these people, and among them was an emir, a Mamluk, who was willing to pay the cost.

I asked him what all this had to do with me. He said that they needed someone who knew the language and could understand the deserters when they left the city. I was speechless. Abd al-Zaher assured me that I would be in no danger whatsoever. All I had to do was accompany one of them from the house where he was hiding to the outskirts of the city.

Monday, 11 November.

I practised a few French phrases with Gaston—common phrases that might help reassure a frightened person.

Wednesday, 13 November.

At sunset, I rode my donkey down the Palace Walk to the Mitwalli Gate at Bab Zuweila, then south to Bab al-Kharq. None of the guards tried to stop me as I passed through the gate. There I waited, heart pounding, hoping that the plan would fail.

Finally, Abd al-Zaher appeared, on foot. He mounted behind me and we rode for a while through an area of old, walled houses. We encountered more wild dogs than people. We stopped in front of a house that seemed to be abandoned. Its stone facade had two storefronts, both of which were closed. Dismounting, Abd al-Zaher looked around, and when he was sure that we had not attracted any attention, he knocked on one of the gates. He knocked once, then twice, then twice again.

The gate opened moments later, and I entered with my donkey behind Abd al-Zaher into a large courtyard. A distinguished-looking man greeted us then led us to a room where we found the Frenchman.

He was of medium height, wearing a galabiya and a turban, from which escaped locks of yellow hair. We discussed his appearance, and decided he should wear woman's clothes and wrap himself in a black abaya that would cover him up and only allow a bit of his blond hair to show.

I explained to him what he had to do and we helped him wrap himself in the abaya. He mounted the donkey behind me, and I bid farewell to Abd al-Zaher and the old man, and we headed west to Abdin, passing by the abandoned houses of some of the beys. The smells of the slaughterhouses and tanneries were making me nervous. At Bab al-Luq, I told him in a low voice to remain completely silent and not utter a word.

The guards at the gate asked me to stop. I almost collapsed from fear as one of them spoke to me, holding a lamp over his head.

—Where are you going?

My wife is ill, I told him, and I was taking her to the Greek physician at Ghayt al-Edda.

—Where are you coming from?

I told him the truth.

—You could have just gone directly from Bab Zuweila, he pointed out.

I told him that I thought this way would be shorter.

I could feel the Frenchman's heart pounding at my back. The soldier raised his lamp over the head of my comrade, but all he saw was a tuft of yellow hair. I imagined that he was going to ask to see his face. But he lowered the lamp and waved us through.

My comrade was shaking. I reassured him that we were fine and out of danger. I turned towards Ghayt al-Edda, fearful that the soldier would want to confirm in what direction I was heading. After a while, when I thought it was safe, I changed direction back towards Bab al-Luq. No one stopped us so we resumed our route, going left until Sheikh Rihan Street. Finally we arrived at the edge of the Nile near Qasr al-Aini and the boat bridge. I dismounted and helped my 'lady' companion down, then we went to the river's edge.

I looked around. The area was quiet. The only light came from the lanterns on the tied-up boats. We stopped and looked around, as instructed by Abd al-Zaher.

Some time passed without anyone appearing. Suddenly a black spectre burst forth. At first I thought it was a demon and I almost pissed myself with fear. He asked me about the Frenchman. I pointed to the 'woman' and he asked if she was ready to board the rowboat. I said yes and explained the situation to the Frenchman. I helped him to dismount and tied the donkey to a tree. I had to help him down to the water and into the little boat. I bade them farewell and left, breathing a huge sigh of relief.

When I got back to Bab al-Luq, the guard asked me about my wife. I said that her condition was such that she had to stay with the doctor, and I would return in the morning. Then he let me pass.

Sunday, 17 November.

I went to her house and found her angry and irritable. She told me Bonaparte had been appointed consul, but only after he had pressured the Conseil des Anciens and tricked them with the help of his brother Lucien who was president of the Conseil. She showed me an article from *Le Courrier* in which the Diwan congratulated him on his appointment as consul. It also contained a plea for unity with the French nation, signed by the members of the Diwan, including Jabarti.

I didn't understand why she was so angry.

—It means he won't come back to Egypt!

I had pretended to ignore the matter of her relationship with Bonaparte, believing that she would forget him while she was in my arms. But all the while she was waiting impatiently for him to return.

I pulled her to the couch. She tried to stop me, but when she saw that I was insistent she gave up and submitted. But she did not respond to me as she usually did.

Thursday, 21 November.

Commander-in-chief Kléber decided to prepare a volume that would contain all the research the scientists had undertaken throughout the country. But the scientists are wary of each other, and some refused to share their work with others.

Abd al-Zaher reported that the Frenchman had arrived safely in Rosetta and later boarded a boat leaving Alexandria.

Tuesday, 26 November.

They assigned a room at the end of the library for the cartographers. Every morning, they file out together, and return later in the day, bearing large swathes of paper. They then set themselves to drawing up maps of the city.

Thursday, 28 November.

Lots of talk about the arrival in Syria of Yusuf Pasha, the Ottoman Grand Vizier. They say the Turks have surrounded the fort of El-Arish which is held by the French.

Thursday, 5 December.

Jabarti confided to me that the French have sent to the English, waiting off Alexandria, to act as intermediaries between them and the Ottomans.

Friday, 6 December.

My teacher said that the Ottoman vizier, Yusuf Pasha, issued a decree before arriving at El-Arish. He addressed it to all the French, calling for two men from among their leaders to come forward for negotiations. So the French sent Poussielgue, the general administrator, and Desaix, commander in Upper Egypt. They have set out for Damietta.

Monday, 9 December.

Fever and cough. Confined to bed. Getting worse.

My teacher suggested bringing a physician from the neighbouring Mansouri Hospital but I refused. Jaafar summoned the barber but my teacher refused to listen to him. He told us the story of Ismail Effendi al-Ruzmangi who was suffering from eye pain, and was prescribed kohl by the barber. However, the barber made a mistake and gave him a mercury chloride that looked like kohl. When Ismail Efendi put it in his eyes, he went blind and later died.

Abd al-Zaher came to visit. He wanted my help in moving another deserter. I couldn't move, so I suggested he ask Hanna. He hesitated, but then agreed and went on his way.

Tuesday, 10 December.

Jaafar mentioned the matter of the Sheikh al-Samanudi, who had a great reputation for spiritual teachings, for being able to make inanimate objects move and for communicating with the jinn. The sheikh claimed to have received a revelation and ascended to heaven the night of the 27th of the month of Rajab, where he prayed with the angels. The angel Gabriel gave him a paper stating that he was a prophet.

Friday, 13 December.

No news from Abd al-Zaher or Hanna. I feel better now, and should be able to go to the Institute tomorrow. My teacher insists I should rest at home two more days.

Monday, 16 December.

I found her very excited. She told me that Kléber agreed to send her back to France. I was shocked.

—You didn't say anything about this. Did you ask to be sent back?

—Of course. Do you imagine that I would leave Napoleon to revel in his glory all alone?

I felt humiliated.

—And what about us?

Her fingers stroked my chin.

—You'll forget about me soon enough.

—That will not happen.

She kissed me on the mouth and I pulled her close, but she resisted. Tears were sliding down my cheeks. She stroked me affectionately.

—What did you expect to happen with us?

—That we would marry.

Her laughter was like an explosion.

—Napoleon asked me to marry him. He intends to divorce Josephine, ever since he learnt from an aide-de-camp that she has taken a lover and that they've both become rich because of their crooked dealings with certain elements in the army. He has promised to marry me so that I can give him a legitimate child, since Josephine could not.

—And you believed him? I asked miserably.

—Of course. He was complaining about her expenses and her unfaithfulness. I don't understand why he married her in the first place. She's older than him, and she was Paul Barras' lover. Everybody knew how many lovers she had and how much money she spent. They used to say she paid her bills from a coffer between her legs.

—But I love you, and want to marry you.

—I am supposed to live with you, in your room, at your teacher's house?

—We can live here at the Institute.

—Do you really think the French would be happy about that? Be sensible, and kiss me before we say goodbye.

She pulled me to the couch and threw herself down. I bent over her and started kissing her like a man possessed.

Tuesday, 17 December.

At sunset I rode my donkey to Hanna's house. His mother said he hadn't been home for a week and she did not know where he was. Maybe he went to the monastery of Abu Sifin in Old Cairo. I was about to leave when it occurred to me to ask:

—Has anyone else come looking for him?

She said no.

At the monastery in Old Cairo, near the Nile, I knocked on an iron-plated door and the doorman opened for me, oil-lamp in hand. I followed him down a narrow passage to another small door leading to the monastery cells. A priest wearing a cassock of coarse fabric, a round black hat and leather sandals told me he had not seen Hanna for weeks.

On to Abd al-Zaher's house near Qanatir al-Sibaa, where I tied my donkey at a good distance from the enclosure where he lives. I was afraid that he had been discovered, and that people might be watching to see who visit.

There was no sign of anyone. I boldly entered the enclosure, went up to the hut where they lived and called for him. His mother answered from behind the door.

—Who's that?

I said my name and she greeted me despondently. I asked about Abd al-Zaher.

—They took him away a few days ago, she said.

—Did they say anything?

—I understood it had something to do with a French deserter. They wanted to know who was working with him.

My voice shook as I spoke.

—What did he tell them?

—You don't know Abd al-Zaher, she said haughtily. He would never betray a friend.

Her voice changed, but she went on.

—This is what I feared. They will beat him and possibly kill him.

I tried to reassure her. I said that the French don't execute without a proper investigation and trial. I promised her to look for him and keep her informed.

Wednesday, 18 December.

Gaston confirms that El-Arish has fallen to the Turks. He was fiddling with some pages that lay before him. He took a cup of coffee and slurped loudly.

—They also uncovered an Egyptian network for smuggling French soldiers, he added.

I froze. Sabbagh looked at me with curiosity.

—Who was leading this network? I asked.

—The Mamluks.

I could hear my own voice rattling.

—And how did they discover it?

—They got wind of a plan to sneak a soldier out and they knew his hiding place so they went in.

—Did they arrest anyone?

—I don't know.

Thursday, 19 December.

The day of her departure. I am confused. Feeling sad to part with her but also feeling a kind of relief.

In the evening, I went to Hanna's house. He has not yet returned.

Friday, 20 December.

Fourier asked me to accompany the cartographers, as their interpreter was ill. He introduced me to Jomard, their chief. We set out on horseback with a Coptic scribe and three guides towards the mosque of Ibn Tulun. There we dismounted and left the horses with the servants. Jomard recorded the names of all the alleys and side streets on a big map, then wrote some observations in a notebook while the Copt took down all the names in Arabic.

Tuesday, 24 December.

A big surprise last night. I was feeling bored and fed up, so I left the house and walked towards the Muski bridge, continuing on to Ataba. I was looking at the shops, and noticed that European goods were scarce.

I crossed the Ruwaii quarter to Bab al-Hadid where the tanners and the carpentry workshops are clustered along with the vinegar makers and the oil pressers and the spinners and weavers and the grain merchants. My feet took me to Ezbekieh, to the house of Pauline. It was dark.

I returned to Ataba and walking past a side street I sensed someone passing by in a hurry. There was something familiar about him. It was Hanna.

I was about to call to him but then I stopped myself and followed him from a distance. At the Red Mosque, he went towards the fortified walls that had been built by Master Yacoub the Copt. There were towers and openings for cannons and rifles, and a large gate with great pillars. Hanna stopped in front of a number of men, clean-shaven and dressed in uniforms that looked like those of the French soldiers, except that they had a kind of headdress with a black band of leather. They carried their rifles just as the French did.

Hanna went up to the door and they let him through. I was just standing there, surprised and perplexed, when I found myself surrounded by four of the men. To my surprise, they pushed me towards the door. I did not yell or try to resist. They shut the door behind me. Hanna waiting for me inside. I had the impression that he had some authority among the guards.

—Welcome, he said.

—Strange way of welcoming, I said.

—Why were you following me?

—I've been looking for you since the day of the French deserter. I was told you were in hiding. So when I saw you today, I wanted to talk but you were in such a hurry that I couldn't catch up.

—Anyway, it's good you are here. I was meaning to pay you a visit. Come with me.

He saw that I was hesitant.

—Don't be afraid. No harm will come to you.

He led me through rooms furnished with mats and carpets and couches and cushions. It was a big house, big enough for a ruler, and full of activity, with hundreds of people moving about. Dozens of scribes from among Master Yacoub's attendants were absorbed in what looked like important matters.

The servants brought us iced orange-blossom water, followed by sirops and coffee. Then they brought three different kinds of cakes and pastries spread out on a large cloth.

I noticed an impressive retinue of servants and orderlies, female servants and slave girls, Ethiopians and Sudanese. They all wore white, and were fully veiled in the Muslim manner.

He smiled when he saw me looking in surprise at the men dressed like French soldiers.

—The Coptic army. I have the rank of lieutenant.

—You're a French soldier now?

—Listen. Egypt needs its own army, for all of us. What we don't need is a bunch of Mamluks always fighting each other. Our Master Yacoub has formed the nucleus of this army from a Coptic unit trained by French officers from the occupation.

—So it was you who arrested Abd al-Zaher?

—It didn't happen like that. We went together to a house in Ghayt al-Edda where the French soldier was hiding. I saw right away that Barthélemy's spies were everywhere. So I decided to leave the spot right away. Abd al-Zaher entered the house alone. Later I was told that Barthélemy's men went in and arrested everyone inside.

I was not convinced, and it must have shown on my face.

—Believe me, that's what happened, he said as he got up. Come with me.

We entered a large hall filled with people. Copts, Syrian Christians, foreigners, Jews, prominent French officers sat together. To my surprise, there were even some Muslim sheikhs. They were all listening to a tall, strongly built man in the centre of the room. I realized this must be Master Yacoub. I would guess he was in his early fifties. He wore a long black robe, and there was no mistaking the respect and awe he inspired. A Muslim sheikh approached, bent over and kissed his hand. Master Yacoub embraced him warmly.

Then a French officer walked in and everybody got up as Yacoub went over to welcome him. The two men embraced. Yacoub took the Frenchman around the room, making introductions, then both of them disappeared into an adjacent room.

Hanna left me standing there for a while, then returned looking very happy.

—Our Master Yacoub would like to see you.

He led me to a room on an upper floor. We waited for a time, then Master Yacoub entered, and I rose to greet him.

—I see you are from Upper Egypt, he said as he shook my hand. I'm from Mallawi.

—I'm from Asyut, I replied.

—Brave and courageous people!

—They don't betray their country.

He smiled.

—Hanna has told me about you. I do not betray my country. I'm not like those sheikhs who go grovelling to Bonaparte every morning! I have joined with the French because I want to help our people. Do you want Egypt to be ruled by these foreign brutes, by Turks and Mamluks? We've got to get rid of them so that Egypt can be in the hands of the Copts and the Muslims.

—But we've fallen into the hands of the French, and they're never going to leave.

—Anybody will be better for Egypt than the Turks.

He was quiet a moment.

—I'm still seeking help for our country from the European powers.

From there, our conversation took a different turn. He asked me about the library where I work, and what books it contains. I discovered that he has read a lot in different languages. He praised Hanna, calling him one of 'our most loyal men'.

In the end, he got up and said, I've enjoyed talking to you, but as you can see, there are many people waiting for me. Perhaps Hanna can arrange another meeting.

Hanna led me outside. I followed silently, not finding anything to say. This was the first time I had ever heard anyone speak about Egypt being independent of foreign rulers.

Wednesday, 25 December.

I told my teacher how I had met Hanna and visited the fort of Master Yacoub, and his first question was: How could you stand the smell of them? I said I didn't smell anything bad.

When I told him what Yacoub said about the sheikhs, he turned a bit pale and did not comment, but upon hearing his speech about Egyptian independence, he waved his hand angrily.

—That's what Ali Bey Kabir tried to do, and he failed. The great powers don't want it to happen.

Friday, 27 December.

In his own notes, Jabarti makes no reference to anything Yacoub had said.

Saturday, 28 December.

Gaston opens up to me, much to my surprise. He began by saying how difficult it is to have any relations with Egyptian women, and went on to tell me of a romantic adventure he had had in Damietta. He lived on a street that led to the city's main mosque, and he would stand and watch the women pass by on their way to pray. A slender woman caught his eye, she looked to be of some wealth. Gaston felt that she was signalling to him with her eyes as she passed. One day he plucked up the courage to give her a kind of military salute, and he saw her place her right hand over her heart.

That evening she sent a servant to him. The servant was a Frenchwoman from Marseille, abducted by corsairs twenty years ago and sold to an Egyptian bey, who made her lady-in-waiting to his wives. The servant told Gaston that her mistress was nineteen years old, and had been married to one of the beys killed in the battle with Bonaparte's army at Imbaba. She fled Cairo for Damietta, taking refuge with a wealthy Turkish merchant, who married her and treated her well. The servant gave Gaston a letter in French from her mistress in which she admitted being in love with him, and asked him to come visit the merchant.

—As you know, said Gaston, we French are as bold and daring in love as we are in war! So I went right away to his shop to purchase some fabrics, and the woman was there, sitting next to her husband. She wore a veil but it was thin and you could make out her features. When the merchant went to look for something, she seized the opportunity and lifted the veil slightly so that I could see her ravishing beauty. I blew her kisses, bought some cloth and returned two days later on the pretext of buying more. The merchant asked me if I could give his wife some lessons in accounting and French grammar, so that she could help him with the accounts and in correspondence with French merchants. Naturally I agreed, and. he led me to a room adjoining the shop where he introduced me to his charming wife so that I could begin the first lesson with her.

I was feeling uncomfortable with this story about love and French lessons.

—You can't imagine how I felt when I saw her face to face, Gaston continued. We could barely speak— only spurts of broken words. We were both in another world. But I managed to teach her some of the basics of arithmetic while she told me her story. She was born in Tbilisi in Georgia and was sold, as was the custom, to an Armenian merchant who took her to Istanbul. Nobody there was interested in buying her as she was too thin, and only fourteen years old. So he brought her to Egypt, where the Mamluk who died at Imbaba had bought her. She did not love him; he was cruel. She asked me to take her with me to France.

Sabbagh had been listening intently; he was clearly fascinated by the tale, eyes fixed on Gaston as he continued speaking.

—We would flirt and steal kisses during the lessons. Soon after, they transferred me from Damietta to Aboukir and then to Cairo. Later I came to know that her family had killed her.

Why did Gaston tell us all of this? I wondered about this for a long time.

Sunday, 4 January 1800.

Around noon we heard a commotion at the door of the Institute. Gaston and I hurried outside to see a postal coach stopping in front.

Pauline was getting out.

She was wearing heavy clothes, and a wool hat that covered her ears. We carried her trunk inside.

Sitting at her usual place, she told us what a rough time she had had. She arrived at Alexandria to board the ship to France along with a whole retinue of Bonaparte's men. When the soldiers learnt of the departure, they rebelled because they wanted to leave, too. Some of them called for surrender to the English. When the ship finally did set out, a British boat blocked it from leaving and forced them all back to Alexandria. The city's governor ordered all of them to return to Cairo.

—So what will you do now? I asked.

—Kléber agreed that I could return to work here until another chance to travel presents itself.

—But where will you stay?

She smiled weakly.

—Here, of course.

Strain and sadness showed in her face. I resisted the urge to embrace her, and soon she went up to her room.

Monday, 6 January.

I moved my seat closer to hers, like before. Gaston smiled inscrutably at us all day. Her scent excites me. She rubbed her leg against my thigh. I waited until Sabbagh and Gaston left, then went upstairs with her. She pulled off her clothes and showed me her naked back. I caressed her buttocks and she told me that Bonaparte loves small backsides.

Friday, 17 January.

I found her overjoyed today. Two messengers of the French to the Turks at El-Arish had returned today. Rumour had it that they had agreed to a truce with the Turks, on the condition that the French leave Egypt.

—Finally, I can return to France!

Saturday, 18 January.

General Dugua, the governor of Cairo, called a meeting of the members of the Diwan, Jabarti among them. He read to them from a scroll outlining the truce and its conditions. The French army will retreat with its weapons and all its equipment to Alexandria, Rosetta and Aboukir, in order to transfer to ships bound for France. After three months, the Sublime Porte will take over control of the country. They will provide the French soldiers with sufficient food and supplies for the period.

People rejoiced at the news of the pact and the imminent departure of the French. Merchants distributed sweet drinks to passers-by.

Monday, 20 January.

Sabbagh did not show up today, and Gaston was preoccupied, so we took advantage of the situation and exchanged sweet kisses. She put her hand on my leg, caressed my thigh. I reached down and pulled up her robe and touched hers, keeping one eye all the while on Gaston. Feeling her flesh I ran my hand up her calf. When I reached her knee she clamped her legs on my fingers and I couldn't free my hand. Gaston unfortunately stayed late, so we could not go up to her room.

Sunday, 26 January.

Beginning of Ramadan. Jaafar returned from the market before the iftar meal, in an agitated state. He had seen Sakita. She was wearing a hijab, but he could tell it was her from the black skin and the upright posture and the way she walked. When he tried to stop her, she disappeared into the crowd. He said that the women who went with the French are putting on the veil now that they've heard the Ottomans are coming back.

Tuesday, 28 January.

Strong winds. A dust storm. The skies went dark and then the rain came. My teacher and I went to the Azhar Mosque for the supplementary prayers. A crowd had gathered at the entrance, and we were told that the Ottomans had arrived. One of their aghas had entered the city in a procession at Bab al-Nasr. We rushed back home for our mounts, and set out again. The streets were packed with people trying to get a glimpse of the Agha. We joined his procession at the Palace Walk. People were lined along the storefront benches and even the rooftops. The crowd was noisy and the women started ululating from the windows. We followed the procession to the house of Hasan Agha, in Suwayqat al-Lala. There the Turkish official got out.

Wednesday, 29 January.

The Ottoman Agha called together a diwan made up of sheikhs, notables and prominent Christians, both Copts and Syrians. My teacher was among them.

On his return, he said that the Agha showed them two decrees from the Vizier, the first stating that he was now the head of the customs at Cairo, Bulaq and Old Cairo, and this meant he would monopolize all the imported foodstuffs and buy them at a price agreed upon with the market inspector, and he would store them. The second decree said that the Sayyid Ahmed al-Mahrouqi was charged with the collection of the enormous sums needed to send the French on their way.

—Straight away they hit us with these two travesties, he went on. The first person they send us is the tax collector and the first order they give is to take away peoples' goods and impose more fines.

Thursday, 30 January.

I am constantly pleading for God's forgiveness. She continues to tempt me. I say that I am fasting.

Friday, 31 January.

Sayyid Ahmed al-Mahrouqi began collecting money from merchants and tradesmen. They started buying and hoarding foodstuffs. Prices rise and peoples' means decrease. Nonetheless, everyone asked to pay, makes the effort to find the money and hand it over without delay, because they know it will help us get rid of the French. A blessed year and a happy time, they chanted, goodbye to the infidel swine! The French, of course, saw and heard all of this. Even the riffraff and schoolchildren led by their teachers would chant loudly 'God help the Sultan of Turkey, may He destroy Barthélemy!' and similar things. When Jabarti heard about this, he did not approve, saying that people were not considering how things might turn out.

Saturday, 1 February.

Jaafar says the French are selling their possessions, along with any surplus mounts and weapons. He suggested to Jabarti that we buy a riding animal, and my teacher asked me to enquire about it when I go to the Institute.

Tuesday, 4 February.

The Ottomans are arriving in Cairo. Every day, another group enters the city, and the people rejoice—as is their custom with new arrivals—hoping it bodes well. They meet them and greet them and bless their coming. The women call out from the windows. The boats come from the north, carrying all kinds of European goods and dried fruits with pistachios, almonds, walnuts, grapes, figs, olives. We had them spread before us as we broke the fast this evening.

Friday, 7 February.

The owner of the neighbouring hammam came to see Jabarti and complained that the Ottoman Turks were sitting at the door to the hammam, insisting that they have a share in the business. He claims they do the same with all artisans and craftsmen, and owners of coffee houses, hammams, tailor, barbers and the like.

Saturday, 8 February.

My teacher went with a group of commoners and artisans to complain to the Governor of Cairo, Mustafa Basha, about what the Ottomans were doing. He paid no attention to them.

Sunday, 9 February.

I looked at the maps that the French had drawn up. It was surprising to discover many aspects of the city I hadn't been aware of. If you approach Cairo from the north, you come first to Bulaq; if you approach from the south, you arrive first at Old Cairo. The Khalij Canal, which begins at the level of the Nilometer at Roda, divides the city into two uneven sections.

The city has three long streets. The first goes from Bab al-Sayyida to Bab al-Husseiniyya; the second parallels the right bank of the Khalij Canal from Qanatir al-Sibaa to Bab al-Shaariyya; the third is al-Azam Street that runs from the mosque of Ibn Tulun to Bab al-Nasr.

There are five wide streets, three of which run from the Nile to the Citadel, and another from Ezbekieh Square to the cemetery of Qaitbay.

The Khalij Canal branches out from the Nile just south of Qasr al-Aini then flows northeast, passing to the west of Birket al-Fil, Darb el-Gamamiz, and finally Bab al-Kharq before exiting the Cairo at Bab al-Shaariyya. Beyond the city, it passes the mosque of al-Zaher Baybars and on to the agricultural lands near Amiriyya.

Friday, 14 February.

According to Jaafar, Ottoman soldiers are taking money and bread from shopkeepers and coffee from the coffee houses, looting whatever they want. They harass women in the markets, and pass off counterfeit dirhams for real ones. They enter villages displaying a paper with Turkish writing on it, claiming that they've come to restore justice and then demanding exorbitant sums for the rights of passage.

Saturday, 15 February.

On my way home from the Institute, I saw an Ottoman soldier sitting in front of the Inal caravanserai. I thought he must be waiting to break the fast. After I had gone in to pray, I heard a great commotion outside. The soldier was standing in the middle of the quarter, shouting. He said his bag was missing, and accused the caravanserai owner and his workers. However, they treated him kindly and offered him another bag to replace the one that was supposedly stolen.

—It's one of their tricks to get money from shopkeepers, the caravanserai owner told me.

Sunday, 16 February.

A group of sad-looking men were gathered by the turner's shop the one who now sold ready-to-eat food. I was told that it was because of the son who worked as a donkey driver. He had rented out his donkey to an Ottoman for a ride out to the desert. The boy ran behind the rider, as the donkey drivers do. But the Ottoman killed the boy, took away the donkey to the market and sold it.

Tuesday, 18 February.

The Turkish Vizier ordered the Mamluk emirs to dress in the Ottoman way. The scribes and clerks and guards had to wear green caps and shorten their sleeves. Jabarti summoned a tailor to have his clothes altered accordingly.

Thursday, 20 February.

I heard a high-pitched scream right after the night prayer. It was the voice of my teacher. I was surprised, it was unlike him. I stood in the courtyard and listened. I couldn't tell what caused the scream, but it had come from the inner gate. Then I spied Khalil heading towards the main door, and I asked him what was going on. He said his father had just been told that Madame Badriyya was going to visit us tonight to betroth his sister, Hanan, to an Ottoman soldier. The sheikh said that he would never be an in-law to the Ottoman military.

—Let the depraved women marry them, he said.

Saturday, 22 February.

Every day we hear about the return of most of the Egyptians who had fled at the coming of the French—aghas, local Janissaries, clerks and scribes.

My teacher says that the Turkish Vizier arrived at Bilbeis, accompanied by Egyptian emirs. They sent for Murad Bey and his associates, but he excused himself, saying he was in Upper Egypt at the time. They did not accept his excuse and insisted he come.

—Did he attend in the end? I asked.

—Murad Bey secretly sought permission from the French, and they let him go to the meeting.

—What about Ibrahim Bey?

—They'll never learn. They've just gone back to their old ways.

He then explained that Ibrahim Bey had asked Sayyid Ahmed Mahrouqi to send him clothing, pants, tarboushes, for himself and the Mamluks. Mahrouqi sent everything, along with tents and shelters. The Mamluks, as always, went to extremes. They had the servants coming and going constantly between the tents of their masters, carrying platters of food covered in coloured silk cloth, while they rode around on mules, horses and sturdy donkeys carrying their precious parcels of expensive cloth and luxurious clothing.

Wednesday, 26 February.

Today is the Eid. I did not go to the Institute.

Friday, 28 February.

I found her reading a book called *Les liaisons dangereuses* by Choderlos de Laclos. It tells of a degenerate aristocrat in the days before the revolution. She told me of the dancing parties at the royal court, and how the ladies held fans attached to their wrists by gold strings, dressed in green taffeta with silver embroidery, diamonds shining around their neck, hair covered in a shiny white powder. As for the men, they wore powdered wigs and jackets embroidered with gold and silver, tight-fitted trousers with lots of jewels.

Gaston was listening to all this with a mischievous smile.

Saturday, 1 March.

She wanted to know if she could look at the pages I was writing at home.

—What for? I asked.

—Just curious, she replied.

I promised to bring her some.

Gaston told us something he heard about a man who beat his wife cruelly, until he drew blood. She went to the French governor, who summoned the husband. In his defence, the man explained that he was trying to get back his possessions that the Mamluks had taken from him. However, her family didn't approve, and so he hit the wife in order to apply the justice of French laws.

The French governor told him that according to their law a person cannot seek justice on his own, and that a woman has the same rights as a man, and her blood is not of any less value than his. He ordered the husband to receive twenty-five lashes.

I still find their attitude towards women very strange.

Monday, 3 March.

My teacher's predictions have come true. There was a clash between the Ottoman and the French soldiers. A Frenchman was killed. Tensions are high. Shopkeepers are shutting their doors. The Ottomans are staying behind barricades they put up near Gammaliyya. Several skirmishes have been reported. A few people killed on each side.

Tuesday, 4 March.

Senior military men mediated between the two sides. The Ottomans took down the barricades, and Mustafa Pasha sought out those responsible for the unrest. There were six of them. All were executed and their corpses presented to the French commander. However, he was not satisfied with that. He demanded that the Turks withdraw to their own camp until the agreed-upon time. If any Turk was to enter the city, he must be unarmed. Mustafa Bey conceded to this demand.

My teacher asked me to report what was happening. So I went to Bab al-Nasr, where some French soldiers were standing outside the gate. When an Ottoman soldier or notable wanted to enter, they stopped him and seized his weapons. Then one or two men would accompany the Ottoman until he had concluded whatever business he has come for, and escort him back out of the city. They gave him back the weapons and away he went.

Wednesday, 5 March.

Gaston stayed late at the Institute. We pretended to study, but we were too excited and aroused to concentrate. We read excerpts from *Paul et Virginie*, a story about two young lovers. It has a tragic ending. Then I read to her from *Anis al-Jalis*, the Companionable

Companion. As soon as Gaston was out the door, we rushed upstairs and shut the door behind us.

Saturday, 8 March.

Pauline was not in her usual place. I waited and worried. When she finally came in, it was from the outside door. She was nervous, and couldn't sit still for more than a minute. She said that a group of French were travelling home tomorrow, among them the generals Dugua and Desaix, the commander in Upper Egypt, and Poussielgue, chief administrator. She had implored General Kléber to give her permission to go along with them, and he agreed.

This news hit me like bolt of thunder. She asked me to help pack her bags. Befuddled, I followed her upstairs. The room was in chaos; her things scattered everywhere. We gathered her belongings and started packing. I saw many things in her room I'd never noticed before, that she must have acquired over the last few days—a pile of muslin cloth, ornamented belts, taffeta, cottons and linens. Tamarind, dates, cardamom, turmeric, opium, red henna, coffee beans, ivory and cinnamon. She said she was going to sell these in order to support herself once she arrived in France.

By sunset everything was ready. She asked me to wait while she washed. She returned in a household robe, her hair wrapped in a towel. She carried a bottle of wine; insisted we drink it together. It made me feel all warm inside. It made me happy, and sad. She noticed this.

—Are you sad because I'm leaving?

—Of course.

—Maybe I'll return, or maybe you'll come to France.

—And how will I find you?

—I don't know where I'm going to live. I'll write to you once I'm settled.

I almost begged her to take me with her, but I stopped myself. I was annoyed. I said I needed to leave.

—Won't you kiss me?

I kissed her on the mouth, and then she pulled me close and my hands were all over her. Then she pushed me to the ground and, standing over me, lifted up her robe. I tried to resist because I wasn't sure what she was going to do. She got on top of me and began to move as if possessed. When it was over, she held me close to her. I kissed her again, then left.

Monday, 10 March.

According to Gaston, the group tried to leave Alexandria but the English forced their ship back to port. Perhaps she will return?

Friday, 14 March.

The Egyptian emirs, the army of Nasef Pasha and a group of Ottoman soldiers arrived at al-Matariyya and are putting up their tents.

My teacher says the French were granted an additional delay of eight days before leaving the country.

Monday, 17 March.

The English allowed Pauline and her group to depart.

Tuesday, 18 March.

I left the Institute at midday and, as my teacher had instructed me, rode my donkey to the bank of the Nile in Old Cairo. I could see the French tents all along the shore, as far north as Shubra.

On my return, I saw their carriages transporting cannons and shot and weapons. I couldn't tell what direction they were headed, nor could anybody tell me. They continued moving all through the night.

Thursday, 20 March.

Groups of French were leaving the city via Qubbat al-Nasr, then disappearing into the surrounding areas. There are now only a few of them left in the city and most people think those are getting ready to depart as well.

Friday, 21 March.

Cannon fire in the morning, and rumours are spreading. People panicking and charging around the edges of the city. We are told that they killed some of the French they came across. At the Friday prayers, which got over swiftly, the Imam prayed for the end of French rule.

We learnt that Kléber rode out before dawn with his troops, cannons and weapons, heading towards Matariyya, where they bombarded the Ottomans. All Nasef Pasha could do was flee, abandoning the tents to be pillaged by the French. The Ottomans nailed shut the mouths of the cannons and left them there.

Jabarti sent me to Bab al-Nasr, where I found crowds of common people and riffraff gathered on the hill just outside. A few were armed; many held staffs and clubs.

In the afternoon, a large group arrived, at the rear were Ibrahim Bey, then Nasef Pasha along with a number of his soldiers. Sayyid Umar Makram and Sayyid Ahmed al-Mahrouqi, and Hasan Bey al-Geddawi, and Osman Bey al-Ashqar, and Ibrahim al-Sinari, lieutenant of Murad Bey, along with their Mamluks and their followers. They entered the city via Bab al-Nasr and Bab al-Futouh, went through Gammaliyya, and I followed them to the caravanserai of Zulfiqar, where they dismounted. Shortly Nasef Pasha stepped forth and addressed the throng:

—Kill the Christians! This is jihad!

They shouted and yelled and moved quickly, murdering any Copts or Syrian Christians they came across. One group went to the Christian quarters near Bayn al-Surayn, Bab al-Shaariya and Muski. I followed them, wondering what would happen to Hanna and his family. I saw the mobs attacking houses, killing any men, women or children they came across. They pillaged the whole neighbourhood and even took prisoners.

The Christians began to fight back, shooting rifles and carbines from the upper stories. The riffraff and the soldiers in the streets and alleys were returned fire.

I did not dare go to Hanna's house, so I returned home and told my teacher the news. He clapped his hands together despairingly and called for the kindness of God.

After dark, the French bombarded the city from their strongholds, concentrating on Gammaliyya. Sheikh Hasan al-Attar came for a visit and told us that the chiefs and notables were determined to leave that night, since they could no longer put up any resistance, given their lack of weapons and the strength of the enemy forces.

My teacher tried to get him to not act hastily and to reflect on the situation. We all went out together to Gammaliyya. We found it and the adjacent areas packed with people jostling to leave the city. Donkeys, mules, horses, sheep and camels laden with their belongings.

Criminals from Khan al-Khalili heard of this, along with some Maghribis of Fahhamin and the Ghouriyya. They came to

Gammaliyya and shouted abuse at those trying to leave. Aided by some Janissaries, they took the emirs' horses and held them in the Qadi's palace and the storehouses. Then they closed the Bab al-Nasr. Most of the people spent the night on the stone benches in front of the shops. Some notables stayed at their friends' homes in Gammaliyya, or just in the side streets of the quarter.

As for us, we returned home. Sheikh Hasan spent the night with us.

Saturday, 22 March.

It wasn't very safe to walk about in the streets, but I went to the Institute nonetheless. It was locked up and closely guarded. They would not let me enter. I went to Hanna's house. They told me he had disappeared and they didn't know where he was.

I met a procession led by Nasef Pasha and some Egyptian emirs. Thousands of Cairenes followed, pulling three cannons. I walked behind them to Ezbekieh, where the lake was all dried up. They marched across it and attacked the house of Alfi Bey. The French troops positioned there fired back. The firing back and forth went on all day.

I volunteered with some others to collect the iron and stone weights used to measure goods in shops. These were to be used in place of real cannon shot.

A group had seized hold of a Christian, so I walked behind them as they made their way to Gammaliyya, where they turned him over to Osman Katkhuda at the caravanserai of Zulfiqar, in order to receive their reward. Some others had killed a Frenchman and brought only his head to claim their reward.

Sunday, 23 March.

We learnt that Muhammad Bey Alfi has arrived. He is staying near the little market by Abd al-Haqq Street near Ataba, along with his men and his Mamluks and some Ottomans.

As for Murad Bey, as soon as he came to know what the French had done to the Pasha and the emirs at Matariyya, he and his men passed over the mountain and fled to Deir al-Tin, behind the churches of Old Cairo, where he will wait and watch how all of this unfolds. My teacher complained about Murad Bey, saying he would not break the truce he made with the French.

Monday, 24 March.

A summons came from Osman Katkhuda for our neighbour the turner. I accompanied him to the house of the Qaid Agha, in the Khurunfush district, off of al-Azam Street.

It transpired that he had called for arms makers, carters, blacksmiths, metal founders and carpenters, in order to build cannons and ammunition, and repair those they have found or scavenged. They brought what they needed—wood, tree branches and metal from mosques. All this is being done in the Qadi's house, and the khan nearby, and in the open space by the mausoleum of Hussein.

Thursday, 25 March.

Jaafar and I spent the day strolling through different parts of the city in order to bring my teacher some news.

The Mamluk beys and the commoners had spread out in different directions. Osman Bey Ashqar manned the barricades in Bab al-Louq and the tanners' district; Osman Bey Tabal manned those at al-Mahjar, Muhammad Bey al-Mabdoul at the Sheikh Rihan Street, and Muhammad Kashif Ayoub at al-Nasiriyya. Mustafa

Bey Kabir was at Qanatir al-Sibaa, Suleiman Kashif al-Mahmoudi at the Souk al-Salah. The youths from the Qarafa Cemetery and the ruffians of al-Husseiniyya and al-Atouf were at Bab al-Nasr and Bab al-Hadid. A group from Khan al-Khalili and Gammaliyya was at Bab al-Barqiyya.

Near Ezbekieh, near Bab al-Hawaa, and in the open space at the Ezbek Mosque and Ataba were gathered Nasef Pasha and Ibrahim Bey along with their troops, made up of Janissaries, Albanians, Kurds and others.

Everywhere you can hear the cries, in Arabic and in Turkish, calling the people to jihad and to maintain the barricades.

In the evening, Khalil returned from the family shop in Bulaq, saying things had flared up. Hajj Mustafa al-Beshtili and men like him were standing firm. They roused the common people, and were prepared to fight. They went out to the encampment abandoned by the French, with only a few guards left to keep watch. They killed whomever they came across and looted the tents and everything in them. Then they came back to the city and broke open all the storehouses belonging to the French, taking whatever they wanted. They made small fortifications all over the city and made ready for war and jihad. Coptic and Syrian Christians living in Bulaq were roughed up, and there was looting.

As for the French, they were secure in their forts surrounding the city, and in Alfi's palace and surrounding houses, and at the home of neighbouring Copts.

Rumour has it that the Vizier has left the city and returned to Syria.

Sayyid Ahmed Mahrouqi and the rest of the merchants and the wealthy took up the costs and paid for the food and drinks. So did all the people of Cairo give of themselves and their property to assist one another. Even the people from the surrounding countryside came, bringing butter, cheese, milk, grain, straw to sell to the Cairenes. Then they went back home.

Wednesday, 26 March.

We heard of a Maghribi, supposedly the one who fought the French near Buhayra, who has gathered together a gang of rural Maghribis and some Arabs originally from the Hijaz. They were spying on the houses of the French and the Christians. Then they would raid the houses, accompanied by a mob of commoners and soldiers, killing the ones they found and looting the place. They dragged away the women and stole their jewellery and clothing. One of them even cut off the head of a young girl because he wanted the gold ornaments she had on her head and in her hair.

Thursday, 27 March.

I was in Gammaliyya when a group of Ottoman soldiers and some other riffraff dragged in Sheikh Khalil al-Bakri. They took his women and children, too. The sheikh was made to walk bare-headed. It was a great humiliation. The commoners shouted cruel insults. Then they mounted him backwards on a donkey and hung bells round his neck. People spit on him and threw filth and garbage.

They accused him of protecting the French and sending them food. I couldn't make out his daughter because the womenfolk were completely veiled. When they brought him before Osman Katkhuda, he was appalled at all this and promised to treat him well. Sidi Ahmed ibn Mahmoud Muharram the merchant took him and wife to his house, treated him well and gave them clothing. There they stayed.

Friday, 28 March.

French troops have surrounded the city and the port suburb of Bulaq. No one can leave; no one may enter. Food supplies are down, prices are rising. No bread in the souks, and you can't buy it from the hawkers any more. The soldiers inside the city are now snatching food and drink right out of the hands of people walking around. The price of water drawn from wells or the public drinking fountains has risen too, such that a waterskin is 60-odd *paras*. As for the river, no one can get to it. The animals are perishing without fodder—no straw, beans, barley or dried clover. Many are calling out to sell a donkey or mule worth 30 *riyals* for 1 *riyal* only, or a 100 *paras* or less. Still they can't find a buyer. The merchants and the well-off are too busy feeding the soldiers manning the barricades.

Saturday, 29 March.

The Coptic grandees, men like Gergis al-Gawhari Faltaos and Malti the Copt, asked the Muslim spokesmen for protection, since their houses were completely surrounded and they feared they would be looted if they fled. Protection was granted, and the Pasha and the Katkhuda and the emirs gave them money and provided them with supplies.

As for Master Yacoub, he was barricaded with arms and soldiers in his stronghold on al-Darb al-Wasii in Ruwaii. Most of Hasan Bey al-Geddawi's fighting was with Yacoub and his men.

Ismail Kashif was in the house of Ahmed Agha Shuwaykar, under which the French had buried gunpowder. This exploded and sent people and children flying in the air, burning every one of them, including Ismail Kashif. The houses, buildings and palaces that overlooked the lake collapsed and fire destroyed every house in Bab al-Mafariq near the mosque of Osman Katkhuda, the entire quarter known as al-Saket, and the open space in front of al-Alfi's house, where the French Commander-in-chief resides. Also the neighbourhood of Fawwala and the houses of Ruwaii up to the Christian Quarter. Nothing left but rubble and ruins.

When my teacher heard this news, he quoted the Quran: *As a result of their evil deeds, their homes are desolate ruins.*

Sunday, 30 March.

They sent to Murad Bey asking him to come, or at least to send the emirs and soldiers that were with him. He excused himself for not attending, and said: Take my advice, seek a treaty with the French, and get out safe and sound.

Murad Bey's response infuriated Hasan Bey al-Geddawi, Osman Bey Ashqar and others. They mocked him: How does that solve anything? We came here, we took possession, and now we are supposed to leave in humiliation? That will never happen!

My teacher says that Murad Bey is responsible for the destruction of the city.

Monday, 31 March.

Firing of cannons and guns and mortars continues day and night, such that people are unable to sleep or rest or even sit for a moment. They are constantly standing and milling about in the souks and alleyways. Most people eat only rice cooked with honey and milk. There is nothing else in the markets.

The French forces are constantly firing in all directions and have captured a number of barricades. The word is passed along among the people that they should go in here or there, to join and assist their Muslim brethren, and off they charge to that quarter's barricades until they are ousted, and they move on to another area and do it all again. It is Hasan Bey al-Geddawi who did most of this work. Each time he hears of French advances in a neighbourhood, he rushes to help its residents.

The call to come and fight is made repeatedly, also by the Agha and the Wali, as well as sheikhs and jurists and Sayyid Ahmed Mahrouqi, and Sayyid Umar Makram. They go around calling the people to fight and urging them to take part in jihad. Some of the Ottomans do the same in Turkish.

Wednesday, 2 April.

The whole city is in chaos. Some armed hooligans managed to infiltrate the Christian Souk. They made it as far as Garden Street, where they closed the big gate and piled up rocks behind it. When the news reached Master Yacoub, he and his supporters rushed over to the oil mills to the east of his house, where they threw open the gates and released hundreds of cattle and buffalo. Herding them to the Garden Street gate, they prodded the animals with the points of their spears to press against the gate, such that they moved the heavy stones. They stormed inside and captured the hooligans.

The Coptic militiamen took turns going up in the towers with their firearms, to fend off the attacks from the riffraff.

Friday, 4 April.

Attacks on the Copts continued yesterday and today until finally the hooligans were forced to retreat. It seems the French assigned special forces to protect and defend Master Yacoub.

My teacher says that efforts are underway to make peace with the French. Sometimes it is Osman Bey al-Bardisi who leads the negotiations, other times Mustafa Kashef Rostam, both of whom are loyal to Murad Bey. The French are demanding that the

Ottomans leave the city, and threatening to destroy it if they do not.

Saturday, 5 April.

The French have set up a tent in the middle of the dried-up lake and hoisted their flag. They ceased firing last night, sending a messenger to the Pasha, the Katkhuda and the Egyptian emirs. The messenger asked to speak with some of the sheikhs, so off went al-Sharqawi, al-Mahdi and al-Sersi and al-Fayyoumi and others. My teacher Jabarti went with them as well.

When he returned home, I learnt that Commander Kléber told them, via a dragoman, what had happened. He had granted amnesty to all the people of Cairo, and the Pasha and the Katkhuda and their troops must leave the city. An agreement was reached with Murad Bey—he would govern Upper Egypt in the name of France, and it was Murad Bey who had indicated that he should burn Cairo to the ground if they did not submit to his rule.

When the Commander asked about the causes of the uprising, the sheikhs told him that it was all the fault of the Turkish vizier, the Katkhuda and Ibrahim Bey and his people. It was they, the sheikhs reported, who provoked the revolt and stirred up the masses and made them false promises, and of course the masses are foolish and have no sense. After much talk, the Commander said, if the Ottomans accept to leave and give up fighting, then let us agree with you and with them and conclude our treaty. We will demand nothing more of you, and one of our dead will be the equivalent of one of your dead.

Sunday, 6 April.

When the Janissaries and the people heard about the agreement, they turned against the sheikhs, insulting and abusing them. They beat al-Sharqawi and al-Sersi, tearing their turbans and spewing the foulest insults at them.

—These sheikhs are apostates! They work with the French! They did it for money!

Sheikh al-Sadat was at the house of al-Sawi and at a loss as to what to do. He tried to slip out by sending ahead a man rallying people to the barricades, just in order to protect himself from the crowds.

The Maghribi was the most vocal of all, calling out in the streets that the peace was not enough, it was time for jihad.

—If the cursed unbelievers didn't think they were going to lose, he cried to the crowds, they wouldn't be trying to make peace and leave! They are running out of gunpowder and supplies!

When my teacher heard this he shook his head.

—That one should mind his own affairs, he said. We have a Pasha and his lieutenant and emirs in this country. Who is this halfwit to say if we should make peace or not?

I could not hide the fact that I was impressed by the Maghribi's boldness.

—What he wants is continual fighting, my teacher said, that's how he can keep looting and stealing and people will give him whatever he wants.

Monday, 7 April.

The French sent one of their own with a note from the Commander-in-chief.

—Amnesty, amnesty! For all!

The people pulled him off his horse and killed him.

Saturday, 12 April.

The French have occupied Faggala.

Wednesday, 16 April.

Dark skies, thunder and pouring rain. The alleys and side streets are filled with mud. People are trying to clear away the mire. The emirs and the soldiers are spattered with mud.

The French are attacking Cairo from every direction; they pay no attention to the rain and mud. The greater part of their attack comes from the direction of Bab al-Hadid and Koum Abi Rish, and from Birket al-Ratli and Qantarat al-Hajib, and from Husseiniyya and Rumayla. They fire from the fort of the Zahir Mosque, as well as the fort at the Qantarat Limon. They lead with cannons; the riflemen follow right behind. Some of them have dipped wicks into oil and tar to make torches which they then throw onto rooftops and through windows and doorways, setting houses ablaze.

Friday, 18 April.

Today the French attacked Bulaq from the Nile and from Bawabat Abu Ela. The inhabitants of Bulaq fought back, throwing themselves into the flames until the Frenchmen overcame and surrounded them from all sides. Some perished in the fires, others were shot. What they have done to Bulaq will turn hair white with terror. Dead bodies are strewn through the streets; buildings and houses burned.

People began to flee when they saw that defeat was inevitable. But by then the French had surrounded the whole area, and prevented them from leaving. They took over the caravanserais, the storehouses, the depots, even the houses and everything in them.

They seized all the money they could find, all the belongings, but also the women, whether old or young, the children both boys and girls, the stores of grain and sugar, flax and cotton, rice and oil and spices. When they find someone hiding, someone unarmed who offers no resistance, they rob him and take his clothes. Then they go on their way, leaving him naked but alive.

Saturday, 19 April.

Someone led them to the Sufi lodge where Beshtili was hiding out; they arrested him and his lieutenant and other men. They kept Beshtili in the lodge but locked his men in the house of the Commander-in-chief. They were kept under close watch, and could not go out even to urinate. After three days they were released. As for Beshtili, they gathered together some of his gang from the commoners. All these were quick to blame their leader Beshtili for everything and said he had refused to consider any sort of truce. Then they released him to his own gang, on the condition that they parade him around the city and then put him to death. They beat him to death with clubs. The people of Bulaq face a fine of 200,000 *riyals*.

Tuesday, 22 April.

People are worn out from the continual commotion, the burning, the endless nights, the lack of food. The poor people and the riding animals suffer the most. The Ottoman soldiers, who just seize whatever they want, are making things even worse. People are even wishing the Ottomans would disappear and things could go back to as they were under the French.

Every day the French advance, and the Muslims retreat. They entered from Bab al-Hadid and Koum Abi Rish, while setting fires with lit wicks. Shahin Agha was there at the barricades, and was injured and had to abandon his position. Those who were behind him retreated as well, and in doing so the people stampeded and trampled each other. It was a disaster. And the French took Koum Abi Rish.

While that was going on, al-Bardisi and Mustafa Kashef and Osman Bey Ashqar worked on the truce and finally arranged a cessation of hostilities. The French would grant the Ottomans and the Mamluk emirs three days to finish their business and to leave the city. They made the Khalij canal the border between the two sides, and none could cross it. Then they put an end to the fighting and put out the fires. The Ottomans, the emirs, the soldiers and the army prepared to leave. The French gave them camels and other provisions.

The Maghribi whom I have mentioned before rode to Husseiniyya to show that he wanted to fight the French and that the arranged truce was not enough. Some of the sensible people of the quarter went to Osman Katkhuda, who had shut himself in the Zulfiqar caravanserai in Gammaliyya, to ask whether they should go with the Maghribi or try to stop him. The Katkhuda ordered them to stop him.

At the same time, al-Mahrouqi passed by the Wood Souk with a crier before him, calling for a return to the barricades, but Nazla Amin Agha stopped him. Then the gate to the storehouse was opened, and soldiers with clubs streamed out, attacking the crowds. Everybody fled, and calm was restored.

Saturday, 26 April.

The Ottoman troops departed to Salhiyya, accompanied by Ibrahim Bey with his emirs and Mamluks, and Alfi Bey with his soldiers, along with Umar Makram, Sayyid Ahmed al-Mahrouqi and many more people of Cairo. Likewise, Ahmed Bey al-Geddawi and his men.

The French have entered the city. The Sheikhs and the notables made the rounds of the souks this afternoon, calling for peace and calm.

Sunday, 27 April.

The sheikhs and the local Janissary command rode out from Bab al-Nasr with a group of Coptic and Syrian Christians, among others. When they had all gathered, they formed a procession and entered the city through Bab al-Nasr, preceded by guardsmen with clubs who ordered everyone to stand as they passed by. Then some Frenchmen on horseback with drawn swords approached, ordering everyone to stand where they were and not to move. So the people remained there, standing up, from the beginning of the procession right to the end, when the French Commander-in-chief appeared, with Osman Bey Bardisi and Osman Bey Ashqar right behind him.

When the procession was over, the French called for flags to be hoisted and the city decorated in celebration. They dressed Sheikh Bakri in sable furs and gave him Osman Kashif's house to live in.

Monday, 28 April.

My teacher tells me that the dust clouds have revealed the wretchedness of the Muslims and the frustration of the hopes of all, those who had fled and those who stayed behind. The clashes, he said, had brought nothing but dust and ruins.

His comments confuse me, as sometimes he rails against the French, and other times against the unruly masses who brought chaos and strife to the city.

Thursday, 1 May.

Murad Bey invited Kléber to pay him a visit at his residence on the island of Dahab. Great amounts of food were spread out for the guests. Murad Bey turned over to the French the sheep, horses and other provisions collected by the Turks. The quantity of goods was astounding. That day the French appointed him governor of Upper Egypt from Girga to Esna.

Friday, 2 May.

Today I visited the Institute. Sabbagh complained about the taxes being imposed. Gaston replied that the only ones who complained about it were the minority, those few who have any money. He also told us that Kléber said they needed to squeeze Egypt like a lemon in order to make a lasting colony of it.

A young Egyptian saw me coming out of the Institute. He spit on the ground as I passed.

Saturday, 3 May.

Following the noon prayer, Jabarti went with the rest of the sheikhs to the house of the Commander-in-chief. He did not return until late at night. I stayed up waiting for him. On his return, he told me part of what had happened. The sheikhs had dressed in their finest attire, each no doubt believing that the Commander was about to give him some great post, or appoint him to the Special Diwan. They had spread out their rugs in the outer chamber, where they were ignored for a long time. No one spoke to them; nobody paid them any attention. When the inner chamber was opened and they were called in, the same thing happened again. They spread their carpets again and sat there again for a long time with no one paying any attention.

Finally, the Commander appeared, with a dragoman and some officers. He sat on a chair in the middle of the room, dragoman and officers standing around him. The local Janissary officers and officials lined up on one side, important merchants and Christians on the other. The Commander spoke for a long time to the interpreter, who then turned and said, The Commander will grant you pardon despite the fact that you deserve punishment, but he demands from you the sum of ten million francs.

—But we joined with the Ottomans only on your orders, protested the sheikhs, because you told us that from the second of the month of Ramadan we would be under Ottoman rule, once again under our previous sultan, the sultan of all the Muslims. We were completely ignorant of what happened between you and them! We just found ourselves in the middle of it, and there was no way to go back.

The dragoman relayed Commander Kléber's response:

—Then why did you not prevent your people from rising up and waging war against us?

—We couldn't do that, we had no authority with them any more. You have heard how they beat and abused us when we told them to accept the peace and stop fighting.

—If that is the case, and you could do nothing to stop the unrest, then what is the use of your supposed leadership? What benefit do you offer, when all you can bring us is harm? When our enemies appear, you are with them and against us. And when they leave, you come crawling back to us making excuses. Your just reward should be that we do with you what we did with inhabitants of Bulaq: kill every last one of you, burn your city and seize your women and children.

Faces grew pale; the sheikhs looked ill. But the interpreter went on:

—But we gave you guarantee of safe conduct and we will not go back on our word. We will not kill you. We are only going to fine you, and the penalty is ten million francs. You will divide it up amongst the population of the city.

Then he demanded that fifteen of them remain as hostages, until the amount be paid. After that, he got up and with his entourage, left the room. The door was shut and heavily guarded. The sheikhs were terrified. They looked at other, with no idea what to do.

Jabarti laughed telling me all this.

—We stayed there completely baffled until it was almost time for the sunset prayer. Most of them had pissed in their clothes, some tried to pee surreptitiously out of the windows. Meanwhile, al-Mahdi tried to discuss with the Christians some means of dividing and distributing the payment. Then they drew up lists of all the groups who would have to pay something: the concession holders and craftsmen, acrobats and merchants, the people of Ghouriyya and Khan al-Khalili, the goldsmiths and the coppersmiths, the slave auctioneers, the measurers, tribunal judges and many more, even the snake charmers and the monkey trainers. Each corporation had to pay a given amount, say 30,000 or 40,000 francs. The same went for sellers of tobacco, soap, metals, perfumes and oil, as well as butchers, barbers and the rest. Holders of buildings and property had to pay one year's worth of rent.

He went on.

—The Sheikhs al-Sawi and Futouh ibn al-Gawhari were being held at the governor's house, and Sheikh al-Sadat was singled out for a large fine. Then they gave Master Yacoub the authority to collect it all. Then the meeting came to an end.

When he finished telling me all this, he instructed Khalil to go the caravanserai and make up an inventory of his wealth and merchandise in order to make the required payment.

Sunday, 4 May.

I did not go to the Institute. I had mentioned the spitting incident to my teacher, and that I was ashamed to go there after what the French had done.

Jabarti was silent for a moment.

—As you wish, he said.

Monday, 5 May.

Sheikh Hasan al-Attar visited us to bid farewell to my teacher; he is leaving Cairo for Asyut in Upper Egypt. We learnt from him that they have imprisoned Sheikh Sadat in the Citadel until his portion of the penalty is paid. He asked to be sent down to his house so that he could arrange the sale of his possessions. They sent him down, and he gave up everything he had, which amounted to 9,000 *riyals*, or about 6,000 francs. Then they estimated the lowest possible values for his gold, silver, furs and clothing, and it came to 15,000 francs. The total of cash and valuables came to 21,000 francs.

The soldiers stuck close to him all the while, not even letting him visit his wife, or anyone else for that matter. After they had finished estimating all his assets, they looked all over the house for what might be hidden, even digging up the ground and opening up the latrines, but they found nothing more.

They transferred Sadat on foot to the governor's house, where they beat him, fifteen blows in the morning and fifteen at night. They locked his wife up with him, and beat him in front of her, as she screamed and cried. This was excessive cruelty.

Some of the sheikhs, Sharqawi and Fayyoumi, Mahdi and others, pleaded that the wife should be taken elsewhere. So she was taken to the house of Fayyoumi, but Sadat stayed where he was.

My teacher added that this was what came of dealing with the French.

—Poor fool. They used to kiss his hand or the hem of his cloak, and when they went away he would ask for the basin and the jug and wash his hand with soap. The Ottomans granted him fifty purses to enlarge his house and another fifty when that wasn't enough to finish the building. Then they appointed him supervisor of the Nafisa and Sayyida Zaynab shrines, and other tombs that bring in a profit, enabling him to buy slaves and slave girls and eunuchs. Proud and arrogant, he took to wearing a high felt hat over his green turban so that he would resemble the big emirs.

Tuesday, 20 May.

They took all the mules, Jabarti's included. The order strictly forbids the Muslims to ride any mules, with five exceptions: Sharqawi, Mahdi, Fayyoumi, Amir and Ibn Muharram. The Christians, whether interpreters or not, are free to ride.

The Eid al-Adha passed without anybody noticing. Jabarti complains about losing his money and not being able to get a loan. He wanted to sell some of his belongings, but could not find a buyer. Eventually, he had to sell some gold and silverwork, but at a paltry price.

Chapter Seven

Sunday, 1 June.

At the Azhar Mosque, one of the merchants had promised to give me a book on medicine so that I could make a copy for him. We had agreed to meet at the mosque after prayers last Friday, but he did not show up. Today, I chanced upon him there and he gave the excuse that he had given it to a young man from Aleppo who earns his living by copying books. We went to the Syrians' residence at the Azhar, where we met a thin, long-faced pale fellow named Suleiman. His hollow eyes had a very grave look.

We sat with him awhile, and he began to talk of jihad and struggle in the path of God. He attacked the vulgarity of the French and the spread of taverns.

—If Egypt is lost, he said, then the Hijaz is lost, and the road to the House of God and the Tomb of His Messenger is lost as well!

His words made a deep impression on me. I will go to see him again.

Tuesday, 3 June.

I went to the Syrians' residence after the night prayer and found Suleiman with two of his friends. He told me about himself. He had long ago decided to devote himself to the study of Sufism and the history of Islam at the Azhar, and this he had been doing for the past three years. But when the French arrived, he decided that he had to assassinate Bonaparte. However, he was too cowardly to act. He left Egypt and found refuge in Jerusalem, where he dreamt of becoming a martyr in the path of God. He had heard that every one hundred years, God sends one person to renew the religion of the Ummah, the Muslim community, and to restore to Islam its brilliance and its vitality.

Friday, 6 June.

I joined my teacher for Friday prayers at the Azhar Mosque today. He says the French believe they are in such a position of strength that they can rule over Egypt for ever.

After the prayers, I stayed behind with Suleiman. He says the angels are preparing to meet him in paradise.

Saturday, 14 June.

French troops are suddenly everywhere. All over the streets, the gates, across the city. It appears as though they are blockading the city and preparing the cannons. People are starting to panic, but nobody knows what exactly is happening.

Saturday, 14 June. Evening.

It turns out that Commander-in-chief Kléber was taking a walk with his chief engineer in the garden of his house in Ezbekieh. An unknown person entered the garden and walked towards Kléber, who assumed it was a beggar and waved him away saying: I haven't got anything. He repeated this to him several times, but the stranger kept coming closer, beckoning him, indicating he needed something urgently. When he was close enough, he reached out as to the Commander if he wanted to kiss his hand. As soon as Kléber extended his hand towards the man, he grabbed him and stabbed him four times with a dagger hidden in his other hand. The Commander, disembowelled, fell to the ground screaming. The engineer yelled out and the stranger stabbed him as well. By the time the soldiers at the gate rushed to the site, they found Kléber breathing his last, and the assassin nowhere in sight. They started beating the drums to alert the troops, and ran out in search of the killer.

It did not take long to find him. The man was crouched in a corner of a garden of the adjacent house, under a collapsed wall. He was arrested and interrogated. He said his name was Suleiman, from Aleppo, and he gave them the names of four friends and associates.

Abdallah al-Sharqawi and Ahmed al-Arishi the Qadi were summoned and detained for most of the night. They were ordered to round up everybody mentioned by the assassin. They rode out to the Azhar, accompanied by the Agha, and asked for the people named. They identified three, but not the fourth. The Agha imprisoned them in the governor's house in Ezbekieh.

When I heard of this from my teacher, I was terrified. Did Suleiman give them my name?

Sunday, 15 June.

I could not sleep last night. Waiting for them to come and get me.

Monday, 16 June.

They have formed a tribunal for Suleiman and his accomplices according to their system of justice. They pronounced the assassin and the other three individuals guilty of murder. This involved the writing of many, many pages, in which the events were described in detail. These were published in French, Turkish and Arabic. My teacher brought a copy home.

I read it carefully. Apparently, Suleiman had at first denied being present in the garden and the assassination. Then they beat him until he asked for forgiveness and promised to speak the truth:

—Why did you come from Gaza?

—To kill the Commander-in-chief.

—Who sent you to do this?

—When the Ottomans were withdrawing from Egypt to Syria, they sent a message to Aleppo, looking for someone capable of killing the French leader and offering a good price. I volunteered.

He told how, in the mosque, he had met Sayyid Muhammad al-Ghazzi and Sayyid Ahmed al-Wali, Abdallah al-Ghazzi and Abd al-Qadir al-Ghazzi, and told them about his plan. He said they all told him not to do it.

After examination of the three Gazans accused of complicity, the judges decreed that Suleiman of Aleppo's right hand be burnt, then he was to be impaled and left until the vultures have eaten his corpse.

They sentenced to death Abd al-Qadir al-Ghazzi, along with Muhammad al-Ghazzi, Abdallah al-Ghazzi and Ahmed al-Wali.

Their heads will be cut off and placed on the ends of sticks while their bodies are to be burnt. All this is to occur in front of Suleiman, before anything happens to him.

I was relieved that there is no mention of me anywhere. However, I am appalled by the judgements, and I tell this to Jabarti. He does not share my opinion.

—Suleiman was a rash young man who came from far away. In any case, the French have no religion but they do adhere to reason when they pronounce judgements. They didn't rush to put him to death as soon as they found him with the murder weapon covered in Kléber's blood. No, they convened a tribunal, they made the killer appear there, they asked him all kinds of questions, over and over,—sometimes under torture, sometimes not. Then they brought the ones whom he had named and asked them questions, both together and individually. Only then did they pronounce the verdict. And they will apply the punishment in strict fashion. It's not at all what we see from our low-life soldiers who claim to act in the name of Islam, pretending that what they are doing is jihad in the path of God, destroying human life just to satisfy their animal desires.

Tuesday, 17 June.

Abdallah Jacques Menou is appointed the new Commander-in-chief. The call goes out to sweep the streets and clean the city.

Wednesday, 18 June.

Officers, notables and a number of Coptic and Syrian Christians gathered to form a funeral procession. A cart carried Kléber's body, in a lead coffin along with his hat and sword, and the dagger that killed him, still covered in his blood. The drums, covered with black cloth, were beaten in a strange way. The soldiers held their rifles upside down, and each of them had a piece of black silk tied around his arm. The box was draped in black velvet. They fired their cannons and rifles throughout the procession.

I was standing in the crowd in front of the Commander's house at Ezbekieh when the funeral cortege came through Bab al-Kharq to Darb al-Gammamiz and was moving towards al-Nasiriyya. When it got to the fort they had built at Tell al-Aqareb, they fired several cannons. Then they brought forward Suleiman of Aleppo and the three accomplices. First, they cut the heads off the Gazans, then burnt Suleiman's right hand. After that, they impaled him on a stake.

I felt sick and almost vomited. But I followed the cortege to Qasr al-Aini, where they lifted up the coffin and placed it on a mound of earth inside a wooden structure they had prepared.

Thursday, 19 June.

I did not sleep last night. Terrible dreams I kept seeing myself tied up on the stake next to Suleiman.

Friday, 20 June.

A few days ago, Commander-in-chief Abdallah Jacques Menou, along with the Agha and the governor, walked around the Azhar Mosque. They wanted to dig holes in search of hidden weapons. When they left, the students began to move their belongings elsewhere, and transferred their books. The residences were abandoned.

The next day, the sheikhs Sharqawi, Mahdi and Sawi went to see Menou in the late afternoon and asked permission to close the Azhar and nail the doors shut. The sheikhs want to protect the mosque and ensure that there can be no doubt or suspicion about what goes on there. The area of the Azhar is vast and there is no way to monitor who goes in and out through its gates. It would be very easy for a student living there to smuggle an enemy inside. The French Commander agreed with this and gave his permission. In the morning, they nailed shut all the doors.

My teacher disapproved of this. since he profits nicely from his lessons there, even if there are only a few students. For one day's lessons, he receives one hundred and fifty pieces of bread.

Sunday, 22 June.

Visions of Pauline and Suleiman keep coming to me in my dreams.

Tuesday, 24 June.

They have decided on new tax of four million: one million is the equivalent of 186,000 francs. Land and property owners will have to pay 200,000 francs; concession holders, 160,000 francs; merchants 200,000 francs; artisans and craftsmen, 60,000. They divided the city into eight districts and imposed on each district a tax of 25,000 *riyals*. The task has been delegated to the sheikh of each quarter.

Saturday, 19 July.

Sheikh Sadat was released and allowed to return home, after having paid the sums demanded of him. They seized his buildings and his farms, cut off his emoluments and prohibited him from meeting with people. He must ask their permission to leave his house, and must curtail his expenses.

Wednesday, 23 July.

The French, along with their Christian helpers, Copts, Syrians and Greeks, are becoming very arrogant towards the Muslims, treating them with contempt. They ordered the Muslims to stand when they pass by, and they are very zealous in this, such that if one of their important men walks down the street, and if someone does not get to his feet, they come back for him and throw him in prison at the Citadel where they beat him. The offender has to spend several days in prison.

Friday, 22 August.

Demands for money continue. A Copt named Shukrallah has been appointed to the task. He is allowed to enter anyone's house to demand payment, accompanied by French soldiers and workers armed with pickaxes. If the anyone does not pay, he gives the order to destroy their house.

Friday, 29 August.

The Nile has risen more than usual this year, and streets are flooded. Elephant Lake has overflown, with the waters reaching all the way to Nasiriyya. Some of the houses overlooking the canal have collapsed.

Saturday, 6 September.

They are destroying houses, building, mosques, bathhouses, shops and mausoleums in the areas of Husseiniyya and outside Bab al-Futouh and Bab al-Nasr. When they tear down a house, they do not let the inhabitants take anything with them. They even stop them from digging through the rubble.

They loot the houses themselves, and take the wood and whatever else might be useful from the debris and use it for their own buildings. The workers tie up the smaller pieces of wood and sell it at exorbitant prices, since there is a shortage of wood for fuel.

The razing has reached from Bab al-Futouh as far as Bab al-Hadid. It is all just one long stretch of rubble. They have walled off the gates: Bab al-Futouh, Bab al-Barqiyya and Bab al-Mahrouq, and constructed a series of fortifications on the Barqiyya hills, now well stocked with men, weapons, supplies and water. The fortifications run from Bab al-Nasr to Bab al-Wazir. They wrecked the upper part of the Nizamiyya Madrasa and its beautiful minaret. They turned it into a fort.

Friday, 19 September.

The Qanibiyya Madrasa, the mosque of the Seven Sultans, the Circassian Mosque near Sayyida Aisha, the Khund Mosque outside Bab al-Barqiyya: all razed. They sealed the Barqiyya Gate and made the adjoining mosque a fort as well, after demolishing its domes and minarets. All the gates of the Maydan are closed off.

And there are more demolitions: houses in Ezbekieh, the Muski arch, and the surrounding area known as al-Ataba al-Zurqa, where sits the Ezbek Mosque. Now you can walk directly from the Muski arch to the Ezbek Mosque along a single, wide-open road.

The Ruwaii Mosque is demolished; a tavern now stands in its place.

Other mosques, like that of Abd al-Rahman Katkhuda, facing Bab al-Futouh, have been completely destroyed such that nothing is left but part of the walls. The Ezbek Mosque has been converted to a market where the French adjudicate taxes and duties on goods.

They broke the stone benches that line the shopfronts and carried away the debris, on the pretence that they are widening the streets to allow their large carts to pass through with building materials. In reality, they are afraid of the barricades people might set up during the next revolt. Shopkeepers now have to sit inside their shops, like mice in their holes, instead of on the benches out front, and this means they have very little space.

Tuesday, 23 September.

All the trees in the gardens of Cairo, Bulaq, Rouda and Old Cairo have been cut down, along with those by Qasr al-Aini, outside Husseiniyya, and in the gardens of Ratli Lake, all for building their fortifications and reinforcing the walls. They use the wood for making carts and barricades and also as firewood. They even took the wood from the boats.

Friday, 26 September.

Imported goods are still very expensive. A pound of soap is 80 *paras*, and a single almond is 2 *paras*. Domestic goods like clarified butter and honey and rice are available and mostly inexpensive. Christian pedlars go through the streets with pots of honey on the backs of donkeys, calling out their paltry prices.

Wednesday, 1 October.

The French imposed regular payments on the sheikhs of the villages. There are three categories. The highest is for those with a thousand acres or more: they must pay 500 *riyals*. The middle category, those who have over five hundred acres: 300 *riyals*. Below that, the payment is 150 *riyals*. They put Sheikh Suleiman al-Fayyoumi in charge of collecting the money.

Monday, 20 October.

The Diwan has a new configuration of nine elders or chiefs. No Copts or Syrians, no officers, no special and general sections, just one single Diwan composed of nine sheikhs. These are Sharqawi Mahdi; Sheikh al-Amir; my teacher, Jabarti; Sawi; Sheikh Musa al-Sarsi; Sheikh Khalil Bakri; Sayyid Ali Rashidi, brother of the Commander-in-chief's wife, and Sheikh Fayyoumi. Also attached to the Diwan are Sheikh Ismail al-Zurqani the judge; Sayyid Ismail al-Khashab as clerk. Sheikh Ali is to serve as Arabic scribe and Qasim Effendi as Turkish scribe, the priest Raphael is named first interpreter and Elias Fakhr al-Shami second interpreter. Fourier is the commissioner delegate.

As a meeting place they chose the house of Rashwan Bey, in the Abdeen neighbourhood. The Diwan is to meet ten times each month.

Monday, 3 November.

Each of the nine members of the Diwan is allocated 14,000 *paras* per month, that is, 1,400 *paras* for each day they meet. They spent the first day choosing the posts of Head of the Diwan and secretary, and as usual, it was Sharqawi and Mahdi who were named.

My teacher says that people are happy about this, because they believe that this Diwan is going to improve the situation and provide some relief.

Tuesday, 18 November.

A man came to the Diwan asking them to intervene in the case of his son, an oil merchant. The French arrested him because a woman had come to him to buy some clarified butter, and when he told her he didn't have any, she accused him of hoarding in order to sell it to the Ottomans. She meant this sarcastically, and he responded: Yes, right under your nose and right under the nose of all the French! A servant overheard this and the news eventually reached the governor, who ordered him arrested.

In the evening, the father came to the house to ask for Jabarti's intervention.

—I'm afraid they're going to kill him.

—No, my teacher reassured him. They wouldn't kill him just for saying something like that. Do not worry. The French are not that unjust.

Wednesday, 19 November.

My teacher heard that they executed the oil merchant along with four others whose crimes nobody knows. He is distressed. I do not dare try to speak with him today.

Thursday, 20 November.

A new charge of one million on artisans and craftsmen: 186,000 French *riyals* each year, in three instalments every four months. Rumour has it that Master Yacoub the Copt will be in charge of extracting it from the Muslims.

Monday, 24 November.

Local Janissary officers, along with some notables and a number of their womenfolk appeared before the Diwan today.

—We have heard that the French want to get their hands on all the tax farms, they told the Diwan.

They asked the French to spare some of the land so that they could earn a living, arguing that it has been passed down from their fathers and their fathers' fathers; if it is taken away from them then they will be ruined and will have no credibility with the people.

Wednesday, 26 November.

A group of concession holders came to the Diwan. They said that they had asked their farmers for what they owed of the land tax, but they refused to pay. The farmers say the French are pressuring them not to pay anything to the concession holders.

Tuesday, 9 December.

Two women were paraded in the streets of Cairo for having sold another woman to a Greek Christian for 9 *riyals*. A judge and crier walked before them, announcing that this was the punishment for selling a free person.

Sunday, 14 December.

My teacher returned from the Diwan in good spirits.

—The tax farmers can keep their concessions. There was no truth to the rumour. If the treasurer said he wanted to seize them, it was either a joke or an interpreter's mistake.

The French have finished constructing a building in Ezbekieh, at the place known as Bab al-Hawa. In their language it is called a *comédie*. It is a place where they gather every ten days in the evening to watch things that entertain them. Each session lasts about four hours. It is all in their language, and nobody can enter without a certain piece of paper and appropriate dress.

Friday, 2 January 1801.

In the Diwan it is said that Commander-in-chief's wife, the Muslim from Rosetta, has given birth to a boy named Suleiman. Fourier told the sheikhs that they should write to congratulate him, which they did, using a very large sheet of paper.

Monday, 5 January.

On leaving the house I saw a rat. Its fur looked wet, and it tried to flee but its little paws were shaking. It let out a short cry and turned in a circle before falling over on its back in convulsions. Blood spurted out of its nose and it stopped moving.

Friday, 9 January.

In the evening, we received a gift of vinegar from Fayyoum from the Emir Rashwan Kashef, one of the mamluks of Murad Bey. He has property in Fayyoum.

Jabarti tells me that he has a monopoly on roses and the rose water extracted from the flowers, as well as vinegar from grapes. He trades in these goods as he pleases, and he rules the whole region as if the land were his property and the people were his slaves.

Chapter Eight

Monday, 26 January.

Near our quarter I saw a man stumbling along, legs wide apart. He sat down on the ground and raised his arms; his shirt was full of holes and you could see his armpits. Passers-by were stopping to stare, so I went to have a look. His breathing gave off a strange whistling sound. Then he vomited horribly.

—I'm thirsty, he screamed. Thirsty!

—It's the plague, somebody yelled.

We all departed quickly.

Sunday, 15 February.

The plague is back and the French are frightened. They sweep their rooms and wash everything, all the clothing and fabrics. They have also instituted a 'quarantine'. Thirty or forty Frenchmen are dying each day. They carry the dead bodies on pieces of wood that look like doors, down from the Citadel to the Qarafa Cemetery, where they throw them into a deep pit and then cover them over with dirt.

Word is spreading that English ships have arrived at Aboukir.

Friday, 6 March.

Members of the Diwan met as usual. The delegate Fourier told them that the ships gathered at Alexandria, about 120 in all, have departed.

The members wanted to know what ships these were.

—They are mostly English, along with a few others, from Malta and Naples. But there are only a few large ships among them.

Saturday, 7 March.

My teacher gathered us all in the courtyard.

—The plague is upon the land, he announced. We must take care to clean everything, purify all the rooms, wash the vegetables with vinegar, and use lots of lemon.

Jaafar said he has heard that those stricken by the disease are taken into 'quarantine' and their families have no news of them because they will be buried in their clothes in a pit and covered over with dirt. And nobody can enter or leave the house of the infected for four days, and all the clothes belonging to him are burnt. A guard stands by the door, and if somebody touches the door or even the outer edge of it, they arrest him and put him under quarantine right away. Their goal is to put the whole city in quarantine!

My teacher said that this was not true. Jaafar suggests nonetheless that we leave Cairo and head to the countryside.

Sunday, 8 March.

Ottoman troops and the vizier, Yusuf Pasha, are said to arrive at El-Arish.

Monday, 9 March.

They took Sheikh Sadat up to the Citadel, without any ill treatment.

Tuesday, 10 March.

In the souks, the criers announce that there is no need to fear the quarantine and that they do not burn all the clothes of the deceased, only those he was wearing at the time of death.

Wednesday, 11 March.

Muhammad Agha, chief of police, has died of the plague. They did not name an official successor, but Abd al-Al will now be in charge of security and market inspection. This Abd al-Al is of very low origins. He used to work as a labourer for one of the Syrian Christians in the Hamzawi caravanserai.

Friday, 13 March.

The French have word that English ships have appeared at Alexandria. Commander Menou has gone there himself.

Monday, 16 March.

Having made certain that the door to my room was locked, I took my inkwell, reed pen and some sheets of paper and began to write:

O Infidel French
Save yourselves before you taste death, be it by the brutal death of the plague, or by the swords of the Muslims
Go back to your godless country
Mind your own affairs and leave us to ours

I then translated this into the language of the French, except that I did not know how to render the expression 'brutal death'.

I copied out the translation onto six sheets of paper, determined to post them in places where the French lived or gathered. I thought suddenly of Alfi Bey's house, but it is too heavily guarded. Likewise, the house of Pauline. In the end, I chose the markets that they frequent, and the gates and bridges they use. I would post one at Maydan Rumayla, one at Bab al-Wazir by the Citadel, one at Qanatir al-Sibaa, and another at the French Institute in Nasiriyya. The remaining three I would post in the northern part of the city: one at Bab al-Nasr, one near the Frankish quarter of Ezbekieh and one at Bab Zuweila.

I prayed the afternoon prayer and then slipped out, pressing the papers against my chest. I headed towards the shrine of Hussein. I walked along Hussein Street and down to Tuffah caravanserai, past the Emerald Palace, to the Saboun entrepôt where Syrian goods are sold. Past the church of the Syrians and the Persian madrasa, past a shop selling balls of ground, grilled meat wrapped in grape leaves and set out on wooden skewers. The minaret of the mosque of al-Hakim came into view, and after a few more turns I was at the Jumblatiyya Madrasa right next to Bab al-Nasr.

From a distance a few local soldiers were visible, along with two French counterparts, gathered by the gate. Walking slowly and looking around, I saw that most of the shops sold textiles. I stopped to buy some chickpeas and lupins.

I had wanted to post the paper where the French would see it easily. The wall of the Jumblatiyya Madrasa? Too far from view, and the pupils would be able to tear it down. I stopped at a shop entrance where a tailor was sewing fabrics of silk, jute and cashmere. There was a brick next to the wall. I took the nail in my hand and got ready.

From the corner of my eye, I could see the soldiers talking and laughing, nevertheless always watching everyone who passed by. A magician appeared. He carried a sort of tube that spouted water, and he could make the flow start and stop at his command. Some kids gathered around him and began to shout and cheer. The French, though, were not impressed by his trick and started to mock him. He took out a sack, and after much jesting and joking, blew into a large seashell he had with him, then lifted the cover of the sack, and there was an egg. He turned the sack upside down, pulled off the cover again, and there was a baby chick. The soldiers now pressed around the magician in a circle, they were no longer watching the gate. This was my opportunity. I picked up the brick, placed the paper against the wall and drove in the nail. Then I dropped the brick and, heart pounding, got away as fast as I could.

Tuesday, 17 March.

I walked in the opposite direction from yesterday. It is not far between Sanadiqiyya and Bab Zuweila, but the street is crowded with people buying and selling and going to and fro. A lot of people with eyes bandaged, due to ophthamlmia. The water carriers jangling their bells to make their way among the animals loaded with goods for the entrepôts. Shops and caravanserais stretch all along both sides of the street, their facades of coloured marble carved and decorated with the names of the sultans and emirs who had built them.

I joined the crowd moving in the direction of Bab Zuweila, past the leather-workers and shoemakers. Nearing the gate, I stopped by the public fountain into which a camel driver had emptied his waterskins.

With a feeling of foreboding I recited the first sura of the Quran, as was the custom of those who passed through the gate above which the Ottomans, 200 years earlier, had hanged the last Mamluk sultan, Tuman Bey.

But luck was with me: there were no guards at the Bab Zuweila. I picked up a rock and started nailing the paper to the wall when a soldier appeared from nowhere and yelled at me.

I ran. The soldier and a number of others were right behind me. I dashed through the open door of a house, and again, luck was on my side: there was another door. I slipped out while they were still waiting for me on the side where I had entered.

Chapter Nine

Tuesday, 24 March.

I am writing in the Citadel prison. I will tell the story of how I came to be here.

The morning after my adventure at Bab Zuweila, I went to the Frankish quarter in Ezbekieh. I managed to post the paper at the entrance to the quarter without anyone seeing me. Then, all of sudden, I noticed some Greeks looking down at me from an upper floor of the house. I made to leave quickly but one of them must have been already on his way down. He grabbed the paper and yelled after me.

I found myself directly in front of a French soldier, his arms stretched wide to catch me. I was too fast for him. Then it was my bad luck to come across three French civilians, one of whom tried to stop me. I gave him a violent shove and he fell backwards on the ground. The other two took off after me. Turning into a dark alley that seemed to be a dead-end, I climbed up the wall of one of the houses. It was empty. I reached the roof and saw that they were still after me. I climbed onto the roof of the neighbouring caravanserai. Unwrapping my turban, I tied it to a nail and lowered myself down into the market. Then I walked out.

Running in the direction of al-Ghouriyya, I saw they were chasing me, so I had to run all the way to Gammaliyya, where I again entered a dead-end alley. I charged through the open door of a house as the owner stood by the entrance watching me as I passed. From the courtyard I could hear the voices of the Frenchmen asking after me.

—He went that way, somebody told them.

They were coming into the alley. The owner of the house told them where I was.

When I heard them coming through the door, I pulled off my clothes and, with them in hand, climbed down the courtyard well. I remained hidden there while they searched everywhere else.

I stayed down there for a while, until it seemed that all was calm above and the people had left. I quietly climbed out of the well, put my clothes back on and clambered to the top of the courtyard wall. The alley seemed empty, so I jumped off falling right into the arms of the new chief of police and security, Abd al-Al, who had been hiding in the doorway of the house.

Abd al-Al took me to my teacher's house. They searched my room but thankfully did not move the trunk. They were looking for weapons, even pulling up the tiles. Jabarti's anger at me was clear.

They took me to the Citadel, where they beat me with horsewhips. They hit me on my hands, my face and my head, demanding to know who I was working with and where I had hidden the weapons. I told them nothing, so they locked me up.

I spent the first night alone, sleeping on the cold floor of the cell. Thoughts of Pauline, and what had happened between us, gave me comfort. By dawn, though, I was shivering, and I had to hop around like a monkey to get the blood flowing.

In the morning, they brought me a piece of hardened cheese and some bread. They needed the space for a new prisoner, so they took me to a bigger room, where there was already a good number of prisoners. Most were accused of causing unrest or provoking opposition to the French. There were wealthy merchants and poor Azhari students, Syrians and Maghribis.

My place was next to a Hajj, a herbalist by profession. He had a strange story. After the revolt, he had gone into hiding from the French. One day Abd al-Al raided his brother's home, arresting the brother and everyone else in the house. They put them all in the governor's place—seven of them and a servant. Then they took them to the Citadel and harassed and abused them, but they released the servant and gave him 50 French *riyals*. They promised him a thousand more if he led them to the Hajj. That's how he ended up in the prison.

I discovered that they have a special lock-up for the Ottoman prisoners; they are not allowed to have any contact with the rest of the inmates.

Around midday, servants brought us some food. Following the evening prayer I talked with a fellow inmate. When he heard I could read and write, he asked me to write a letter to his family which he would send with a servant of one of the merchants. He brought me paper, ink and pen, and I wrote out what he told me. I asked if I could keep the writing materials, he said yes. I wanted to continue to record events as they occurred, and so I wrote about what happened to me. When I finished, I folded the paper and hid it in my clothing. Inkwell and pen I put under my bedding. Luckily, the guards and soldiers were so preoccupied with the stream of new arrivals that they did not make any searches of bedding and belongings.

Wednesday, 25 March.

Some people heard about the letter I'd written, and now everybody is asking me to write for them, and offering to share their food in return.

Thursday, 26 March.

New prisoners arrived at the Citadel after midday. We learnt from them that the Ottomans had reached Gaza, with the vanguard as far along as El-Arish. The French had summoned the members of the Diwan: they would be taking some notables as hostages, in accordance with the rules of war.

A guard tells us that they took four sheikhs: first, Sharqawi, Mahdi and Fayyoumi, bringing them to the Citadel in the middle of the night out of respect. The sheikhs have been installed in the Sariya Mosque in the Citadel. Sheikh Sadat soon joined them. Each has a servant who can come and go and bring them whatever they might want from their homes. They are also allowed visitors from friends and family they need written permission from the governor.

Friday, 27 March.

A strange surprise: three prisoners transferred from the Rahmaniyya fort, and one of them is Abd al-Zaher. I put his bedding next to mine and we spoke of all that had happened to us. He confirmed what Hanna had told me about his arrest, although he still suspected that it was Hanna who had informed on him.

He commended me when I told him how I had posted the papers. Then I recounted my story with Pauline, and he recited to me some parts of *Wiles of Women* by al-Batatouni al-Busiri, that tell how women are ignorant of the Sharia, how they are filled with a sexual desire that knows no bounds, that they are mentally inferior and that they try to lure innocent men into the crime of adultery. And it was a woman who was responsible for the slaughter of the Prophet's cousin and son-in-law, Ali ibn Abi Talib, and of Ali's son as well.

Saturday, 28 March.

I have noticed continual movement in the Citadel grounds. At first I thought it was just the arrival of new prisoners, but it went on all day. One of the rooms has a window rimmed with spikes, through which you can look down onto the grounds of the Citadel, next to the Azab Gate. From this window, I could see the French bringing in their possessions, supplies and ammunition, on the backs of mules and camels. This went on all night.

Sunday, 29 March.

Abd al-Zaher still complains about the shamelessness of women and how they display themselves in public and mingle with the French. He said that women have started to promenade by themselves or with others of the same age, their servants or guards walk ahead armed with sticks, clearing people out of the way. As if the women were rulers! As for the black slave girls, they go to the French in droves, informing them where their masters are hiding, as well as where they stashed their money and possessions.

Wednesday, 1 April.

I have befriended one of the guards, a Copt. He is from Upper Egypt, like me.

Thoughts of Pauline are with me constantly, especially at night.

Friday, 3 April.

The guard tells me he has heard of fighting between the French and the English at Alexandria. A disaster for the French, many troops were killed and they had to withdraw to the interior of the city. He also says that Hussein Pasha, captain of the Turkish fleet, was off the coast at Aboukir, and his men have already disembarked. The French soldiers are normally very reserved and do not betray emotion, but now one can see in their faces the reaction to this news.

Tuesday, 7 April.

No more ink, no more paper. The man who had them tried to get me some more, but the soldiers wouldn't allow it. The Coptic guard promised to bring me some in secret.

Friday, 10 April.

The guard fulfilled his promise and brought me a supply, after the prayers. So I have started writing again. We pass the time playing chess, cards, checkers and backgammon. I learnt about mancala, played by two people on a board with two rows of six holes each. The players try to get each a pebble or stone into each of the six holes.

Tuesday, 14 April.

One of the carpenters has made nineteen little statuettes for playing tab. It is a game for two people, played on a grid drawn on the ground. Each player takes four small sticks, black on one side, white on the other. They throw the sticks at a knife stuck in the ground, and depending on the combinations of black and white, they move the statuettes around the grid.

Thursday, 16 April.

The word is that the English and the Ottomans have occupied Rosetta.

Sunday, 19 April.

One of the Syrian interpreters who attended the Diwan is imprisoned with us. We asked him for the news, and he told us that at the last meeting, the general treasurer, Estève, had asked those present to speed up the collection of the agreed-upon half a million in order to provide for the soldiers. Then Estève told them that the French do not like to lie and are not used to lying, and that is why the members of the Diwan must believe everything they tell them. Someone interjected that only hashish-eaters were liars, and the French did not eat hashish.

—Know that the French will never give up Egypt, and they will never leave, the treasurer went on. It is now their land, under their rule, and even if they should be overthrown, they would only retreat to Upper Egypt and then return to reconquer Cairo.

The Hajj said that this Syrian interpreter may well be a spy sent to inform on us.

Monday, 20 April.

My friend, the guard, tells me they have surrounded Hasan Agha's house because they found a French boy hiding there. The boy had converted to Islam and shaved his head. The guard also reports that Taher Pasha has arrived at Abu Zaabel with an army of Albanian Ottomans.

Monday, 27 April.

Rumour in the prison is that Murad Bey has died of the plague, somewhere in the south. When the French were on good terms with him, they had granted him the emirate of Upper Egypt, paying his wife Nafisa 100,000 *paras* per month. Then they reduced it to 50,000 *paras*.

I discovered that my friend Hajj Ali knew Murad Bey personally. He tells me that he was lighter-skinned and blonde, like the people of the Caucasus, in his fifties, stocky of build, with Circassian features: pale face, thick beard and fiery, cruel eyes. According to my friend, he was a cruel tyrant, arrogant and conceited. But he was fond of scholars and listened to what they had to say. He tended to favour Islam and the Muslims, and enjoyed the company of eloquent and cultured men. He also liked to play chess and listen to music.

Hajj Ali recounted Murad Bey's story. He had been a slave belonging to Muhammad Bey Abu Dhahab, who freed him just a few days after having purchased him. He made Murad an emir, granted him valuable feudal estates, made him part of his circle. He loved him. Then he married him to Sitt Fatima, widow of the Emir Salih Bey, and Murad moved into his former palace on Kabsh Street.

When Muhammad Bey Abu Dhahab died, the powerful emirs decided to grant authority to Ibrahim Bey and not Murad Bey. The latter took as a second wife the widow of Ali Bey, Sayyida Nafisa, a beautiful Georgian known for her power and her fortune. He lived a life of opulent ease in Giza, and didn't set foot in Cairo for six years. Murad enjoyed life in the palace he had built in Roda, and another in Jazirat al-Dhahab, and the one in Qaymaz near Adliyya. All the while he shared power and revenue with Ibrahim Bey.

Murad Bey moved between these palaces and spent much of his time hunting and had built for himself a great arsenal. Artisans made cannons and bombs, cannon shot and rifles. He even ordered the construction of new gunpowder factories, to add to the other gunpowder factories in the area. For this he not only made use of all the blacksmiths, carpenters, smelters but also used up almost all the available iron, lead, coal and wood.

He brought people from the Qalyunjiyya and Greek Christians and shipbuilders who built for him a number of warships and galleons, all equipped with cannons and arms like the Turkish fleet. A Greek named Nicolas he appointed as commander. Nobody knew the reason for all these expensive preparations. In any case, all the arms, weaponry and powder remained in the storehouses until the French seized it all.

Saturday, 2 May.

This afternoon we sensed that there was some sort of uproar inside the Citadel. We knew that the wife of Commander-in-chief Menou had left Alfi Bey's house and come up to the Citadel with her brother Ali al-Rashidi, for reasons of security.

Wednesday, 13 May.

Rumour in the prison has it that English and Ottomans have arrived at Rahmaniyya and seized its citadel and all nearby fortifications.

Sunday, 17 May.

Continuous uproar outside. Climbing onto Abd al-Zaher's shoulders to look through the opening, I could see a number of millstones being brought in, followed by water tanks and chests of gunpowder and sulphur. There seemed to be stores of wheat and grains, along with bedding and other supplies.

According to the guard, they are putting up barricades and digging trenches to the north and east. Anyone available is being put to work. At Imbaba, huge rocks and watercraft are placed so as to stop any boat getting through. The river bank is fortified from Bab al-Hadid to the Limun Bridge, to Sebtiyya, all the way to Shubra.

Saturday, 23 May.

We heard that the eastern armies have made it to the Nile at Banha and Talha, and that the English and their allies have the French surrounded at Alexandria. They have breached the seawalls and flooded the surrounding villages and farm land with salt water.

Monday, 25 May.

Jaafar visited me, bringing fruits and other food. He said that the police chief Abd al-Al came to them, disguised in women's clothing. He searched the entire house, looking for a woman named Hawa, former wife of one of the emirs. This woman had been acting strangely. She was married to Nicolas the Greek and had lived with him for some time. But now she had gathered her clothes and somehow managed to come down from the Citadel on a donkey. Her belongings were carried by a second donkey. She rode into a side street and paid the donkey drivers their fare, then dismissed them and disappeared.

Sunday, 7 June.

We heard cannon fire in the distance this morning. They say that the Ottoman vizier has arrived at Shalaqan, to the north. Also,

English soldiers were at Warariq, on the western side of the Nile, near Imbaba.

Sunday, 13 June.

Another visit from Jaafar. He brought some food. He apologized for the fact that the markets were short of meat and butter and cheese, and that the French had requisitioned all the oil presses. The shortage of sheep and livestock meant that meat was very expensive: one pound cost 9 *paras*. Clarified butter, 35 *paras*; onions, 800 *paras* per hundred pounds, and a pound of soap was 160 *paras*.

Jaafar told me that Jabarti wanted aniseed for an infusion, and had sent him to buy some, but he could not find it anywhere. He was told that there was none to be found, except with a merchant who was selling one ounce for 13 *paras*. After much effort, he managed to get from the merchant two ounces at that price.

I asked him about the cannon fire of the morning. He told me that my teacher had gone to the Azhar that morning and climbed to the top of the minaret. With the aid of a spyglass, he had seen English soldiers setting up their tents on the outskirts of Imbaba.

Tuesday, 16 June.

We heard a loud call outside, and only after we heard it several times did we understand they were announcing the punishment giving information to the Ottomans or the English. Subsequently, the guards told us that Abd al-Al had killed a man at Bab Zuweila who was carrying a letter from some women to their husbands in the Ottoman camp. They also said that the Turks had arrived at Adliyya and their encampment extended all the way to Minyet al-Sirg.

Saturday, 20 June.

The forces on the eastern side advanced and are now near Qubbat al-Nasr.

Ibrahim Bey camped at the Sufi lodge of Sheikh Demirdash. When a group of Ottomans approached the city near the slaughter-houses, the French fired on them from the forts of al-Zahiriyya, Najm al-din and al-Tell.

Sunday, 21 June.

Rifle and cannon fires exchanged between the two sides from morning to mid-afternoon.

Monday, 22 June.

More fighting, all day. According to the night guards, about 25 Ottoman soldiers entered al-Husseiniyya. They sat on the coffee-house benches, ate cakes and bread and boiled beans, drank coffee, then returned to their camp.

The soldiers on the western shore have now advanced as far as Giza.

Tuesday, 23 June.

Around midday the fighting ceased. The English have spread out south of Giza, preventing any boats from crossing to the eastern side of the Nile. Therefore, food arriving from the south does not reach Cairo: melons, vegetables, cucumbers, clarified butter, cheese and livestock. Costs are rising even higher: a chicken for 40 *paras*; no meat in the markets.

Wednesday, 24 June.

The guards suddenly burst in on us this morning. They searched through all our clothing and possessions. Frenchmen stood by giving orders as the guards fell on us in a fury, thrashing us with horsewhips. I noticed my friend the Coptic guard was among them. He pretended not to see me. They confiscated all our games, papers and ink. I managed to keep my notes under my clothes. By the afternoon, things had calmed down.

Thursday, 25 June.

The Coptic guard brought me some ink. He said there were negotiations ongoing between the French and the invaders. We heard no cannon fire.

Monday, 29 June.

The Ottoman prisoners in the Citadel are released. Each received some cloth and 15 piastres. A group of Bedouins and fellahin was also freed. I am hoping that it will soon be my turn to leave.

After sunset, I heard the cannon fire. According to the guards, it had come from the fort of the Zaher Mosque.

Tuesday, 30 June.

The guards say that the Ottoman flag flies over the Zaheriyya fort, and that the Muslim soldiers are occupying its ramparts. The cannon fire we heard last evening was announcing its surrender. Word is spreading of the release of the sheikhs held hostage along with the rest of the prisoners.

Wednesday, 1 July.

They released the rest of the imprisoned sheikhs, among them Sadat, Sharqawi, Amir, Muhammad Mahdi and Hasan Agha, the market inspector.

Thursday, 2 July.

Abd al-Zaher was released today.

Friday, 3 July.

They set me free, and I ran out of the Citadel Gate and kept running until I reached the Azhar. There I saw all kinds of soldiers: Janissaries with their long caps hanging down their backs, and a split feather in front; Mamluks wearing embroidered kaftans, their swords hanging on their right from wide belts, their daggers visible, turbans wrapped around their high hats; Albanians sporting the short white kaftan they call the tannura, tarboushes with long tassels, and leather pants.

Khalil, Jaafar and the other servants welcomed me home. Jabarti was at the meeting of the Diwan. I took some clean clothes and went to the bathhouse. My teacher was waiting for me on my return. He told me about the Diwan, where they discussed the conditions for peace: The French army must leave Cairo and its fortifications and proceed by land to Rosetta, and from there by ship to their own country. This was to take place within 50 days. The English and the Ottomans would cover the expenses and supply them with the necessary provisions, camels and boats.

We ate fresh moloukhiyya for lunch, with ragout and cucumbers. After the meal, word came that English officers, accompanied by Frenchmen, had arrived in the city. They were taking a tour, looking at the souks. Khalil, Jaafar and I hurried out and followed them to the mausoleum of Hussein. As we watched, some of the Ottoman officers entered while the French remained outside.

Monday, 6 July.

A messenger brought my teacher an invitation to a meeting of the Diwan.

—Come with me, he said.

—Is that wise? I asked. People are not kind to those who attend these meetings.

—It's the last of the meetings. We have to attend. And you must take note to remember well everything that is said.

All the sheikhs and important merchants were there, along with the treasurer Estève, the Commissioner-delegate, Fourier, and the interpreter. Carpets were spread out and everyone sat. The Commissioner took out a sealed letter from the Commander-in-chief Menou, and handed it to the chief of the Diwan, who opened it and passed it to the interpreter who read it aloud.

Then Estève the treasurer spoke.

—I shall not speak to you of the reasons for our departure from Egypt. My concern is rather with political affairs. I come to tell you how difficult this separation is for us. Each and every one of you has witnessed the love and the brotherhood that exists between the people of France and the people of Egypt. The army and the people were like one people. The name of Bonaparte, the First Consul, is as dear to you as it is to us. This great brave man, of unrivalled genius, deserved to be your ruler for ever! Since the day he was obliged to leave us because of the difficulties facing him in his own country, you have always been present in his thoughts, and he still hopes that through him Egypt will have the equitable administration that he promised you when he was here, as well as the justice that was denied you by previous rulers . . . One day we shall return to Egypt to complete the good work that French rule has begun but which we were not able to complete. Do not imagine, O sheikhs, O learned men, that our absence from these lands is anything but temporary. Of this I am certain. Our two countries will soon renew the ancient bonds that link us together.

At the end of this speech, the Diwan dispersed and. the sheikhs went on to greet the Ottoman Grand Vizier, Yusuf Pasha and the Egyptian emirs who were with him.

I sensed that Jabarti was worried about something. He kept biting the side of his moustache.

—Pray to your Lord that the Vizier will receive us and not have us all thrown in prison. They will not forgive all those who took part in the Diwan.

When we arrived at the tent, we greeted Ibrahim Bey, who came with us to see the vizier. As we entered, they ordered the sheikhs to remove the shawls from around their head and shoulders, before meeting the Grand Vizier. What Jabarti had anticipated was correct: the Vizier did not rise to greet them. We sat there for a while, then left.

Wednesday, 8 July.

Word is that the French will leave and hand over the fortifications by midday tomorrow.

Thursday, 9 July.

We passed the night listening to the racket made by the Ottoman soldiers, as they shouted, marched and talked loudly. By morning, it was clear that the French had left during the night and given up the Citadel and the other forts and barricades. They went to Giza, to Roda, to Qasr al-Aini. No trace of them in the city, in Bulaq, Old Cairo or Ezbekieh.

Sunday, 12 July.

Boats arrived from the north, laden with Turkish goods, along with nuts and dried fruits: pistachios, almonds, walnuts, grapes, figs and olives.

Wednesday, 15 July.

The French have departed, leaving Qasr al-Aini, Roda and Giza and heading north towards Warariq. The Captain Pasha and most of the English go with them.

French rule over the lands of Egypt lasted three years and twenty-one days.

—Glory to He whose rule will never end, and whose power will never be lost, said my teacher. Their expedition started with forty thousand men. Only half of them were left at the end.

I went with him to watch the great departure from the bridge that the French had built to Roda Island. It was a solemn procession, with hardly a sound other than the horses' hooves on the ground. General Belliard at the front on the back of his grey-speckled steed; Master Yacoub following, dressed as a French general and displaying his badges and decorations, sword at his side. Next to him: his mother, his wife, some relatives and followers. I did not see Hanna among them.

Thursday, 16 July.

The call went out that the procession of the Grand Vizier Yusuf Pasha was on its way. People of all stations and nations came together. They paid exorbitant prices to rent floors in buildings that overlook the street; they sat on rooftops and in rows before shopfronts.

The procession carried on from early morning until almost midday. I followed them as they entered the city from Bab al-Nasr till it reached the middle of the city. In the lead were the Janissaries and the Albanians, behind them were the Syrian soldiers, the Egyptian emirs, the Maghribis, some marines and Muhammad Pasha, the governor of Egypt. There were scribes, and the chief secretary, the deputy of the Sultan and the great aghas, accompanied by drums and tambourines. The military judge and his deputies, Egyptian scholars and Sufi sheikhs and dervishes.

The Grand Vizier, preceded by couriers and runners, wore a sort of feather tiara, studded with diamonds. Two men behind him and two at each side threw white silver coins, minted in Istanbul, to the onlooking men and women. Behind him also were a number of his subordinates and his special Turkish musicians, then came the cannons and ammunition carts. There was much firing of cannons throughout the whole procession.

As was their custom, the people rejoiced and celebrated their arrival, in their persistent belief that this will all turn out for the better. They greet and welcome and bless the newcomers; the women chatter from windows, and in the souks; noise, shouting, children everywhere, and voices calling: *God give victory to the Sultan*!

After the procession, Ottoman soldiers, from all different nations, sat on street corners and at neighbourhood gates, at coffee houses and bathhouses. They asked people for food, for drink, for coffee, and there was no refusing them. They even invited themselves into peoples' homes.

In the souks, bread, meat, butter and oil are now plentiful. Stores are well stocked, and prices are down. Lamb sells for 8 *paras*, goat for 7, water buffalo meat for 6; clarified butter is 180 *paras* for ten pounds, having earlier sold at 300 *paras* for the same amount. All vegetables are sold by the pound, even lemons and radishes, and a pound of bread can be bought for 1 *para*. A waterskin is now

10 *paras*, down from 20. Fruits, too, are abundant: grapes, peaches, watermelon. Most of this is due to the Turks and Albanians who buy at low prices from the farmers who transport it overland or by boat, then resell it in Cairo or Bulaq at a handsome profit.

Friday, 17 July.

Soldiers are hereby to cease their association with tradesmen and traders, except in cases where the latter are willing and consenting. Most of the soldiers continue to make demands on the people anyway.

Sunday, 19 July.

No one is to harm or injure any Christian or Jew, be he Copt, Greek or Syrian, for they are the Sultan's subjects.

My teacher is angry because the new rulers have sent decrees to the provinces and villages of Egypt stating that nothing should be paid to the concession holders, but only to collectors sent by the state. He slapped his palms together furiously.

—How are we going to manage without that money?

Tuesday, 21 July.

Sheikh Bakri has lost his dear Mamluk, the one the French ruled was his to keep. Osman Bey al-Tonburji had made a complaint to the judge who summoned Bakri and the merchant who had sold the Mamluk to him. Osman Bey testified that the young man was meant for Murad Bey, but Bakri, with pressure from the French, had forced the merchant to give him the Mamluk instead, and did not pay the full value. The judge ruled that the Mamluk should be taken away from Bakri who had already given him both his freedom and the hand of his daughter in marriage. They annulled both the emancipation and the marriage contract. Osman Bey took the Mamluk and paid compensation to Bakri. He also paid the merchant the remainder of what was due.

Sunday, 26 July.

A new decree states that Christians must wear only blue and black. Guards were watching out for them, ready to snatch away their tarboushes and their red shoes, leaving them only their skullcaps and blue belts. The Christians complained, and the authorities heeded their pleas and ordered that no harm should come to them.

Monday, 27 July.

The Grand Vizier asks the merchants for 110 purses as an advance to be paid from the tithe on spices.

Saturday, 1 August.

Today the latrine was cleaned and emptied and the copper polished for the first time since the murder of Kléber.

Sunday, 2 August.

Hasan Attar has returned from Upper Egypt. He showed Jabarti a letter Master Yacoub wrote to some Coptic notables. The Orient has reached such a disgraceful state, Yacoub writes, that there is no alternative but to seek deliverance from foreign lands. The conscience of the great nations like France and England cannot accept that the cradle of wisdom, the lands of the prophets, should remain in such a condition. It was necessary to convince the English and the French of the necessity of helping the people of Egypt to break free from the Mamluk and Turkish rule. Without the cooperation of the English, there could be no independent authority for Egypt. It is in their interest to exert their influence over an independent Egypt, and by that influence Egypt shall regain its prosperity.

Tuesday, 4 August.

Sheikh Bakri's daughter was brought to her mother's house after sunset. They summoned Sheikh Bakri, too, and then they asked her about her flirtatious behaviour with the French. She said she has repented for what she did. When they asked her father's opinion on that, he said he disowned her. Then they broke her neck.

Wednesday, 5 August.

The soldiers continue to buy and sell different kinds of food supplies and extorting money each day from shopkeepers, taking bread from the bakers and coffee from the coffee houses without paying anything. There are even some who enter peoples' houses and order them to leave so they can live there. If people complain to their chief, he says, why will you not welcome the mujahideen who fought on your behalf and who saved you from the unbelievers? The soldiers outside the Christian quarter demand not just food and lodging, but pocket money and the price of the bathhouse as well.

Thursday, 6 August.

The Ottomans are now demanding donkeys. The forced a merchant from the Inal caravanserai off his mount and took it to the souk to sell it. The merchant followed and had to buy back his own donkey.

People are so afraid that they have begun to hide their donkeys. When the soldiers came to us today, we told them we didn't have any. But then they stood outside the door after we closed it, waiting. Knowing they were still there, we quietly hoped that our animals would keep silent. When the soldiers didn't hear anything, they started to make donkey sounds themselves, and eventually one of ours started to bray in response and the game was up. They knocked on the door and demanded the donkey. Jaafar at least managed to get a bit of money out of them.

Tuesday, 18 August.

We are told that the French have departed from Aboukir.

Monday, 24 August.

Christians and Jews are now guaranteed security. They must pay four years' worth of the jizya, the poll tax on non-Muslims.

Thursday, 27 August.

The wage of a mason is now 80 *paras*.

Sunday, 30 August.

A group of Upper Egyptians have come to see Hasan Attar, fleeing the tyranny, taxes and plundering of Alfi Bey, recently named governor of the region. They say that when the Turkish soldiers arrive in a village, they demand money even before they come to eat the food offered them.

Monday, 31 August.

I found my teacher sitting in his usual place, in front of a pile of papers containing all that he had written since the arrival of the French, along with some poetry and some prose that were the work of Hasan Attar. He was reading it over carefully, page by page, moving his head and speaking under his breath. Finally he asked me to bring the inkwell, a pen and some blank leaves of paper, and to take down what he was about to dictate.

He took the first page from the pile, and examined it carefully.

—Write this, he said:

> The year 1213 was the beginning of the time of great battles and momentous events, a time of crisis and calamity, when evil was everywhere and trials and tribulations upset the equilibrium of the age. A time when natural dispositions were disrupted, when horrors went on uninterrupted when our fortunes were reversed and the good order corrupted. Destruction reigned and desolation spread throughout the land, and *Yet thy Lord would never destroy the cities unjustly, while as yet their people were putting things right.*

These were the same words with which he had begun his book on the beginning of the French occupation of Egypt, so I assumed that he simply wanted a new copy for a friend or somebody who wished to buy one. But he went on:

—Write this title at the top of the page: *The Manifest Glorification of the Awaited Termination of the French Occupation.*

—A new book? I asked.

—Old and new at the same time.

—I don't understand.

—Can you imagine that the Ottomans would accept that I praised the French and condemned the Turks? The Grand Vizier has asked me to write the history of the French occupation. I need to clear myself from any accusation of collaboration with the French.

—I've read what you wrote. What you say is the truth.

—Do you think the Turks will accept that?

—So what will you do?

—A new book. Same as the old one, but I'll remove whatever could get me in trouble with them. And I'll dedicate it to Yusuf Pasha, the vizier.

This made me think about what I had written. Would I have to do the same?

I continued writing as my teacher dictated:

> I have written here, on these various and unordered pages, all that took place since the French occupied Egypt up to the arrival of the Grand Vizier, and often have I thought of gathering them together and arranging them in proper order so that this may serve as a history of the wondrous and strange events of the day, one which will enlighten the intelligent man and serve as reminder for every generation to come.

Sources and Acknowledgements

Historical sources on the French occupation of Egypt are plentiful, and at the top of the list is the great chronicles of al-Jabartī, *ʿAjāʾib al-āthār wa-tarājim al-akhbār* (The Most Wondrous Achievements: Biographies and Reports of Events) edited by Abd al-Raḥīm ʿAbd al-Raḥmān ʿAbd al-Raḥīm in 2003 [In English translation: ʿAbd al-Rahman al-Jabarti, *History of Egypt*, 4 VOLS, edited by Thomas Philipp, Guido Schwald and Moshe Perlmann, 1994]; then there is the *Description de l'Égypte*, composed by members of the expedition (2002, translated by Zuhayr al-Shāyib); as well as an Arabic translation of its tenth volume by Ayman Fu'ād al-Sayyid which contains a detailed description of Cairo and the Citadel.

There is also the excellent study by the American scholar J. Christopher Herold, *Bonaparte in Egypt* (1962), translated into Arabic by Fu'ād Andrāws (Andraos); and the biography of *ʿAbd Allāh Jāk Mīnū* (Abdallah Jacques Menou) by the Egyptian historian Muḥammad Fu'ād Shukrī (1952).

In 1989, the French orientalist Henry Laurens published *L'Expédition d'Egypte, 1798–1801*, which differs from the work of Herold only in matters of detail but lacks the latter's enchanting style and its anti-racist, humanistic perspective. It was translated into Arabic by Bashīr al-Sibāʿī.

Recent years have seen the publication of important documents from the accounts of the French expedition's officers, such as the *Mémoires sur l'expédition d'Egypte* of Captain Hauet, translated by Bātsī (Patsy) Jamāl al-dīn (2005); and those of Joseph-Marie Moiret (1984), Arabic translation by Kāmīliyā (Camélia) Ṣubḥī (2000).

More general sources on the French occupation and the history of the eighteenth-century Egypt are as follows:

- ʿAlī Mubārak, *al-Khiṭaṭ al-tawfīqiyya* [the famous multi-volume topographical history of Cairo], 1969[1st EDN, 1888];
- ʿAbd al-Raḥmān al-Rāfiʿī, *Tārikh al-ḥaraka al-qawmiyya* (The History of the Nationalist Movement, 1979);
- the writings of Nelly Hanna, *Habiter au Caire: la maison moyenne et ses habitants aux XVIIe et XVIIe siècles* (Living in Cairo: The Average House and Its Inhabitants in the 17th Century, 1991) translated in Arabic by Ḥalīm Ṭūsūn (1993); *In Praise of Books: A Cultural History of Cairo's Middle Class, Sixteenth to the Eighteenth Century* (2003), Arabic translation by Raouf Abbas (2004); as well as the articles, also translated by Raouf Abbas under the title, *Tujjār al-qāhira fī l-ʿaṣr al-ʿuthmānī* (Merchants of Cairo in the Ottoman Period, 1997).

One must also mention André Raymond's *Artisans et commerçants au Caire au XVIIIe siècle* (Artisans and Traders in Cairo in the 18th Century, 1973), translated by Nāṣir Ibrāhīm and Bātsī Jamāl al-dīn in 2005.

In 1974, the Egyptian Association for Historical Studies held a conference on ʿAbd al-Raḥmān al-Jabartī; its proceedings appeared in 1976, edited by Aḥmad ʿIzzat ʿAbd al-Karīm.

Most sources mention Pauline Fourès (née Bellisle), mistress of Bonaparte in Egypt. They report that he refused to meet her after her return to France, but he gave her a residence in Paris and gifts of money on several occasions. That same year, she married an officer named Pierre Henri de Ranchoux, for whom she obtained a number of mid-level consular postings. She published a novel, *Lord Wentworth*, and took up painting. After the Restoration, she divorced her husband, sold her furniture, and travelled to Brazil with a former officer of the Imperial Guard. They became wealthy, importing French goods and exporting exotic wood back home. They travelled back and forth between the two countries until 1837, when they settled in Paris, where she wrote another historical novel and lived to the age of ninety.

As for Master Yacoub, the Coptic leader, he died six years after leaving Egypt by boat for France.

Al-Jabarti lived to the age of seventy, through the first twenty years of Muhammad Ali's reign. He lost his eyesight, and grieved for his son Khalil who had died in mysterious circumstances. It was rumoured that Muhammad Ali was responsible for his death.

The French expedition has drawn the interest of a number of Egyptian authors: ʿAlī al-Jārim, *Ghādat rashīd* (The Lady of Rosetta, 1960); Majīd Ṭūbiyā, *Taghrībat banī ḥatḥūt* (The Exile of the Bani Hathut, 1977); Muḥammad Jibrīl, *al-Jawdariyya* (2006). There is also the play by Alfrīd Faraj, *Sulaymān al-Ḥalabī* (1966); and the film by Youssef Chahine, *Adieu Bonaparte* (1985). The same is true of some Francophone writers, for example, Gilbert Sinoué's *L'égyptienne* (1991), among others.

*

The author is indebted to professors Layla ʿInān, Nelly Hanna, Raouf Abbas, Nāṣir Ibrāhīm and ʿAlī Muḥammad for their assistance. He would also like to thank the novelist Aḥmad al-ʿĀyidī for the conversions from the Islamic to the Gregorian calendar, and the poet Ḥamza Qināwī for his linguistic expertise.

Cairo, 21 December 2007

*

*

*